Braided Secrets

Theresa Schimmel

This is a work of fiction. Names, characters, places, and incidents either are the product of the author's imagination or are used fictitiously. Any resemblance to actual persons, living or dead, events, or locales is entirely coincidental.

Cover illustration created by Dennis Lavorato

www.tamstales.net

ISBN: 1530431972
ISBN 13: 9781530431977

Dedicated to sisters everywhere, to the special bond they share

Acknowledgements

I would like to thank the many people who have helped and supported me in the process of writing and publishing **Braided Secrets**. To my husband, Steve, thank you for believing in me and encouraging me every step of the way. Thank you to my proofreader, Robert Stiepock and my editors, Yvette Beau and Ehren Schimmel, whose professional expertise and input was invaluable in the revision process. Thank you also to Judi Scott who provided editorial guidance with the initial draft and formulation of the discussion questions at the end of the book. Thank you to Forrest Sklar, Carolyn Hansen, and David Christener for reading and critiquing my manuscript and providing valuable and enthusiastic feedback.

Petey

My sister Maggie told me that we can sit on the clouds. Wouldn't it be perfect to be able to sit on those cotton puffs and drift away from the problems of the world? I believed anything Maggie said. I believed her when she said that footprints in the moist sand by our house came from Indians in the woods. I believed her when she said the gooey sap dripping from the sweet gum trees was unsweetened molasses. I believed her when she said that she had stopped seeing Jimmy Makowski.

I had long discarded most of Maggie's imaginative tales — that summer I turned thirteen. Little bumps were budding on my chest while Maggie, at fifteen, wore a 34C bra, had long, wavy blonde hair, a Pepsodent smile, and hips that swayed in her white shorts. We had just moved to the Village, a low-income housing complex of duplexes, small cape and ranch houses. My father said it was only temporary, just until the latest layoff at the loading docks was over. Mom took a job at the town newspaper office.

There were five of us, all girls. Maggie, the oldest, was the only one not given the name of Our Blessed Mother. She was named Margaret Eleanor. Mom liked St. Margaret, and gave her a middle name after her deceased mother, Eleanor. They didn't even have a girl's name picked out for me because Dad was sure I was going to be a boy. I was supposed to be Peter, named after St. Peter's Church where we went every Sunday for Mass. When they saw I was a girl, they gave me my grandmother's name, Agnes, with the middle name of Mary. But everyone calls me Petey. My three younger sisters were Genevieve Marie, nicknamed Genny, Mary Louise, and Clare Maria, the preemie, who was still small for five.

I tried my best to be a boy by playing ball with the guys, riding my bike, and climbing trees. My one female vanity was my hair. I keep it in a ponytail or braids during the day, but before bedtime, Maggie sits on the edge of my bed and brushes it while we talk. It's our nightly sister ritual. Maggie is the one who braids my hair, intertwining colored ribbons into the long wavy chestnut strands. She taught me how to play jacks and jump rope. She held my hand and walked me to school the first day. Her homemade chocolate chip cookies are the best ever. She's the big sister everyone adores and will always be my best friend.

The new neighborhood swarmed with kids. Maggie and I put flyers in mailboxes offering babysitting service for thirty five cents an hour. We figured if we undercut the going rate of fifty cents an hour we'd get more business. The phone rang constantly. We worked almost every night that summer. On Thursdays we walked together to separate jobs on Oak Street. Maggie sat for the Ganesh girls who liked to read and do their homework, politely say goodnight, and go to bed. She'd watch television and munch on freshly bought pastries. I, on the other hand, had to rein in the four little Lopez monsters. The last time I babysat them, the two oldest were rolling on the ground clawing at each other and I had to spray the hose on them to get them to stop. I bathed the mud-covered scrappers while the other two brothers raced around the house screaming. By the time I got them all to bed, I was exhausted.

It was on one of those Thursday nights that I first noticed the guys following us.

"Who are those boys Maggie?" I asked. Maggie glanced at the two boys a few yards behind us, and flashed a smile. I poked her and she turned back around.

"So? Who are they?" I asked again.

Maggie shrugged indifferently. "I don't know. Don't they play ball with you or something?"

I leaned towards her and whispered, "Those guys are older. One of them even has a mustache." I glared back at them, trying to scare them off. "I don't like them following us."

Maggie pulled my arm and locked elbows with me. "Just ignore them. That's what I usually do."

As I said goodbye to Maggie entering the Ganesh walkway, I noticed our followers had stopped at the corner. It became a regular thing, boys following Maggie, although not always the same ones. There seemed to be an underground network of boys passing the word around about where Maggie babysat each night. Something about it gave me the creeps, but it didn't seem to bother Maggie.

With the babysitting money we made, Maggie and I sometimes would take the city bus to the beach. The summer of '63 was a hot one. Our nickels plinked in the bus coin collector. The driver pulled the handle to shut the door behind us, and we grabbed the bars to keep from falling over as we stumbled down the aisle. Our shorts stuck to the vinyl seats. Mom had lectured us about talking to strangers, but Maggie smiled at everyone, and people were always smiling back, even the old and grumpy-looking passengers. Sometimes Maggie would say "Hi" and answer their questions. I'd poke her with my elbow, but she didn't pay any attention to me.

The bus dropped us off at the beach entrance, where we showed our passes. Our flip-flops smacked on the hot asphalt parking lot as we made our way to the boardwalk. There it was. The ocean! I longed for the cool water to engulf me, making me feel carefree and alive. Pulling off my flip-flops, I jumped onto the sand and ran as fast as I could, leaving Maggie to pick out our beach spot. I paused briefly at the waters' edge, took a deep breath, and plunged in. My arms pulled hard amid the waves as I swam to the raft. Pulling myself up the ladder, I sat alone on top of the bobbling wet planks. I marveled at the deep blue all around, the hazy shimmer in the distance, and the sun-sparkled ripples. Wasn't God more present here than at church? I licked the salt on my lips and threw my head back, staring into the sky. A large wave jostled the raft and my stomach churned. Time to take a breath, dive back in, and head to shore.

Unsnapping the strap of my swim cap, I gingerly stepped onto the pebbled shore. I saw our blanket spread out, about fifteen feet above the water line. Shielding my eyes with my hand, I scanned the beachfront, looking for Maggie. Then I heard her laugh. With her toes burrowing into the sand, she stood next to a tall, tanned lifeguard at chair #4. His legs were spread wide, his whistle hung low on his sun-bleached chest. I dropped onto the beach towel and rolled onto my stomach, shading my eyes to look up at them. She was smiling at him, and nodding her head. I tried to get her attention, but her eyes never left his. Soon, it would be time to go home and she hadn't even gone in the water with me. As the sun lowered, I angrily stuffed our towels into the beach bag. She sprinted back to the blanket, all smiles. I shoved the beach bag at her.

"What are you doing talking to the lifeguard?"

She set down the beach bag, hands on her hips. "What's your problem, Petey? We were just talking."

"You never even went in the water."

Maggie shrugged. "Next time."

Summer was almost over. Didn't she know that? I glared at her. "Pick up the other end of the blanket, Maggie."

She took the other blanket end and we shook it lightly. I looked at Maggie and said, "He looks awfully grown-up to me. Does he go to Gravor High?"

"No", she countered quickly. "He's in college. A senior."

I dropped the blanket. "A senior in college! Jeez, Mags. He's old! What would Dad say? He doesn't even want you going out with guys until you're sixteen."

Maggie lifted up the blanket. "Oh, for heaven's sakes, I was just talking to him. That's all. And he's not old. He's twenty-one."

My mouth dropped open. "Twenty-one!" I shouted.

"Ssshhh, he's coming over." We finished shaking and folding the blanket as the lifeguard approached. He seemed even bigger up close. I tried not to stare at his muscles. Maggie looked like she was in some kind of trance. I wanted to clip her aside of the head like Mom sometimes did when we were doping off and not listening to her. Instead I poked her with my elbow till she said, "Oh, this is Petey, my sister."

He looked at me and said, "Hi. You're a good swimmer, kid. I was watching you out there."

I tucked the blanket under my arm. "We gotta go. Our parents are expecting us home soon." Digging my heels into the sand, I trudged forward, glancing back as I went. They stood across from each other, their faces almost touching. I shouted, "Hey, c'mon Maggie!" She ran to catch up, waving back at him. He flashed a smile and yelled out "I'll call you!"

I kept my face turned to the window all the way home. Why couldn't she have just gone swimming with me instead of hanging around some guy? Twenty-one was old, all right.

After supper, I noticed that Maggie ran to the phone every time it rang, but Dad and Mom didn't seem to notice. Dad had his feet up on the hassock, listening to the baseball game. Since the layoff, a friend got him a painting job. It was hard work but not as exhausting as loading and unloading crates at the dock warehouse. On those days he stripped off his grimy work clothes and took long soaks in the tub to soothe his aching muscles. I wondered how much longer the layoff would last. The last time this happened, the car had been repossessed. We did get another one, an old Plymouth station wagon. There was a slight dent in the side and it made a strange "shushing" sound like it was telling us all to be quiet. Mom joked that the car must be possessed by St. Frances de Sales, who counseled silence. Dad started calling the car "Frank." When the phone rang at ten o'clock, Mom, Dad, and my younger sisters were already in bed. Maggie jumped up and ran to the phone.

Dad yelled out from the bedroom, "Who's calling at this hour?"

"It's just a friend, Dad."

"Maggie" he called out from the bedroom, "I've told you before not to have your friends call this late at night."

"Yes, Daddy." Her tone was sweet and compliant as always, but the whispered phone conversation went on long after I heard my father snoring. It was him, the lifeguard. I was sure of it. I pretended to be asleep when she finally came to bed.

"Petey, I know you're awake. Why don't you sit up and let me brush your hair?"

I rolled over to face the wall. "Maybe I'm too tired tonight."

"Oh, come on. Don't pout. You know you like me brushing your hair. 'Sides, we haven't talked much tonight."

I pounded my pillow. "How could we? You've been on the phone all night."

"C'mon," she pleaded, leaning over to kiss my cheek.

Reluctantly, I sat up and flipped my hair over my shoulders. Maggie began pulling the brush through my thick tangles and chatting in her usual perky way. "It was Jimmy, the lifeguard. He's *so* nice. He can really talk, you know, about all kinds of things. Not like those dorky boys in school with me. She hesitated, then added, "He asked me out."

I spun around and looked at her. "He what?"

"He's a really nice guy, and I think he's ..."

"Dad will never allow it and you know it."

"Well, it won't really be a date, ya know. We'll meet at the beach and then get some ice cream after he gets off work." Maggie gently turned me around and continued brushing. "What do you do to get your hair in such a mess?"

I shrugged. What was so special about this guy? Beach days were for family, not boyfriends.

"Tomorrow is Sunday," I said. "We're all going to church. It's supposed to be hot, and Dad said he might take us all to the beach."

She brushed harder. "Maybe Dad can meet him then. He'll see how nice Jimmy is and let me go out with him."

"Fat chance."

She set the brush on the night stand. "It will all work out. You'll see."

I slumped back onto the bed. "Turn off the light. I'm ready to go to sleep."

"Okay. Your hair sure is pretty, Petey. You should wear it down more often."

I pulled up the covers, turned stone-faced towards the wall, and mumbled, "It gets in the way when I play ball."

"How about I clip it back with some barrettes?"

I ignored her and instead silently counted the miniature rosebuds on the wallpaper. It worked better than counting imaginary sheep.

Maggie sighed. "Well, good night, sleep tight, and don't let the bed-bugs bite."

I clutched the sheet tightly, pulling it around my neck, letting my hair fall into my face. Within minutes I could hear Maggie's soft snoring as I counted my two hundredth rosebud.

Maggie

From the time I was little, I'd run to the door as soon as I heard Daddy's car pull up in front of the house so I could be the first one there. He'd kiss me on the cheek and say, "How's my Sunshine?" Petey got her usual big rough bear hug. Genny would squeal when he tossed her into the air. Daddy calls her "Genny-Bug." About the only time she sits still is when she's plopped in front of the TV. He would tousle Mary's thick curls. Daddy nicknamed her "Mop-Top." Even after Mom brushed Mary's hair, the curls had a mind of their own and would spring out in all directions. Then of course, there was Clare. She was Daddy's "Little One." Most evenings you could find her curled up on my father's lap, until it was time for bed when he would hand her over to me. I bathed her and helped brush her teeth, before reading bedtime stories. Fairy tales are her favorite, especially Cinderella, which I've read hundreds of times. But she likes my made up fairy tales the best. Mom says I get my gift of story-telling from Dad. I remember him telling me lots of stories when I was Clare's age. Now I tell some of the same stories to my sisters.

When Daddy came home from work today, I thought about telling him about Jimmy, but he was in a grumpy mood. He snapped at Mary when she spilled her milk at the table. I guess this work layoff is getting to him. Besides, I'm not sixteen yet. For ages now he's been telling me that I have to be sixteen before I can date. Guys call a lot, but most are just pests. I did kind of like talking to Russ Bersconi, but for some reason Dad axed that friendship when he learned what his name was. Jimmy is different. I can't wait to see him again. Petey says that Dad won't let me date Jimmy even after my birthday 'cause he's twenty-one. I hope she's wrong. Daddy can be kind of strict sometimes though. I remember the first time he saw me wearing lipstick. I was thirteen.

"Maggie, is that lipstick on your mouth?"

"Just a little Daddy."

"Take it off." Dad had that menacing glare that made me hesitate to argue.

"But, Daddy, all my friends. . ."

"I don't care about what your friends do. I said, Take it off!"

"*Daddy, please...*"

His eyes softened. "Maybe next year, when you're in high school."

"But ..."

"Next year, Sunshine. You'll grow up fast enough."

He kept his word. As soon as I started high school, he bought me a tube of pink lipstick. I have others now too, but the "Pretty in Pink" from Daddy is still my favorite. It might take a little pleading, but as soon as I turn sixteen, I'm going to have Jimmy come over. Daddy will love him. He's *so* mature. And smart too. Daddy talks all the time about how important it is to go to college. He didn't go but he reads a lot and Mom always says that he's the smartest man she knows. I can just picture him and Jimmy sitting on the front porch talking about all kinds of things. I'll have to ask Jimmy what ball team he roots for. I hope it's the Red Sox. Oh, God, what will I do if he likes the Yankees? No, he isn't a Yankee fan. I'm sure of it.

Jimmy is lifeguarding tomorrow so I've already hinted to Daddy that Sunday is going to be a perfect beach day. He said maybe we would go after church. I wish Daddy would let me buy one of those new bikinis, but I guess I still look good in my blue checkered two piece.

I can't wait 'til tomorrow.

Petey

Looking back, I wish I could erase that Sunday when it all started. It proves that days that start out bright and sunny don't necessarily end that way.

Mom was getting the younger kids ready for church and hollering at Maggie and me to get moving. There was only one bathroom, so sometimes I had to sit outside and wait for it to be free. My stomach was rumbling, but we couldn't eat before Mass. I didn't want to drink water either, or I'd have to pee before Mass was over, and I hated climbing over everyone in the pew. Everyone knew where you were going. Criminy, what was taking Mags so long in the bathroom? When the door finally opened, Maggie stepped out in her slip, her hair swept up in a French twist, and she was wearing lipstick.

"It took you long enough." I snarled.

"I had to use a lot of bobby pins to get my hair just right. Do you like it?" She twirled around to show me the back of her head. It did look pretty, with a yellow bow ribbon artfully hiding the pins.

"It makes you look old, but it's nice, I guess."

Maggie smiled. "Thanks. Do you want me put your hair up? I have some matching ribbon for your hair."

I liked it when our hair ribbons matched but nature called. I pushed past her, slamming the door behind me.

"You didn't answer, Petey. Do you want me to put your ..."

"Maggie, for Chrissakes, I'm on the toilet. We have to leave in just a few minutes!" I snapped.

Mom knocked on the door. "Petey, I heard that. You know better than to use Our Lord's name in vain! And don't take too long in there. Others still have to use the bathroom."

"Yes, Mom." I flushed the toilet and pulled up my nylons, cursing under my breath. The slip strap kept falling down. The nylons itched like mad, and the garter belt straps pressed into my thighs. Why did I have to wear all this stuff? Maggie said I shouldn't complain because my legs looked great in nylons. Who'd be looking at my legs, anyway?

Church was always a big ordeal at the Donovan house. Dad would shine his shoes and pick out a tie. Mom would help Genny, Mary, and Clare get washed, dressed, and brush their hair. By 8:40, we were all in the car except Mom. The tip of Dad's large ears would turn red as he honked the horn and clenched the steering wheel.

"Damn. What's taking that woman so long? Doesn't she know all the parking spots will be taken?"

We'd all be as still and quiet as we could. Truth is, Mom left her preparation till last. But when she came out, wearing her Sunday finest with hat, gloves, and high-heeled shoes, she always looked gorgeous!

Sitting on St. Mary's side in the fifth row, we took up one full pew at church, just behind Mr. and Mrs. Zucchero and their twin little boys, Eddie and Dominic. Eddie spent most of the Mass kneeling on the pew seat staring at me. When his mother wasn't looking, he would stick his tongue out or make silly faces. I wanted to stick my tongue out at him, but the one time I did, Mom gave me such a dirty look that I learned to just ignore him.

This morning Monsignor Neelan was saying the Mass. He wore a gold cassock. A satiny white stole with red crosses on either end was draped around his neck. I didn't like his neck. It was thick like a bulldog's. A red cap sat on top of his pumpkin-shaped head. He raised the host:

"Behold the Lamb of God. Behold Him who takes away the sins of the world."

Voices responded in unison.

"Lord, I am not worthy to receive you, but only say the word, and my soul shall be healed."

Eyes remained riveted on the host as I tapped my chest with closed fist to the three chimes from the altar boys' bells. Parishioners filed forward for communion. The repeated clunking of kneelers resounded throughout the church. Only Clare, who wouldn't make her First Communion until next year, remained in the pew. Maggie's black mantilla brushed my cheek as I stepped out into the aisle behind her. I had forgotten to wear my hat again so Mom had clipped a tissue on my head with one of her bobby pins. My tongue quivered as I waited for Monsignor to place the host there with his thumb. Sucking in my cheeks to make saliva I swallowed the tasteless wafer, made the sign of the cross, and proceeded back to the pew. I never knew how long to kneel saying my post-communion prayers. Maggie seemed to kneel forever, so I didn't try to outlast her. Besides, Clare was fidgety by then, and I would draw her attention to the colorful pictures in her children's missal. Sometimes we would color together in a coloring book, even though Maggie said it was sacrilegious to be coloring Mickey Mouse in church.

After Mass, we went to the church hall for doughnuts. Dad stood near the exit, sipping his coffee. He tucked a napkin into the top of Clare's dress and handed her a jelly doughnut. Genny and Mary stood by Mom as she chatted with friends. I scratched the back of my leg. Damn nylons. Fifteen minutes. That was all the time Dad allotted Mom to socialize before giving her the signal. We could then head home, and I could change my clothes.

We must have used up at least five of those minutes when Monsignor Neelan approached Maggie who was standing with a group of friends. The girls parted to let him enter the circle. He smiled directly at Maggie and said, "You're looking lovely, as usual, Margaret." He was good at remembering everyone's name. Mom said that her father and Monsignor Neelan had been high school friends, so they went way back.

I asked her once why Gramps never mentioned Monsignor Neelan, but all she said was that her father wouldn't ever talk about him, and she didn't know why. Sometimes Mom invited Monsignor Neelan over for dinner, but he hadn't been to our house since we'd moved to the projects. I was just as glad. Mom gushed over him, like he was God or something. And he kissed us right on the mouth! Yuck! I didn't even kiss my parents on the mouth. I always wiped it off right away. Once I complained about it to Mom. But she only said, "Oh, that's just his way."

I spotted the red cap now coming towards us.

"Good morning, John." He extended his hand to my father.

"Morning, Monsignor." I could see my father's jaw tighten.

"Agnes, you're growing up fast." He patted my head. "Where is your mother? I'll have to weasel an invitation to come over for one of her delicious pot roast dinners. It's been awhile."

Dad responded and nodded toward my mother. "She's talking to Mrs. MacDonald, Monsignor."

Monsignor Neelan looked across the room. "Oh, yes, I see her now." He turned back to us. "How's that jelly doughnut?" He bent down to pinch Clare's cheek before walking over to my mother. A big blob of jelly squirted onto Clare's dress as the Monsignor walked away.

I clucked my tongue. "Jeez, Clare, look at you!"

Dad was getting impatient. "Go clean her up, and on your way, get your mother's attention. Let her know that I'm ready to go."

As I scooped off some of the jelly and licked my fingers, I asked, "Dad, can we go to the beach when we get home?"

"We'll see. I promised to finish up that painting job later this afternoon, so if we go it'll have to be short. Now get Clare washed up and then find your mother."

I took Clare by the hand and weaved through the jabbering crowd.

Mom stood in a circle of women. She turned immediately when I tapped her on the shoulder and spotting Clare's mess exclaimed, "Oh, my, what happened?"

"Jelly doughnut. Dad says he wants to go."

"Okay, okay. Tell him I'll be there in a minute." She reached into her pocketbook, pulled out a few tissues. "Here, get some water to clean her up." She turned back to her friends, and I caught the end of her laughter as I ducked under some guy's arm and headed to the water fountain.

Dad was corralling the younger girls into the car when Mom and Maggie showed up. Mary and Genny immediately started to fight over who would sit next to Maggie. I rolled my eyes in exasperation. "Just sit, for Chrissakes!"

"Petey, what did I tell you about your language!"

"Yes, Mom."

"It's okay, Petey. I'll sit in the middle." Maggie climbed in the back, and Mary and Genny sat on either side. Clare curled up on Maggie's lap. Mom squeezed next to Dad up front to make room for me. I rolled down the car window, staring into the heat-filled haze, thinking how delicious the ocean water would feel. Soon I heard giggles from the back seat. Maggie was teaching them some new tongue twisters. Dad began to chuckle at Clare's efforts to get all the words out. He then repeated the words very slowly for her to say after him, "How much wood would a woodchuck chuck if a woodchuck could chuck wood?" We all clapped when she finally got it.

After fixing a big breakfast of scrambled eggs and bacon, Mom got busy making sandwiches and giving everyone orders about what to pack for the beach. I helped Clare find her flip-flops.

"I think I saw them sitting by the bathtub, Clare." Genny yelled over while stuffing towels into the beach bag.

The bathroom door was shut except for a slight crack. The phone cord stretched under the door to the phone sitting on the hall floor. "Maggie, is that you? We need to get in the bathroom. C'mon." I knocked on the door.

"I'll be just a minute."

"You don't have to be in the bathroom to use the phone! Clare needs her flip-flops."

The door opened slightly and two pink flip-flops came flying out.

"And her sand bucket."

She set the sand bucket out and closed the door again.

"You better hurry up, Mags. We're going to leave in a few minutes."

"All right, all right. Hold your horses, Petey."

As we squeezed into the back seat of the car with Genny and Mary, I whispered to Maggie, "Who were you talking to?"

She gave me a big smile and whispered back. "Jimmy is on duty today at the beach."

I looked up at Dad. He was busy talking to Mom.

"You have to tell Dad about him."

She shrugged. "Sometime."

I gave her a stern look and whispered firmly. "Today!"

Mom turned around. "What are you two arguing about?"

"Nothing Mom." I said.

"You just came from church. You know better than to argue." Mom chided.

"Yes, Mom," we both replied as I elbowed Maggie and repeated, "Today!" She just stared out the passenger window.

Dad pulled into the parking lot, and everyone grabbed something to carry. We always placed our beach blanket just a few feet from the water. I was anxious to swim, but helped with the set-up first. Maggie peered down the beach. Jimmy was on duty, not in the nearest chair this time, but further down. Maggie turned to my father.

"Dad, can I take a walk over to the jetty?"

Dad questioned her, "By yourself?"

"Yeah, I don't feel like going in yet."

"All right, but don't be too long. Your mother packed sandwiches for all of us, and we're going to eat soon."

"Okay, Daddy."

I watched her stroll down the beach, hoping my father was watching too. But Genny and Mary were busy pulling him toward the water. They loved to stand on his shoulders and jump into the ocean. All the Donovans were real fish. Mom had taught all of us to swim. This summer she'd been giving Clare lessons.

I wanted to tug on my father's arm and point down the beach, but I wasn't a tattletale. As I suspected, Maggie didn't walk to the rock jetty.

Instead, she stopped at lifeguard chair #2. I was the only one who noticed how long she was gone. She barely got back when Dad announced it was time to go. I didn't want to leave. We'd been here less than two hours, only enough time for one swim and lunch. As I started rolling up the beach towels to stuff into one of the beach bags, I heard Maggie pleading with our father.

"Daddy, it's such a gorgeous beach day. Can't Petey and I stay for the full afternoon? There's a late bus that we can catch."

"Your mother will need help with supper," he replied.

Maggie turned and begged Mom.

"Oh, let them stay John. I'm just going to cook hot dogs and beans, since you're heading off to work soon anyway. There's only one more week before the start of school. Let them enjoy the last days of summer."

Dad hesitated but finally acquiesced. "I guess it's okay. Remember, you two stick together. Even though you're both good swimmers, I don't want one of you going in without the other. Got it?"

"Yes, Daddy." Maggie smiled and gave him a big hug.

After they left, I jumped up from the beach blanket, beaming. "Let's swim to the raft! I bet I can beat you!"

"Maybe later, Petey." Maggie reached into the beach bag and pulled out a hairbrush. Head thrown back, she brushed gently.

I put my hands on my hips and exhaled. "Puuh -You haven't even been in the water yet! What are you waiting for?"

"I *said, maybe* later. I'm going up to the boardwalk to get an ice cream. Wanna come?"

"I didn't bring any money. I'd rather go in the water." I said pouting.

Maggie responded, "You don't need any money. Jimmy said he'd treat."

"Jimmy?"

"Yeah, he's off duty in fifteen minutes and said he'd buy us an ice cream."

"Margaret Donovan! That's why you begged to stay! What about me? I want to enjoy the beach, not hang around some old lifeguard."

She tossed her hairbrush back in the bag, stood up, and snapped, "He's *not* old. Suit yourself. I'm going to have chocolate chip on a sugar cone."

With my palm over my eyebrows, I squinted at her as she walked away. Maggie's painted toenails crisscrossed the sand, her long hair bouncing with each step. She tugged at the bottom of her bathing suit and began to jog as Jimmy came closer. I turned around and ran toward the water only to remember my father's words. Damn it. Now I was stuck on the beach blanket until she got back. Ice cream sure sounded good but I wouldn't chase after her.

On the bus ride home Maggie talked non-stop Jimmy. I told her I didn't want to hear it. She just smiled and said, "Okay, Miss Prissy. In another year when some hot guy catches your eye, you'll understand."

"Don't think so."

"Did you take another swim?"

"Couldn't. Dad said we had to be together, 'member?"

"Oh, right. Sorry. You 'coulda come for ice cream. They even had your favorite — butter pecan."

I began to salivate. "Maybe there's some in the freezer at home."

"Naw, Dad finished it up last night."

"Shoot." I crossed my arms and stuck out my lip.

"Stop sulking. Here's our stop. C'mon." She stood up to pull the cord, and I followed her down the steps, hoping to never hear the name Jimmy again.

Maggie

There was a tug on my blanket. I rolled over and opened one eye. "Maggie?" Clare was standing next to my bed rubbing her eyes, clutching her purple stuffed bear.

"Mypurba can't sleep again?" I asked. Clare's head bobbed up and down. In toddler language, "my purple bear" had become "mypurba." I flipped the blanket over to let her crawl in. The stuffed bear now had only one eye, a stitched- up left ear, and a thread- bare belly. "Did you have another bad dream?" I asked. She wiggled up against me, the bear between us. "Do you want to talk about it, Clare?"

Her blond ringlets brushed my chin as she lifted her head to answer. "A big man was watching me. He was eating a jelly doughnut, and he kept coming closer and closer, and then..."

She dropped her head and squeezed her bear. "And then what, Clare?"

"The jelly squeezed out. It was all over me and I was all purple, just like mupurba."

I stifled a laugh. "Hmm. No jelly here. Just you, me, and Mypurba." I kissed the top of her head, smelling the lingering scent of Johnson's baby shampoo.

"Can you sing to me, Maggie?"

"Okay, but not too loud. We don't want to wake Petey." She nuzzled closer and I began to sing. "Hush, little baby, don't say a word, Papa's going to buy you a mockingbird." Puffs of warm breath tickled my neck, as her breathing slowed. I stopped singing, watching her chest rise and fall. Light filtered through the curtains as the trill of a songbird broke the silence. I lay awake listening to the melody. Could it be? Yes, it was a mockingbird! Mom loved mockingbirds. She said they were God's morning gift.

Dawn is my favorite time of day. Everything seems new and fresh. I'm headed back to school today. My books are sitting in a stack on the floor. Chemistry will be tough, especially if I have Sister Paula Marie. Everyone says she's a tyrant. She sometimes strides down the halls at school, towering over everyone, never smiling — the total opposite of Sister Marian, whom I adore. I hope I have her again for English. She made the romantic poets of the Elizabethan era come alive. How can anyone not like the beautiful poem about Genevieve by Coleridge? Sometimes I try to write poetry but I never seem to find just the right words. If I were to write a poem about Jimmy, how would it start? My darling love? It would be heavenly to spend the day sitting in the sunshine with a pad of paper clutched to my chest dreaming of him and finding those words. Instead I'll be doing Algebraic equations and looking at Chemistry formulas. Ugh.

Clare's head bumped my chin as she stirred. Ah, to be five again. Fingering one of Clare's ringlets, I whispered "Enjoy kindergarten, little one." Lifting her arm from around my waist, I slid out of bed and headed to the shower, just as the alarm blared, and Petey's hand slammed down on the clock.

Thank goodness the water was hot this morning. Piling my hair on top of my head, I poured on the shampoo and lathered my hair. Would Jimmy meet me after school? He said he might. I wished I could wear my indigo sweater -- the one that everyone says matches my eyes. Instead it's our school uniform, the plaid skirt, white button down blouse, and ugly gray wool blazer. Some of the girls roll the tops of their skirts up to make them shorter. Why bother? You always get caught by one of the nuns when they take out their rulers to check skirt lengths.

Petey was banging on the bathroom door. "Hurry up. I gotta go!"

"Okay, hold your horses." Turning off the water, I wrapped a towel around me and opened the door. "Morning, Petey." She pushed past me and slammed the door.

Downstairs I heard the familiar shuffle of Mom's scruffy slippers on the kitchen floor followed by the clanking of the coffee pot and water gushing from the faucet. Mom was starting Dad's breakfast and making our sandwiches. I hope she remembered that I liked mayonnaise, not mustard. Or maybe she'd fix my favorite, peanut butter and fluff.

Clare was now awake and sat watching us get dressed. Petey pulled her wet hair into a ponytail and dashed downstairs for breakfast. I sat under the hair dryer until it was dry enough to flip into a pageboy like I'd seen on television. I held up two small flower hairclips. "What do you think, Clare? Red or pink?"

Hopping off the bed, still holding her bear, Clare replied emphatically, "Red."

"And lipstick?"

Our eyes locked in the dresser mirror. "Pink," she said.

Clare toddled after me down the stairs. Mom handed me a glass of juice and some toast. I sprinkled some sugar and cinnamon on it.

Petey yelled from the door, "Maggie, hurry up. We're going to miss the bus."

"Just a minute!" There was no need to rush. The bus was usually late. I grabbed my stack of textbooks, dropped the toast on top, and took a swig of juice. I thanked Mom as she handed me my lunch.

She gave me a quick kiss on the cheek. "Have a good first day, Maggie. And keep an eye on your sister. First day of high school is a big day for her."

I gave a quick kiss and hug in return, smelling her rose-scented lotion. "She'll do fine. You know Petey, Mom. She's always the brain of the class."

Mom crossed her arms, her eyebrows furrowed. "I know she's smart, but socially...I still wonder if we did the right thing having her skip a grade. She's ... Clare, stop pulling on me, what is it?"

Clare stood tuggi___ at ___ ___bathrobe, ___ I can't find Mypurba."

Leaning over my ___ pile of ___, ___ ___ a tear from Clare's cheek. "You left him in my ___ La___ nie ___

I turned to go b___ ___ ___ ___ that wo___rried look on her face. "Gotta catch the bus, Mor___ ___ ___eat___

"Just. . .take c___ ___ ___ ___ ___

"Like I said, Mom, sn___ ___ ___ fine." I ___adn't really thought much about Petey. High school can be rather intimidating that first year. I wondered if she'd have Sister Dragontooth. Of course that wasn't her real name, but no one could help staring at her. She had this one extra-long bucktooth that stuck out over her bottom lip. It gave her a bad lisp. Thank goodness she taught Algebra, where she did more writing of equations than talking.

Petey was already down the street waiting on the corner for the bus. Taking the city bus was new for her. For eight years she walked to St. Peter's Elementary School.

"Hey, Petey, you look nice in your uniform."

"I guess. Better than the blue jumper. What took you so long?"

"It's only seven-fifteen. The bus doesn't come for another five minutes."

"Cutting it close, as usual, *Maggie*."

"Worrying as usual, *Petey*. I took the bus for two years, and it never came early. Don't sweat it." I pulled out a lipstick tube from my blazer pocket for a retouch and asked if she wanted some.

Petey dismissed the question. "You know I don't use that stuff." She pulled a folded piece of paper out from one of her books. "What's this on my schedule? EC Specials? I thought I had Biology fourth period?"

I looked at the list of Petey's courses and her daily schedule. "Oh, yeah, EC-Specials." I explained that was only for the first day. "They talk to you about all the extra-curricular activities you can join."

"Well, I have that babysitting job after school on Tuesday and Thursday. 'Sides, unless they have sports for girls, which I know they don't, I'm not interested."

I tried to think of a sport for girls at our school. "I think they may have started a girls' basketball club."

"Humph. They had that at St. Peter's. It was stupid. They had special girls' rules for basketball, where the guards had to stay in the back-court, and the forwards were the only ones who could shoot the ball. They weren't even allowed to dribble. Is that stupid or what? Nothing like the *real* game of basketball. *And* I had to wear these really dopey gym uniforms, with skirts."

"Oh, yeah, I think I remember those. They *were* dopey! There's other cool clubs though."

"Like what?"

"Well, I'm in the Sodality Club."

"The *what* club?"

"It's a devotional club of girls dedicated to praying to Our Blessed Mother. Last year we made rosary beads and scapulars and delivered them to nursing homes. We always have Kool-Aid and cookies and stuff, and you know, just hang out. Sister Alfred is our club director. She's kind of old, but nice. We do all the planning for the Coronation of Our Blessed Mother in May. The whole school comes out to watch. And one girl from the Junior Class is chosen to be May Queen to crown our Blessed Mother. Wouldn't it be wonderful if it were *me* this year, Petey?"

I envisioned myself climbing the stairs to the statue of the Blessed Virgin out in the center courtyard, setting a crown of flowers on her head while everyone watched.

The bus pulled up. The doors folded open. "Hi, Mr. Benson."

He flashed a broad grin and said, "Hey, Maggie. Who's this?"

"My sister, Petey."

Nodding, Mr. Benson said, "First day?"

"Yup. She's a freshman." I stepped up and Petey followed.

The doors swung shut and we grabbed the bar overhead as the bus lurched forward. I pressed my chin on the top book to keep the stack from falling onto the floor and slid into the first available seat.

Petey was staring at me. "Why did you lie?"

"What? What are you talking about?"

"I heard you talking to Dad last night. You didn't tell him about Jimmy."

"What are you talking about? I didn't lie."

Petey shifted her books again and turned towards me with that same grimace she gave Mary and Genny when she scolded them. "Dad asked about the phone call. You told him it was one of your friends. I *know* it was Jimmy."

"So? That's not lying. Jimmy is my friend. I just didn't tell him it was my boyfriend."

"Boyfriend!"

I unzipped the inner pocket of my handbag to return the lipstick and pushed the top book of my stack back in place. "Well, not really my boyfriend yet, but I think he will be. He said he might swing by after school. Do you think you could manage to catch the bus yourself on the first day?" I looked over at my sister. "Don't look at me like that, Petey Donovan! You're as bad as Sister Paula Marie. I haven't committed a mortal sin, you know."

"Not yet." Petey slammed her books on the floor, placing her feet on top.

"What's that supposed to mean? I know right from wrong, Petey. I haven't done anything wrong."

"And what am I supposed to tell Mom when I get home? That you're cruising the countryside with your new *boyfriend*?"

"Don't be so sarcastic. You don't have to say anything. By the time you get home from your babysitting job, I'll be home. She won't know that I'm late."

"I'm not lying for you, Maggie."

"I didn't ask you to. Just don't mention Jimmy yet. I'll be sixteen in a few weeks, and then I'll remind Dad that he said I could date." Petey was still glaring at me. "Don't look like that! Please? You know I can't stand it when you're mad at me." Juggling my books, I reached for Petey's hand and gave it a squeeze. The bus brakes squealed as it came to a stop.

It should have been a perfect day. Seeing my old friends, thinking about Jimmy, checking out new teachers, but Sister Paula Marie ruined everything. I'd hoped I wouldn't have her this year. But there she was, standing by the door of Room 101 with her ruler, measuring the skirt lengths. She grabbed my shoulder as I walked past.

"What's that I see on your face, Margaret Donovan?"

"What?" I said sheepishly.

"You know better than to wear eye make-up to school."

"But I'm not wearing eye make-up."

"Don't lie to me. Go to the girl's room and wash that dark eyebrow pencil off."

"But, Sister, I ..."

She turned me around and gave a shove. "Go."

I stood over the sink, not sure what to do. How could I wash off something that wasn't there? My eyebrows had always been dark, despite my blond hair. Maybe if I rubbed them with warm water, it would look like I had done something. Turning on the faucet, I cranked out a rough brown paper towel, and began scrubbing. A little pink tinge appeared around my brows. Maybe that would appease her. I returned to the classroom. Everyone had taken their seats, and Sister was passing out the Chemistry books.

"Margaret, you are in Row Three," she directed.

"Yes, Sister." I ducked into my seat, keeping my head down. I could hear the wooden rosary beads clicking against one another as she approached. The white habit brushed my shoulder, as the Chemistry book fell with a thud on my desk.

"Look at me, Margaret." I glanced up. "Just what I expected. Come with me." She pulled me to the front of the class. A lump thickened in my throat as I held back the tears. She opened a desk drawer and took out a bottle of hydrogen peroxide and a rough sponge. She scrubbed my eyebrows, as if trying to wipe spots off a dog. I winced but refused to cry. Finally she put down the sponge. "Humph. Go sit down, Margaret."

My eyes were stinging and my forehead throbbed. The Periodic Table in my book became a blur. My friend, Samantha, who sat behind me, patted my back sympathetically.

When the final bell rang, I rushed out the door, and hurried to my locker. Girls babbled as boys whipped off their sweaty blazers, shoved each other, and slammed lockers. The pungent odor of adolescent perspiration and wool filled the air. Pushing my way through the mass of red and gray, I fumbled with my lock.

"She sh-sh-sh- shouldn't do th-th-th-that. Not t-t-t to you, M-m-m-Maggie." Billy Jenkins was rocking on his toes, eyes hidden behind thick lenses, his acne-pocked face even redder than normal. In first grade I had let him show me his bug collection during recess, and in fifth grade I'd shared my history book with him when he'd left his at home. Ever since then, he'd been my shadow, one that I wanted to shake. Somehow I never had the heart to tell him to get lost, like everyone else did. Scooping the books from my locker, I turned and smiled.

"Thanks, Billy."

He continued to stare at me, even as Samantha's arm encircled my waist, pulling me away. "She's a witch, you know. Everyone says so." Our arms cradling thick textbooks, we walked out of the school. Holy Redeemer Academy stood atop a high hill, crested with barrel-chested oaks and vibrant maples. I blinked repeatedly in the bright sun, my eyes smarting. The statue of Our Blessed Mother stood in the center of the large brick courtyard. Samantha and I mumbled our requisite Hail Marys as we walked past her to the sidewalk. Petey was already waiting for me on the street corner. When Samantha finished telling her what had happened, Petey's face looked like an all-day sunburn.

"How could you let her do that, Maggie!"

"She's a nun, Petey. What was I supposed to do?"

"Tell her to go to hell, that's what I'd do!"

I shook my head at her. "No, you wouldn't."

"Yes, I would. You can't let her get away with this! C'mon, you gotta go home and tell Mom."

"I can't!"

"Why not? That witch needs to be reported."

"To who? She's a nun. Mom won't do anything. Just forget it." Ever self-righteous Petey. But I had to admit she always stood up for me. It's one of the things I loved about my sister.

We walked a full block before I saw him. Grinning at me with his arms folded, Jimmy was leaning against a green Chevy parked on the corner of Broad and Thames Streets.

"Hey, Maggie."

"Jimmy!"

Petey and Samantha hung back as I rushed to the car. He was here! I'd thought of nothing but him all day, wondering if he'd come. Without his bathing suit, he looked kind of different but still *really* handsome. A belt cinched his Bermuda shorts. The tied sleeves of his blue sweater hung loosely over his yellow shirt. His ankles were crossed and I could see hairs on his legs that curled like gold rings over his tan. I knew Samantha was watching, so I stopped a few feet in front of him, but his arm quickly reached out and pulled me forward. His touch dizzied me for a moment, so I didn't hear Samantha, who then repeated herself.

"I *said*, remember me?"

I turned around and apologetically made the introductions. "Sorry, Sam. This is Jimmy."

"The lifeguard?"

Jimmy smiled. "That's me. Sam, was it? Nice to meet you." He shook Samantha's hand, then encircled my waist and said, "Ready for a spin, Maggie?"

I hesitated for a moment as I caught Petey's gaping mouth and remembered Mom's words about watching out for my sister. "Sam, can you make sure Petey catches the right bus?"

Samantha grinned. "Sure. See you tomorrow. C'mon, Petey." She motioned for Petey to follow but my sister stood motionless on the sidewalk with eyebrows furrowed and mouth open, as if she'd just witnessed a traffic accident.

"Go on, Petey." I said. "I'll be home soon."

"But, but, what will I tell Mom?"

"Don't worry. I'll be home before Mom. Stay with Samantha." I watched Sam tug on Petey's arm and attempt to pull her away even as she stood there and continued to stare at us.

Jimmy opened the car door and I slid across the front seat. "Nice car, Jimmy."

"A friend sold it to me. It's eight years old but in mint condition." He looked at me with a quizzical expression. "Hey, you okay? You look like you've been crying or something."

I told him the whole story about Sister Paula Marie and the eyebrows.

"Has this nun picked on you before?"

"Well, sort of, but not this bad. It was *horrid*, everyone watching and...." Remembering made me teary-eyed again. I hung my head and started to turn towards the side window, but his arm reached over and touched my chin, bringing my eyes back to his.

"Yeah, and everyone knew that she was only making a fool of herself, not you."

"But why, why did she do it?"

He wiped away my tears with his thumb. I took a deep breath and exhaled.

"She's jealous," he said simply.

"Jealous?"

"Think about it a minute. I bet she only picks on the pretty girls, right?"

"Well, I don't know. She did pick on a couple of others that are pretty, yes."

"See. She's just jealous, and assumes that all you pretty girls are sluts, or worse."

"Jimmy!"

He was looking at me with those clear eyes, like blue shaved ice. "You're an angel, Maggie. Anyone who spends any time with you knows that. So you've got to just ignore this nun, and stay clear of her."

He turned the key in the ignition.

"How can I do that? She's my chemistry teacher."

"Are you good in science?"

"I do okay, but I've heard she's pretty tough." He turned to check for traffic, before pulling onto the road. There was a small mole on the back of his neck, just above his shirt collar. Would it be warm to the touch?

"I'll help you if you need it. I'm majoring in Bio-Chemistry."

"Really? What made you pick that major?"

He laughed. It was the kind of laugh that spread over you like a warm blanket.

"You'll probably think this is funny, but I got one of those chemistry kits for Christmas one year as a kid, and loved it. You know, the crazy kid that experiments with stuff in his parents' basement? That's me. Might even go into medicine someday."

"Be a doctor? Wow!"

He laughed again. "Maybe, but research interests me more. Dr. Salk is my hero."

"Who?"

"Dr. Jonas Salk. You know, the guy who invented the polio vaccine."

"Oh, right. My sister Genny has a scar from her vaccine."

"Small price to pay."

"Yeah, I know. There was a boy in my elementary school with polio. He had leg braces."

We were headed down Ocean Avenue. The beach parking lot was only a block away. He turned to me and asked, "You want to take a walk on the beach?"

I knew he wanted me to say yes, but it didn't seem right. Not yet. "I'd be kind of hot, in my uniform and all. And it's getting rather late."

"We'll just take a drive by the shoreline then." We took a left onto Shore Road, where we saw an occasional sand dune peeking up. The roar of the surf was so loud that Jimmy had to raise his voice. "So how about a movie this Saturday?"

"Um, that'd be nice, but…"

"But what?

"I can't really date yet."

"What do you mean? You've never gone out with a guy?"

I shook my head, and fiddled with the silver cross pendant at my neck. He swung the car to the right and parked on the side of the road. He was leaning against the door with one arm draped over the driver's seat, the other still on the steering wheel. "Move over, Maggie."

"Why?"

"You're too far away."

I edged closer to him. His warm fingers curled around the back of my neck, his thumb slowly rubbing up and down.

I lowered my head and began twisting the Claddagh ring on my finger. "You see, it's my Dad. He says I have to be sixteen before I date. But I'm *almost* sixteen."

"How soon is almost?"

"A couple of weeks."

"So? What's two weeks?" His thigh pressed against mine and I dared to look up.

"You don't know my Dad. He's an ex-Marine, kind of strict. Rules are rules, he says. You know." I fidgeted with the edge of my blazer, wanting to peel it off. How could I be so hot with the ocean breeze blowing through the open car window?

"Ex-marine, huh?"

"Yeah, but he's a sweetie, really. You'll see. I know he'll like you, but we've got to wait until my sixteenth birthday."

Brushing my hair behind my ear, he bent down and kissed me before I knew it. A soft, gentle kiss that made my heart pound. I wanted him to kiss me again but I was afraid. Would just one more be enough? I inhaled the musky scent of his after-shave, absorbed the warmth of his breath, desperately wanting to press my lips against his. Instead I moved back to my seat.

"We better get back. My mom will be home from work soon."

He put his hands back on the steering wheel, started the car, and then peeled out onto the road.

I bit my lip. He was quiet, his eyes straight ahead. Was he mad at me?

"You understand, don't you?"

His smile made me feel all marshmallowy inside. "Sure. I can wait."

When we drove up, Petey was just bringing my sisters into the house. Jimmy leaned over and gently touched my chin with his fingers. His lips were so warm. The second kiss was just as delicious as the first. "Tomorrow after school, same time? I want to see you as much as possible before classes start."

"Okay." I slammed the door and waved as he drove off. Petey was waiting for me on the front porch with her jaw clenched, her hand on her hip. She opened her mouth, but I cut her off.

"Don't start, Petey. It was just one quick kiss, that's all." But I knew there would be more, lots more. For the first time, guilt seeped in and I prayed that Petey would stay quiet.

Monsignor Neelan

He untied the purple fascia from around his waist, unbuttoned the black cassock and hung them in the oak wardrobe. Standing only in shorts and an undershirt, he surveyed his reflection. For sixty-two years his body had held up well. The weight room helped. And he always walked the golf course instead of riding a cart. So, despite his love of rich food and fine drink, he remained taut and trim. Maybe not the physical specimen he was as a high school star quarterback, but no middle-age paunch, no sagging underarms.

He stepped closer to the mirror and fingered the thinning hair. Thank goodness his biretta covered most of it. He detested his baldness, but remembered once being told that he looked like Yul Bryner. That pleased him. After putting on his shirt, he tied on the rabat which covered his chest and attached to the chafing Roman collar. Jutting his chin out, he slid a finger behind the starched collar and tugged. Why couldn't they make the damn things in a larger size? The creased black pants and jacket slid from the hangar. Finally he reached for the taffeta lined box on the shelf behind his desk. Carefully lifting out the biretta, he brushed the red tuft with his fingertips and blew on it to ensure there was no trace of dust. Unlike the cassock with its red piping and purple fascia, the clerical suit had nothing to distinguish his status. Only his biretta did that. Positioning it on top of his head, he gave himself one last approving look before leaving the rectory for the weekly Sunday visit to his mother.

He was late, which meant she would be in a foul mood. His mother expected punctuality. But it took time to make the rounds after Sunday Mass. He had to chat with the regulars, fuss over the ladies' Sunday finery, kiss the babies, shake hands and talk sports with the men. Greg Campbell kept him pinned at the door with his incessant complaining but given the amount of money the egotistical jerk put in the collection basket each Sunday he couldn't afford to dismiss him. Then there was the Ladies'Auxiliary President, Marian Fistner, who in her ever-solicitous manner, rattled on about how new altar linens needed to be purchased.

His black Cadillac pulled into the long boxwood lined driveway. Turning off the engine, he stared at his childhood home. The large, meticulously maintained house had been built over a hundred years ago. With a Rapunzel-like tower and large wrap-around porch, it was an impressive example of Victorian architecture. Last summer Mother had the roof shingled and the exterior painted, keeping the original pink and white colors. Before he even reached the top step, Mrs. McIntyre opened the door to greet him. With hands clasped over her ample stomach, she curtsied. Despite his efforts to explain that this was unnecessary, she continued to treat him like some sort of royalty.

"She's upstairs in her room, Monsignor. Would you like me to take your hat?"

He waved her outstretched hand away and replied. "Biretta. No thank you. How is she today, Bertha?"

"The same. Hard to know, really. You know how she is."

He nodded. How could you judge the seriousness of the woman's physical condition when every visit brought a litany of complaints? Abundant pillows propped up her frail body. Her snow white hair had been combed and twisted into the usual tight bun at the nape of her neck. Her eyes were closed and her mouth was slightly agape. His steps wakened her.

"Robert? Is that you?"

"Yes, Mother."

"Come closer, so I can see you. It's dark in here."

Instead, he turned to the large bay window and drew open the curtains. "It's a beautiful day, Mother. You should let the sunshine in."

She clucked, "What difference does it make? Rain or shine, I'm stuck in this bed."

"You know that's not true. I bought you a wheelchair and have offered to take you out whenever you want wherever you want."

"You think a ninety year old woman should be gadding about?"

"The doctor said it would be perfectly fine for you to go out. He advised it in fact."

She straightened up and tugged on the covers. "The doctor! Did you know that he's only in his thirties? You really think I should listen to someone who could be my grandson?"

He winced, surprised that the old woman would make that reference. Had she forgotten? His mother was both grieved and shamed when his unwed sister Betsy died giving birth prematurely. The baby, a boy, could not be saved. He was in Rome at the time, but rushed home as soon as he received the cable alerting him to the sad news. He had stood at his mother's side listening to the Bishop celebrate the Requiem Mass. Somehow ritual and memory had taken over and he was able to recite the prayers. The loss of Betsy had been a turning point for him. She was his only confidante, the only one who listened to him. Mother never mentioned his older sister or the grandson that died with her.

"You're late, Robert. Isn't your final Mass at eleven? Why should it be a problem to get here by two?"

"Mother, you know that there are a lot of people expecting my attention. It's hard to get away."

"Your mother expects some attention too."

He sighed. How many times had they had this conversation? "Greg Campbell asked after you." He attempted to divert her from perennial self-pity.

"I bet he did. He wants to know how soon he'll see me in my coffin. I haven't forgotten how rude he was to your Uncle Ned. He may have a lot of money, but the man has no class, none whatsoever." She paused to catch her breath. "Did anyone else ask about me?"

"Of course."

"Well, don't just stand there. Pull up a chair and tell me."

He sat in the overstuffed armchair and crossed his legs. Fingering the doily on the arm rest, he turned to his mother and replied, "All sorts of people. Would you like some coffee, Mother? I'll ring for Bertha."

She waved her hand in the air dismissively. "I've had enough coffee. Didn't she offer you some?"

"No, but I'll have my usual brandy, if you don't mind."

"Suit yourself. You know where it is."

He walked to the liquor cabinet, opened it, selected one of the snifters, and poured the brandy. "Rose Donovan asked after you."

"Who?" She straightened up in bed.

He set the bottle back and clicked the door shut. Turning around, he said, "Rose Donovan."

"The police chief's daughter?" She folded back the comforter, turning towards him. "Can't say as I remember her too well, but I remember Joe. Quiet sort, but he managed to make something of himself. Is he still a widower?"

"As far as I know. Haven't seen him in years." He swirled the brandy and took a sip. His mother was staring at him.

"It was for the best you know."

"That she died?"

"No, no. I didn't say that, Robert. I may not have liked Eleanor, but I never wished her dead."

He wasn't so sure. When he'd first told his mother about Eleanor, his mother's reaction was visceral. Called her a gold-digger who was only after his family's money. Never mind that Eleanor's family didn't need their money. With his mother it was always about money and prestige. Before he knew it, she'd arranged for him to go to Rome to spend the summer with Uncle Ned, a priest who worked at the Vatican.

Seeing his distress over the prospect of leaving Eleanor, Betsy had implored him to stay and do what he wanted. But he had never resisted his mother before and could not do so now. Once in Rome, he was introduced to a world he'd never seen before, a place where purple-cloaked men with gold crucifixes walked with impunity, comfort, and power. He wrote Eleanor a letter to tell him of his decision to enter the seminary. She wrote back to tell of her engagement to Joe Kelley. His course had been set. Eleanor was lost to him.

"And what do you hear from the bishop these days?"

He turned, shaking off his reverie. "What do you mean?"

"You know what I mean. Has he submitted your name to Archbishop Finnahan yet? My God, Robert, you're 62. You should be on your way to Rome by now. You're not even a bishop yet. Do you want me to call your Uncle Ned? Even in his retirement he has some pull."

"No, Mother. Don't call Uncle Ned."

Her eyebrows rose. "Don't be stupid, Robert. A little phone call can only help. I'll call tomorrow."

He jumped from the chair. "Mother, I said don't call Uncle Ned!"

She tsk-tsked in reply, "My, my, aren't we getting testy in our later years. Well, it's your life. Now, get Bertha for me. It's time for my medicine."

Obediently, he walked down the stairs. He knew that she'd call Uncle Ned despite his objections. But the bishop would not be sending his name to the archbishop's conclave. Not with the information in his file.

Petey

The leaves crunched under my footsteps as I stomped and muttered their names "Maggie and Jimmy." First she leaves me with her friend like I need babysitting or something. *She* was the one who was supposed to be with me at the bus stop. Now I have to walk to Mrs. Manoletti's house to pick up my sisters. She was supposed to do that too. Not to mention that Dad and Mom know nothing about this thing with Jimmy. It just isn't right. But I can't tattletale on her. I just can't. Maggie needs to end this. She doesn't need a boyfriend, especially not an old guy. Maybe I shouldn't worry about it, but *someone* had to.

Mrs. Manoletti was rocking on her front porch with her usual skein of yarn, knitting needles clicking and her glasses perched at the end of her nose. Clare sat at her feet looking at a book, while Genny and Mary jumped rope on the sidewalk. Clare was the first to see me.

"Where's Maggie?" she asked.

"She had to stay late. She'll be home soon," I answered, while smiling at Mrs. Manoletti.

She pouted, "But I wanted to show her my book."

Mrs. Manoletti patted her on the back. "You'll see Maggie soon. C'mon, give me a hug and go with Petey now."

The girls ran ahead of me into the house, which was a good thing because they didn't see *him* drive up in his fancy car, grinning like the Cheshire cat, and then kiss *my* sister! Before I could say anything Maggie jumped out of the car and ran inside. Clare was already chattering away and shoving a book in front of her face. I yelled at Genny and Mary to get started with their assigned chores, which were posted on the refrigerator.

When Mom got home I was peeling potatoes in the kitchen. I heard her greeting the little ones with hugs and kisses before entering the kitchen. Pecking me on the cheek she asked "Where's Maggie?"

I shrugged. "Upstairs, I guess."

"Did she vacuum the living room yet?"

"Yeah, I think so."

"Just let me take off these heels, and grab an apron and I'll help you."

I was a pretty speedy potato-peeler. Mom quartered them and dropped them in a pan of water after I passed them to her.

"So, tell me about your first day."

"It was okay. Mostly just learning the schedule and all." Then she asked about my courses, even though I'd already told her all that before.

Mom salted the water, reached in the cupboard for another pot and began opening a can of corn, while I finished the last of the potatoes. "You left some skin on this one," she said, passing me a potato. "You see any of your friends from St. Peter's there?"

"I sat with Sherlin Wang at lunch."

"How are they doing? I haven't spoken to Connie in a long time."

"They're moving soon."

"To a new house in town?"

"No, to New York."

"New York? After all they put into that restaurant? Moving after all these years. Wonder why."

"Yeah. It was kind of weird when I asked her about it."

"Weird?"

I shrugged. "I mean she didn't say why, or anything. She just said that it was a family decision, and wouldn't say any more."

"Hmm. I wonder if Monsignor Neelan knows about this. He was fairly close to the Wang family, Went over there for Sunday dinners sometimes, just like he comes here. He raved about Connie's dumplings. Don't they have five girls, just like us?"

I scooped the peels from the sink and nodded. "Sherlin is the third oldest."

"Well, maybe I'll talk to Monsignor about what the parish can do to help. Genny! Come set the table. It's your night." Genny needed constant reminding.

Mom bent down to get the frypan from the lower drawer. I saw a snag in her nylons. I knew she'd be mad about that. She was always complaining about how much her nylons cost and if they could send a man to the moon, why couldn't they make nylons that didn't run.

Since Mom was asking about friends, maybe this would be a good time to tell her about Barbara. She was going to Gravor High and was going to try out for the softball team.

"Mom, you remember my friend Barbara?"

"Who?"

"Barbara. We just got to be friends last year. She came over once."

"Barbara. Sorry, Petey, I don't seem to..."

Genny came running into the kitchen. "Mom, tell Mary to give me back my yoyo."

Mary appeared in the kitchen doorway, pressing a yellow and blue yoyo against her chest. "I had it first."

"Did not."

"Did too. Give it back." Genny reached for the yoyo, yanking at it as Mary pulled back. The string snapped in her hand. Mary yelled at Genny, "See what you did."

Mom sighed as she wiped her hands on her apron. "Give the yoyo to me girls. Genny, get started on the table, and Mary, get out your reader. You're supposed to read one chapter a night to me, remember? Petey, you've got dinner under control, right?"

"Yeah, I guess. What did you want me to do with the pork chops?" Why can't they ever give Mom a moment's peace or let me finish a conversation?

stories about the teachers at Holy Redeemer. My side began to ache from laughing. Finally, we knelt to say our prayers and crawled into our twin beds.

Through the curtains I could see the soft glow of a full moon. I'd always loved gazing at the moon. My earliest memory was a night that Mom and Dad stepped onto the porch to do just that. Mom held me in her arms while Dad lifted Maggie onto his shoulders. Mom pointed to the moon, and said "See the face on the moon." Then she rattled off a rhyme. "I see the moon, and the moon sees me. God bless the moon and God bless me." Mom and Dad both beamed and clapped when I repeated it. That's how I got my other nickname. Dad pinched my cheeks, and called me his little "Moonface." Now our President was talking about sending men to the moon. That didn't seem possible. I tried to imagine the moon as a place to walk. I knew it wasn't like earth, but what was it like? And would we ever really go there?   My mind resisted sleep. So much to think about.

I rolled over and looked at Maggie, who was already asleep, her breathing slow and steady. Her long blond hair swept over the pillow. Her dark eyebrows were perfectly arched, her full lips in a slight smile even in slumber. It had hurt to see her crying today because of that awful nun. She so rarely cried. When I thought of Maggie, I thought of smiles and laughter and imagination. Genny, Mary, and Clare all clamored for her to tell stories. The neighborhood kids came running when she joined us in play, knowing that she would come up with some imaginative new game. I was once told by a friend that it must be so cool having her as a big sister because being with Maggie was like having a party. Why did she want a boyfriend?

I dreamed of Jimmy that night. He was sitting in his lifeguard chair watching me. Where was Maggie? How come she wasn't there? I looked down the long expanse of empty beach. I was alone, except for the occasional seagull flying overhead. The sun's brilliance blinded the horizon. Instead of my usual sprint into the ocean, I entered slowly, one cautious step at a time. I looked back at Jimmy. One arm draped over the back of the chair, the other twirled his whistle. He smiled directly at me, as if to urge me forward. Once the water reached my chest, I dove in. Turning my face to the left in a crawl, salt water seeped over my lips. Then I switched to a breaststroke. I didn't see it coming, the wave that swallowed me. My body twisted and turned. A vacuum of water sucked me under. I called out to Maggie, but it was Jimmy who appeared. He was lifting me out of the water. Sputtering with my head resting in the crook of his arm, I blinked. Stretched out on the sand, I saw his face close to mine.

His breath was warm. "Are you okay, kid?"

Maggie

My birthday is tomorrow. Sixteen. The only thing that I really want for my birthday is for Dad to say that I can start dating Jimmy. That's all I can think about. Today is the day. I'll ask him at the breakfast table after church. With everyone there and my birthday coming up, he'll say yes for sure. Won't he?

I genuflected at the end of the pew and grabbed Clare's hand as we left the church. Dipping my hand into the holy water, I heard Dad whisper to Mom not to take long chatting with friends. He wanted to get home and finish breakfast before the Red Sox came on. He never missed a game. I didn't know who they were playing today, but Petey would. She and Dad always listened to the games together. We filed into the packed church hall. Genny and Mary dashed to the doughnuts while Mom immediately spotted Mrs. MacDonald. Monsignor Neelan eyed me from across the room and headed in my direction. Fortunately, Clare chose that moment to ask me to take her to the bathroom. I hadn't listened to a word of the sermon today. If he asked what I thought I'd have to lie. I hated lying.

Clare and I emerged from the bathroom to see Dad corralling everyone out to the parking lot. Petey, Genny, Mary and I squeezed into the back seat. Clare sat up front with Mom and Dad.

Mom turned and smiled at me. "Someone has a very special birthday tomorrow." I smiled back.

"You want your usual lemon cake with buttercream frosting?"

"Of course."

"I'll have to make it today, as I have to work late tomorrow and won't have time. Anyone want to help?"

"Me, me, me!" A chorus of voices responded. What they really wanted was to lick the bowl.

Mom glanced over her shoulder. "Maggie, do you know Kileen MacDonald?"

"Just from church. She goes to Holy Redeemer, but she's older than me. I think she graduated last year, maybe."

"I was talking to her mother. She was supposed to start community college this fall."

I looked out the window as we drove past the park, wishing Jimmy and I were one of the couples stretched out on the lawn under one of those brilliantly colored maple trees. Maybe by next weekend we would be.

"So now instead of going to college, she's getting married. Her mother said that she got terrific grades in high school. Now all that is wasted."

I turned away from the window. "Kileen what?"

"Didn't you hear what I said? I swear, Maggie, your head sure has been in the clouds lately. She met some boy this summer, and now is getting married next month. Surprising. She never seemed like the boy-crazy type to me."

I could see Dad's frown through the rear view mirror. "Sounds like a shot-gun wedding to me."

"Well, I don't know about that", Mom said, "but the guy is in the service, twenty-four, I think."

"That explains it."

"Explains what?"

"Rose, guys that age are interested in only one thing. It's not like high school puppy love."

My stomach tightened. Why this conversation today, of all days?

"What's puppy love, Daddy?" Clare asked.

"Well, uh, just kids liking each other a lot, in school and all."

"Oh. Then I have puppy love at my school too. With Katie, and Julie, and Matthew. They're my bestest friends."

"Silly. That's not what Daddy meant." Genny poked Clare.

"Hey. Don't poke me. That is too what it means, right Daddy?"

Mom turned towards Dad and rolled her eyes. "See what you started."

"Well, my point was not to explain puppy love, but that girls in high school, if they date at all, should date boys their own age." He caught my eye in the mirror.

I glared at Petey, certain that she had spilled the beans, but she shrugged her shoulders and gave me a bewildered look. How could I ask about dating Jimmy now? So I chickened out and let the day go by without saying a word until Petey and I were getting ready for bed. With her back turned toward me I brushed my sister's hair vigorously.

"Ow, that hurts!" Petey yelled.

"Sorry." I lifted the brush, uncertain how to confront her. "Petey, you said something to Daddy about Jimmy, didn't you?"

"Of course not."

"You *must* have said something. Why did he look straight at me when he was talking about older guys and dating?"

"Cross my heart and hope to die. I didn't say a word."

I sighed. Petey never lied.

"But how am I going to tell them about Jimmy now?"

"You can just stop seeing him."

"No, I can't."

"Yes, you can. Just tell him that he's too old and that your father said you can't see him anymore." She plopped on the bed, her arms crossed.

"Petey, look at me," I coaxed.

Petey pushed her bangs back, her hazel eyes glaring at me. How do I get her to understand? "I can't just *stop* seeing him. I think I love him."

"What! That's crazy! You've only known him a few weeks. You don't just start *loving* someone after a few weeks."

"Oh? And how do you know that?"

She shrugged. "I just do."

"You don't get it, do you? You don't know how it is between a man and a woman. Someday, you'll see."

"But you're not a woman. You're a kid."

"No, I'm not. It doesn't take long to know you're in love with someone. Don't you remember Dad telling us about how he fell for Mom after only one date?"

"Well, yeah, I guess, but they weren't in high school."

"Don't you see, Petey? It doesn't matter how old you are. You can't just walk away from someone you love." I wanted her understanding and sympathy. Instead she was acting like a stubborn child, closing me out.

"I don't want to talk about this anymore." Petey slid off the bed and stomped across the room to the bureau. She yanked out a drawer and took out her pajamas.

I tugged on her shoulder, spinning her around. "But *I* want to talk about it. You know that you're more than my sister. You're my best friend. *Please* understand." How could she not see how important this was to me? Tears rolled down my cheeks, but Petey didn't see them. She was already putting on her pajamas and climbing into bed. Her face was turned to the wall with the covers over her head. I loved her but sometimes she made me want to scream!

I went to the bathroom and shut the door. Splashing the cool water on my face after the Noxzema, I stared into the mirror. What did Jimmy see when he looked at me? Lightly touching my lips, I tried to reclaim his kiss, remembering its warmth. I unhooked my bra and raised my arms through my lavender nightgown. The outline of my breasts showed through the thin cotton. I touched them lightly. Tomorrow I would see Jimmy again.

to my forehead. "How are you? Feeling a bit better? I wish I'd been here for you, dear."

"Maggie helped me."

"I know. You're lucky you have such a caring big sister. I have to start dinner now. You going to be okay?" I nodded. "I'll bring up a dinner tray if you're still feeling poorly."

I heard the front door slam followed by shouts of "Daddy, Daddy!" As usual, my sisters were all running to greet him. I threw the covers off and swung my feet out of bed, hoping to join them. But a sudden wave of cramps came, and I lay back onto the bed.

"Where's Petey?" he asked. There was mumbling from below, then footsteps on the stairs. Looking up, I saw my father in the doorway. Dad was not a large man, at least not compared to many, but his body was taut, compact, and muscled from years of hard labor. To me, he was big. He walked to the bed slowly, and sat on the edge. He lifted the cloth on my forehead and kissed me and I smelled the sweat and grime of a hard day's labor.

"Rough day, Petey?"

I nodded. He pushed damp bangs from my forehead and then took my hand.

"It's hard to be a woman, Petey. I guess you're finding that out from the start."

"But I don't want to be a woman, Daddy. I'm only thirteen."

"I know, sweetie. No matter how old you are, you'll always be my little girl." His rough hand reached for mine under the covers. "What's this?"

"Oh, I was starting to feel a little bit better. So I pulled this photo album off the book shelf and was looking at the pictures. I don't think I've ever seen it before."

Dad picked up the small cloth bound binder and flipped it open. "My, my, this goes back a ways."

"I know. They're all black and whites. Is that you and Mom in this picture?"

"Yep. Before we were even married. Standing in front of my folks' house."

"Mom was really pretty, wasn't she?"

He touched the photo. A slow smile crept across his face. "Still is."

"You're in uniform."

"I'd just gotten out of the Marines."

I pointed to a picture of a petite woman leaning against a tree, hair tucked behind her ears. "Who's that, Daddy?" His smile disappeared, even as he stared at the photo. Downstairs I could hear Mom rattling the pots and pans, getting supper started, yelling at Genny to start setting the table. Dad's eyes were fixed on the picture. "Daddy? Don't you know who she is?"

"She's your Aunt Charlotte."

"I have an Aunt Charlotte?"

"My sister."

"But Daddy, I thought you just had two brothers, Uncle Philip and Uncle Frank. Why didn't you tell us about your sister? Where is she?"

His chest rose and fell as he slapped the album shut. "Long gone, Petey. Long gone."

"How did she die, Daddy?"

He stood up and set the album back on the shelf. I stared at his back and noticed for the first time the speckling of gray hairs on his head. The chime of the wall clock broke the silence. His hand still touched the binder of the album. I waited, and then asked again, "How did she..."

He turned around and answered abruptly. "She didn't."

"But you said . . ."

He sighed. "It's a long story, Petey."

"But I want to know, Daddy. Won't you tell me?"

He gazed into my questioning eyes. "I suppose you're old enough to know. Charlotte was the baby of the family. Pretty and vivacious. I was supposed to walk her home from school, keep her out of trouble. But, well . . ." The bed creaked as he sat back down next to me. I reached for his hand.

"What, Daddy? What happened?"

His head bowed for a moment before he answered. "Russ Fiarotta. That's what happened. I told her he wouldn't stick around, and he didn't.

When she got pregnant, my folks sent her away, or at least tried to. They put her on the train to go to a place, you know, where they'd take care of her, put the baby up for adoption, and then Charlotte would come home. But she never did come home. She never even went to that place. I don't know where she went."

I hesitated to ask more, seeing the sudden stoop of his shoulders, the drop of his head.

"What happened to the baby?"

He turned back towards me. "What?"

"The baby, what happened to the baby?"

"I don't know, Petey. None of us do." He leaned over and kissed my brow. "Now close your eyes and rest." His calloused hand held mine as I drifted into a fitful sleep.

Maggie

Jimmy was right. I would have to talk to Mom and Dad. I'd put it off long enough. But I knew it would not be easy. I hadn't seen him since his college classes had started. I didn't know it was possible to miss someone so much in one week. He called me from a phone in his dormitory and we agreed to meet Friday after school. Staring out the classroom windows at the cloudless turquoise sky, I couldn't wait for the day to be over. When I saw him waiting for me at the bottom of the hill, I had to hold myself back from running all the way.

He hugged me tightly, whispering in my ear. "God, it's good to see you. I couldn't wait for Friday to come." He opened the car door, and I slid across the seat, tossing my blazer in the back. We smiled at each other as the engine ignited. "Thought we'd take a drive down to the beach. It's such a nice day."

"Sounds good." My cheek rested against his broad shoulder, feeling the fuzz of his navy blue sweater. Steering with his left hand, he draped his right arm around me and pulled me close. His thigh rubbed against mine, causing a tingling sensation. Perspiration broke out under my arm. Was it the day's heat or something more? When we pulled into the beach parking lot, I was disappointed to see so many cars.

Jimmy must have thought the same for he quickly said, "I know a private spot. I brought a blanket and some soft drinks. C'mon."

My shoes and bobby socks dangled from one hand as we ran along the beach laughing. Jimmy took my other hand as we climbed over a rock jetty and then up a tall sand dune. Hot sand granules pushed through my toes. Then I saw it, a sloping alcove hidden between the dunes. A few logs of charred wood sat as evidence of previous nighttime occupants. But presently it was deserted. Jimmy spread out a plaid bedspread. Stretching my arms up to the sky, I breathed in the sweet smell of beach roses and salty sea air and then looked over at Jimmy on the blanket. He was staring at me.

"What? Why are you staring at me?"

"You're just so beautiful, Maggie."

I blushed and dropped onto my knees on the blanket. "Tell me about your classes."

"Must I? I wasn't exactly thinking of my classes right now."

I laughed and again felt the warmth come into my face. "But I want to hear about them."

He smiled back at me. "Biochemistry is going to be demanding but I love it. I have some ideas for an independent research study. Professor Stein is very encouraging and lets me use the lab whenever it's free. My only non- science class is my elective in Black History."

"I never heard of Black History but I love history. Some of my favorite books have been historical novels. If I become a writer, that's what I'd like to write."

"You want to be a writer?"

"Maybe. I fantasize about acting too."

"I could see you in the movies. No one could take their eyes off of you." He reached for me then, pressing his mouth to mine. We had kissed before, but nothing like this. An intense heat surged from within. His lips were warm and soft. My body leaned back onto the blanket. The sun's rays created a shimmering white halo around Jimmy's head. I squinted to look up into his eyes, and said his name only once before he was kissing me again. My hands reached around under his shirt, pulling him close. I felt his backbone cradled between thick muscled flesh, warm to the touch. His leg slid over mine, his knee pushed up my skirt. I drew in a breath as his mouth moved to my neck. His fingers unbuttoned my blouse and then reached under my back to unfasten my bra. I pulled one arm out of the sleeve and let him push the bra to the other side. My breasts were now exposed. I opened my eyes to see round white mounds, circled with brown, nipples pointing toward the sun. Jimmy's kisses moved downward, his mouth closing over them. With each moist suck, my nipples hardened. Pushing my hips upward, I closed my eyes and took a deep breath. Suddenly, a dog barked. My body tensed, and I sat up. Reaching for my blouse, I clutched it in front of me.

"It's okay, Maggie. No one can see us from the beach."

But I was already fastening my bra, and slipping my blouse back on. Thoughts now came flooding into my head. What was I doing? How could I be lying here, half-naked? "Jimmy, I can't do this. I mean, you know. . ."

"I know." He sighed. "You're just so beautiful, Maggie. I've thought of nothing but you all week."

Circling my knees under me, I leaned towards him, gently kissing his cheek. "I thought of you all week too, but you know. We have to be careful."

He rolled onto his side, propped on his elbow. "We'll take it slower from now on, I promise." Tenderly, he tucked a stray hair behind my ear and kissed it. Transfixed with the warmth of his breath, I watched him grab two bottles of Coke, pop open the bottle caps, and ask, "Have you told your parents about me?"

"Huh?"

"Your parents. Did you talk to them?"

"Not yet, but I plan on telling them tonight. Honest." He stretched back onto the blanket, but I remained sitting up, my back to him, trailing my fingers in the sand. His hand pressed against my back, and I tensed, unsure of his next move. I kept sipping the Coke, willing myself to stay sitting.

"Why don't I take you home? You can introduce me to your parents today."

"Today?"

"Yeah, why not?"

"Well, I don't know. I think it'd be better if I tell them first. You know, not surprise them."

"You're sure?"

I nodded, but I wasn't really sure of anything. What had just happened to me? Inside I was throbbing, charged like those electric currents in that science class experiment. I tried to refocus, think clearly, but not of Dad and Mom. No, thinking of my parents was not what I wanted to do right now.

"C'mere. Give me another kiss, Maggie. Then, I promise we'll go."

I turned around and bent down half way, but he pulled me on top of him and I let the bottle drop, dribbling coke into the sand. We kissed some more. He rolled over on top of me, leaning on his forearms. The tiny blond whiskers on his cheek reflected the sunlight. I reached up and touched them gently.

"Jimmy, I wish we could stay, but ..."

"I know. We'd better go."

He drove me to the bus station to catch the next bus, which arrived fifteen minutes late. I assumed that was why Dad and Mom were waiting for me in the living room when I got home. Mom was perched on the edge of the couch, arms crossed, squeezing them tight. Dad, still in his work clothes, stood beside her and barked at me when I entered, "Where have you been?"

"Sorry, Daddy, but the bus was running late. Remember, I told you, Mom."

Dad's ears were turning red. "Who were you with?"

"Let her finish, John."

I bit my trembling lip. "I - I... had something after school. Remember?"

"Yes, but you didn't say what, Maggie. Sit down, your father and I want to have a talk with you." She reached for Dad's hand and pulled him down next to her on the couch.

I sat in the chair across from them and looked around for Petey, wondering if she'd told them. But there was no sign of my sister.

Mom turned to face me. "I picked up your sisters today at Mrs. Manoletti's house."

"Oh. Were you expecting me to do that? I'm sorry. I thought Petey would be home to do that."

"Petey stayed late for yearbook club."

"That's great. She needed to join something. I've been talking to her about some of the special..."

"It's not Petey we want to talk about, Margaret." My father's voice was terse. The look in his eyes scared me. What did he know?

I pushed back into the chair, and looked up at the ceiling.

"Mrs. Manoletti told us she saw a young man drive up to the house last Friday afternoon. She asked your mother if he was your boyfriend, since she saw you kiss him before getting out of the car. You want to explain yourself, young lady?"

The water stain on the ceiling seemed darker and larger than before.

"Look at me when I'm talking to you!"

I looked at my knees instead, willing them to stop shaking, but they didn't. I gripped them and glanced at my father, whose eyes still bore into me. For the first time, I found myself at a loss for words. What could I say now that would make them understand? This wasn't how I wanted to tell them about Jimmy. "Well, Petey was sick, remember? She didn't want to walk all the way to the bus station. I thought she might faint, really, so I asked a friend to take us."

"Who is he, Maggie? You're not supposed to take rides from strangers. You know that." Mom had that slow even tone that she used when she was trying to control her anger.

"Like I said, he's a friend, not a stranger."

"Obviously, if you are kissing him in broad daylight!" Dad's face was now completely red. His left temple pulsated and I stared at the blue vein coursing through it. I knew what that meant. How could I keep my father from exploding further?

Mom placed her hand on my father's knee, squeezed gently, and spoke. "Maggie, you know we love you. We're only thinking of your safety."

"I was going to tell you about Jimmy tonight. He's a great guy. I was just waiting until my birthday, you know, so I would be sixteen, and could date like Dad said."

"Your birthday was two weeks ago, Maggie. When did you meet this guy?" Dad asked.

"Well, it was at the end of the summer, but like I said, I was waiting..."

"We heard what you said. Now I want to know who the hell he is, and why you were sneaking around behind our backs. We have to find out about him from Mrs. Manoletti. Your poor mother didn't know what to say to her. She felt like an idiot."

"I'm sorry. I thought, you know..."

"No, we don't know. It's true you weren't sixteen when you met this boy, but your father and I aren't blind. We know boys are interested in you, that you'd start wanting to go out. I don't think your Dad would have been rigid about the exact date."

"I guess."

Mom leaned towards me and asked, "Is there something about this boy you want to tell us, Maggie? Is he a junior at Holy Redeemer Academy?"

"No."

Mom looked crestfallen. "So he goes to Gravor High then?"

"No."

"He's not a drop-out, for God's sakes, is he?"

"No, Daddy, he's not a drop-out. He's at the university."

"He's in college! How old is this guy?"

For one brief moment I thought of lying. But I had never lied to them before, and knew they would eventually find out. "He's twenty-one."

"Twenty-one! Did you hear that, Rose? Our daughter is sneaking around with a twenty-one-year-old college guy that we've never met! Kissing him in front of our house for the entire world to see, and God only knows what else!"

I blushed with flashbacks of Jimmy and me on the beach blanket.

Dad stood up then, and walked over to me, glaring. "I don't want you seeing this guy, this *man*, ever again, do you hear me?"

"But, Daddy."

"Don't 'But Daddy', me. He's far too old, and obviously can't be trusted if he's driving my daughter around before being man enough to come into the house and meet us."

"He wanted to meet you. It was me who told him to wait. Please, Daddy. Let me see him. You'll like him; I know you will." Dad stepped back. If I reached out and clung to him, would his anger dissolve? But my hands stayed pressed together.

"The subject is closed. You'll call this guy... what's his name?"

"Jimmy."

"You'll call Jimmy and explain that your parents do not approve of you dating someone much older, and that you won't be seeing him anymore. You got that?"

I looked over at my mother, my eyes pleading for sympathy. But she looked down at the carpet, her lips pursed. I called out to Dad as he turned away. "You can't do this!" My eyes flooded with tears. This couldn't be happening. I had to stop him. "Please, Daddy! You didn't even give him a chance!"

He glared at me, making me want to crawl away like I was some kind of insect. "I don't need to give him a chance. And you, Margaret Eleanor, will do as you're told. I don't want to hear another word about it. You're to come straight home from school every day until you've earned our trust again. Your mother will tell Mrs. Manoletti what time to expect you for picking up your sisters." He shook his head at me, turned and announced, "I'm going to take my bath now before supper."

"But Daddy . . ."

He stormed out of the living room and slammed the bathroom door.

Facing my mother, I pleaded, "Mom, can't you talk to Dad, make him understand?"

She had once told me about how hard she'd fallen for Dad. She must remember what it was like to be in love. Why was an older guy different? I thought about what Jimmy and I did at the beach. Was he afraid I'd go all the way, maybe even get pregnant, like Kileen? I was afraid too, but we had stopped, hadn't we? Didn't Dad have more faith in me than that? I should be able to have a boyfriend, especially one as great as Jimmy.

Mom stood up. "Do as your father says, Maggie." Why didn't she look at me? Instead, she just turned her back to me and walked out. Alone, choking back the tears, I sank into the couch.

Petey

Everyone knew there was something wrong, even little Clare who usually chattered all the way through dinner. When Dad was angry it was often quieter at the dinner table, but tonight the only sound was the scraping of silverware on plates. I'd overheard enough of the conversation with Maggie in the living room to know what it was about. They knew about Jimmy. It wasn't until Maggie and I were alone in our bedroom that I heard the whole story.

"Dad wants me to call him tonight and tell him it's over. I can't just stop seeing him, Petey. I can't." She hiccupped between sobs.

I handed her some tissues. "I think you have to, Maggie."

"If they would just give him a chance!"

"Shh, they'll hear you!"

She blew her nose, and whispered, "You know, Petey. You've seen how nice he is. What difference does it make that he's older? Do they know how stupid and dorky the guys my age are at school?"

Shrugging my shoulders, I opened my mouth to respond but Maggie kept talking.

"Jimmy isn't like that. He's smart — and handsome — and really cares about me. He was so happy to see me today." Through the tears, Maggie blushed a deep red.

I bit my lip, uncertain what to say. Maggie's sobs became louder as I fidgeted on the bed. Tentatively, I said, "Maggie, I know you like Jimmy, but lots of guys like you, and you'll meet someone else."

"No, I won't. Not like Jimmy. How can they do this to me?"

I put my arm around her. She burrowed her head against me. Hot tears moistened my shoulder. This wasn't the Maggie I knew. It was me who cried and went to my older sister for comfort or consolation. Maggie was the one who usually put things right, helped me to see the bright side of everything. But I didn't know how to make things right for her. I had never been in love before and was beginning to think I never wanted to be. So I just held her and let her cry. Finally she lifted her head and went into the bathroom. The water faucet ran for a long time.

I tapped on the door. "You all right, Maggie?"

"I'll be out in a minute."

Finally she came out. "I'll have to call him. Do you think Dad and Mom have gone to bed yet?"

"It's ten o'clock. They're usually in bed by now."

Maggie went downstairs to use the telephone. I lay in bed a long time, waiting for her to return. I thought that she might want to talk some more. But when she finally crept into bed, she didn't say a word. I heard a few sniffles.

"You okay?"

"I'm all right. Go to sleep. It's late."

I rolled over, anxious to do just that. Six o'clock would come soon enough. I prayed to God that Maggie would be all right in the morning and that she would forget all about Jimmy. Secretly, I was relieved that Mrs. Manoletti had told Mom and Dad. Now, Maggie could go back to being herself, and I could stop worrying about whether Dad would find out about some secret boyfriend. I was so naïve.

Maggie

Jimmy and I hadn't worked out the details, but we knew we couldn't end it. I had never disobeyed my parents before, but they were just plain wrong. And I knew they would come around eventually. The problem was — how could I possibly see Jimmy without my parents' knowing? His classes had started so he wouldn't be driving home until the weekend. I'd call him from the payphone near school during the week.

It was my friend Samantha who was our savior. She had been asking about Jimmy ever since she met him that first day. When I told her what my parents did, she screamed into the phone.

"They *what*?"

"Forbid me to see him."

"Christ, Mags, how can you not see him?"

"I know. I mean, I think I *love* him, Sam."

"Really?"

"I think so. I can't stop thinking about him."

"You and Jimmy are kind of like Shakespeare's star-crossed lovers."

"Who?"

"You know, Romeo and Juliet. We read it in English, remember? Well, anyway, you two are destined to be together, just like them. So we just have to find a way, that's all. I'll be like the friar and make all the plans."

It was a long week. I went through the motions of school, picking up my sisters, doing my homework and household chores, but my mind was always on Jimmy; remembering the deep richness of his voice, or the touch of his lightly stubbled cheek against mine. At night my body ached and I did not know why. I'd heard the term "lovesick" and always thought it to be a silly notion, but now wondered if there was an actual disease with physical symptoms. I couldn't wait for the end of each school day when I could call Jimmy at his dorm. He ended each call with kisses in the phone, but that wasn't the same as the real thing.

Samantha was the first of my friends to get her driver's license and had no problem borrowing her mother's car. I told Mom that Sam and I were going shopping Saturday, and then over to Sam's house. The real plan was for Jimmy to meet us at Smitty's Grill, a local diner. Lying caused more guilt than the disobedience.

Sam and I did do a little shopping before meeting up with Jimmy. It lessened my guilt some, having told a partial truth to Mom. I saw him walk through the door before he spotted us. My heart beat faster. He stood at the entranceway scanning the room, his hair neatly combed, his crisp shirt collar folded over a pull-over sweater.

Sam leaned over and whispered. "God, he's gorgeous." She waved her hand in the air to get his attention and pointed over to me.

Grinning, he bounced down the steps, strode to our booth and slid in beside me. His eyes fixed on mine. I let them consume me.

"Ahem." Sam finally got our attention.

We looked over at Sam. "Hi, Sam. This is sure nice of you. Have you ordered yet? It's on me."

We sat drinking cherry colas before Sam said goodbye, saying she'd meet us back here at 3:30.

Our original plan was to go back to our spot on the beach, but the weather had turned gray and chilly. Jimmy suggested we take the hour drive to see his campus. I hesitated briefly, thinking of what my parents would say of me going to his college campus. But then, no matter where I went with Jimmy, they wouldn't approve. So, why not? We didn't talk too much on the way. He drove with one hand on the wheel, and the other on my thigh. Even through my dungarees, I could feel the warmth of his fingers.

We toured the campus a little, stopping at a small duck pond to rest. The grass was still moist from this morning's shower. Sitting on Jimmy's jacket, I leaned into him. A pair of mallards swam toward us, ducking their bills into the water for food.

"They look so content, don't they?" I asked.

"Who?"

"The ducks, with all the time in the world together."

His hand took mine, our fingers intertwined. "Maggie, I know I said we'd take it slow, but these two weeks have been an eternity. I just have to..."

I lifted my face to his and kissed him, long and hard. I didn't care who was watching.

He took my hand, pulled me to my feet, and said, "Come on." I followed blindly. His dormitory was only a two-minute walk from the pond. His room was on the second floor. I could have stopped him but I didn't. The door pushed open and before I knew it we were on the bed. He shoved some books to the floor before unsnapping his dungarees. I watched them fall and puddle around his ankles. He stepped out of them and I saw his erection. I should stop him now, before we...

He looked at me and said softly, "Take off your shorts."

I obeyed. My legs began to quiver, even as they spread apart. His hips were hard, his abdomen flat. His tongue enveloped mine, and then moved to my neck.

"Jesus, Maggie."

It was the Lord's name that stopped me. Jesus, my Lord and my Savior. I pushed Jimmy back.

"What's wrong?"

"I can't. That's all. I just can't."

He sighed. "You sure?"

I nodded.

He sat up on the bed, as I stood and pulled on my Bermuda shorts. "I'm sorry, Jimmy. I just, you know."

"Yeah, I know." He grasped the back of his neck, pushing his head down. "You're driving me crazy, you know that?"

I stroked his hair.

Lifting his head slowly, he sighed. "I probably shouldn't have brought you here." His arms circled around my waist as he looked up at me. "I think I'm falling in love with you, Maggie Donovan."

I held my breath. Love; he said it. He was in love with me. I wanted to fall back on the bed and feel him inside of me. Instead I said, "It will be all right. Just got to take it slow. My parents will come around." I stroked his hair lightly.

He gazed up at me. "You sure?"

My fingertips touched his cheek briefly before I took his arms from my waist and said, "We'd better head home."

"Yeah, I guess so." He stood and kissed me softly.

It was all I could do not to pull him closer and never let go. When I was with him, there was no shame. Only later, when I went to confession was I forced to think of sin.

Monsignor Neelan

He recognized her voice as soon as he pulled back the screen. "Bless me Father, for I have sinned. It has been a week since my last confession." Sweet Margaret. Soon he would hear of her impatience with her sister, her small vanities, and occasional selfish thoughts. How old was she now? She had grown into a beauty, even more ravishing than her mother. Last Sunday, while serving communion, his hand wavered on her tongue. Her soft hair had brushed his finger and he froze momentarily as she made the sign of the cross, rose from the kneeler, and stepped back. After Mass he had searched her out, anxious to be near her again. He had enjoyed the lilt in her laughter when she talked with friends. Now that same voice faltered from behind the screen.

"I spoke once to my sister harshly, and I ..."

He waited. "And what, my child?"

She whispered, "I disobeyed my father."

Disobedience. That was a rare one for Margaret. "You must remember the Fourth Commandment: Honor thy Father and thy Mother."

"Yes, Father, but what, what if..."

"What if what?"

She was mumbling something. He pressed his ear to the screen. "Speak up, my child."

"What he says — it doesn't make sense. I don't see why I can't..."

"Can't what? The Fourth Commandment is not to be ignored."

"Yes Father." She was sniffling.

He shouldn't have cut her off. She was about to tell him more. What had been her transgression? Margaret was the apple of her father's eye, but John could be strict.

"Tell me more, child. Have you committed other sins?" He grew impatient as she remained silent, almost blurting out her name. He asked again, "Are there any other sins?"

"I have had impure thoughts," she whispered.

Bingo. He knew it! A boy. Her Dad must be putting the clamps on some boyfriend. He licked his lips and smiled. "Hmm. Are these general thoughts, or about someone specific?" No answer, just the sound of her knees fidgeting on the kneeler. "Can you tell me?"

"Someone specific."

"I see." He wanted to hear more. How much should he press her for information?

"I'm ready for my penance and absolution, Father."

Perhaps now is not the time for details. He would find out somehow. "Say a full rosary, and try to remember Our Virgin Mother when you have such thoughts." He rambled off absolution with the Sign of the Cross. He listened to the remaining confessions with half an ear. Too many questions in his head to focus. Who was Margaret seeing? Was there more than impure thoughts? Had there been kisses, or maybe even more?

Petey

For a while, life seemed normal. I began to enjoy learning how to do algebraic equations, conjugating French sentences, and dissecting frogs. But I missed my sister. Like driftwood slowly going out to sea, she was moving away from me. Maggie no longer regaled me with stories or chatted about the day's events. I could tell her mind was somewhere else. One night as she brushed my hair I asked if she thought about Jimmy or missed him.

I felt the brush stop mid-stroke. "Why're you asking me that?"

I shrugged. "Just, you know. You really liked him, but now you don't even mention his name."

"What's there to say? Dad and Mom won't let me see him."

"Yeah."

She stopped brushing for a moment and reached around to look at me. "Did you agree with it, Petey?"

"What?"

"Forbidding me to see Jimmy?"

"Kind of. I mean he *is* too old. And they didn't really meet him or anything."

"Exactly. And for the umpteenth time, Petey, he's not too old. He's only five years older than me. Do you know how many men are five years older than their wives, or even more?"

My suspicions were right. She had been thinking of Jimmy. "No. I never thought about it."

"Well, the answer is plenty. It was just one of those times that Dad blew his stack, and Mom had to go along with it, that's all."

I turned around. "Maggie, you're not still seeing him, are you?"

She pushed my head forward. "Turn around. I'm not done yet."

"Maggie? Are you?"

"I said I wouldn't, remember?"

"Yeah, I know, but if you are seeing him, you should end it. It would only mean trouble."

"'Cause you'd tell?"

"I've never been a tattle-tale, Maggie. You know that. Even with Genny, who's constantly getting into trouble."

"Yeah, remember that time she put glue instead of mayonnaise in Mary's sandwich because she was mad at her?" The hairbrush shook as Maggie laughed before she added, "Or the time she hit Robbie over the head with her lunchbox because he was spying on her?"

I laughed, remembering the look on our neighbor Robbie's face. It was good to be talking about something else. That night, I lay awake thinking about the row that Maggie had with our parents, wishing that I could make things right between them. I tried saying Hail Marys and rocking back and forth. That usually helped put me to sleep but not tonight. Gently lifting the covers, I slipped my feet into my Bugs Bunny slippers, trying not to scuff them on the floor as I walked across the bedroom. Tiptoeing downstairs to get some warm milk, I stopped at the bottom step when I heard my parents' voices. I sat very still and listened.

"John, I'm not sure we did the right thing."

"What do you mean? Maggie's not seeing that man anymore. She's out of danger."

"But she's not happy, John. She barely speaks to us anymore. And you don't say much to her either. Don't you think she sees that? She's still the same Maggie, the little angel you fell in love with the moment you laid eyes on her."

I heard my father sigh. "Yes, I know, Rose. She looked so much like you when she was born, the same golden hair, deep blue eyes, and big smile."

"I think she looks even more like my mother. Even though she died when I was born, I've seen pictures. I sometimes wonder if my father avoided me because I reminded him too much of her."

"Do you really think that?"

"He loves me in his own way. But I wish we had the kind of bond that you have with your daughters. It's a precious thing. You don't want to lose that."

"Don't you think I know that, Rose? Maggie will come around. You'll see."

"Perhaps. But she's in love, and that doesn't go away easily."

"She *thinks* she's in love, but you and I both know she's way too young, and he's much too old for us to encourage this."

"You were older than me when we met. My father didn't want us to date but he didn't stop us from seeing each other."

"How can you compare that to this? I was just back from the war and you had just finished high school. Your Dad didn't want me to marry you because he didn't think I was good enough for you, and he was right about that."

"Oh, John, that's not true."

"I didn't have much to offer, Rose. No education, no job. I was just lucky that a friend got me in at the loading docks. Not that I made much money. I've never provided for you and the girls like you deserve."

"We deserve a loving husband and good father, and that is what we have."

"A good father protects his daughters, and that's what I intend to do."

"Maggie's a good girl John. She certainly is a devout Catholic. Look how she goes to daily Mass so often and says her rosary. I know we've raised her to do the right thing."

"Rose, you try to remind me what it was like to be in love. But I think you're the one who has forgotten. I never met anyone more faithful to the Church or more devoted than you. But we still came close, remember?"

For a minute I thought my mother was mad or something, as there was no response. I didn't know what my father was talking about. The bed squeaked as someone rolled over. "We came damn close. Remember? Fortunately we held off until after the wedding. You are not just the most devoted woman I ever met, Rose. You're also the most passionate, and I suspect our daughter takes after her mother."

"You're making me blush."

"So, we're going to stand together on this one, right? We don't want Maggie repeating Kileen MacDonald's mistake, do we?"

This time it was my mother who sighed. "Okay, John. We'll give it time."

I skipped getting the milk, tiptoed back up the stairs, slipped into bed, and lay awake, tossing and turning long into the night.

— —

I don't know if I would have done it if it wasn't for the Mission priest. Perhaps it's not fair for me to put the blame on him. But Father Gunther's words kept pulsing in my brain like a bad headache.

About once a year, a Mission priest came to St. Peter's. Sometimes, they came from some far-away country where they had worked with the poor and unbaptized. We heard stories of poverty, ignorance, and need, and were asked to donate so that little African or Chinese babies would not grow up as pagans. But other times, it was a priest from our own country whose mission was to spread God's word through inspiring homilies. Mom had heard that Father Gunther, the new missionary priest, was a terrific speaker, and would be leading an "All Souls Day Novena" after First Saturday's confession and communion. He was also scheduled to speak at Holy Redeemer Academy. I would miss my last two periods of the day, biology class and study hall, which I wasn't too happy about. Biology was my favorite subject, and I had lots of studying to do for midterms. For some reason, he was going to speak to only the girls on one day, and the boys on the next.

We filed into the auditorium right after lunch, long rows of red plaid skirts and gray blazers. Seniors, in red blazers, sat in the front rows. There was the usual chatter as everyone took their seats. I spotted Maggie next to Sam in the third row. He strode onto the stage, stepping to the very edge. He was not dressed in the usual black cassock of a priest, but rather a long brown robe with a hood resting on his broad shoulders. Rocking back on his heels, he clasped the long wooden rosary beads tied to a rope at his waist. We waited for him to speak. Instead he reached into his robe and pulled out a cigarette lighter. With a quick flick it was lit. He held it aloft.

"Fire, one of the many gifts from God, for man to use for creative purposes. But when touched to the human skin, it brings untold suffering." A huge gasp went up from the audience as we watched him place his hand over the fire. He didn't even flinch. But I swear I could smell flesh burning as his voice boomed into the audience. "God has given us many such gifts that man has repeatedly misused. It is only fitting that fire, the element of greatest pain, is the reward for those who break God's commandments." He pocketed the lighter and paced back and forth across the stage, stopping to speak.

"You have all memorized the Ten Commandments since you were young children. But have you embraced them? You are now entering a time in your lives when Satan beckons you in new and exciting ways. He will entice you with the fruits of the flesh. Even now, you have sinned, as your thoughts become impure."

Suddenly he jumped down into the center aisle. With a slow steady gait, he strode forward, eyes burrowing into each girl he passed. "God has given us the gift of sexual union for the purpose of creation. But just like fire, it can destroy the holy temple of your body when used for other purposes. You must clear your mind of every unchaste thought and return to the womb of the Lord. Your bodies are Temples of the Holy Spirit and must remain so. Do not tell me you are without sin! I see it in your eyes, the way you walk. I know the secrets you harbor! Unclean and evil! Our Sixth Commandment, *Thou shalt not commit adultery,* is not only for those who are married. No, it is a call for the unmarried to remain pure until the Sacrament of Matrimony."

For almost two hours we listened. I had never before felt so small and so unclean, even though I'd never even kissed a boy, unless you can count the time when I was eleven and playing hide-and-seek with Robbie and his sister. We'd hid behind a tree and he kissed me. It was gross and I told him so. I kept spitting on the ground, trying to get his saliva out of my mouth. He just laid there staring back at me, like *I* was the one who was weird! I didn't really want to kiss Robbie, so it shouldn't count, right? I mean, why was I feeling guilty? We filed out in total silence, clammy with sweat, trembling inside.

In the hallway, I saw Maggie and Samantha huddled by their lockers. Samantha had been coming by the house a lot lately. She and Maggie were off somewhere almost every Saturday and sometimes on Sundays too. Mom was always telling me how nice it was that Maggie had such a good friend. She'd often pester me to make more friends. I didn't know how to tell her that not *everyone* had to be popular.

It was true that I hadn't any really close friends. I guess I always thought of Maggie as my best friend. But lately, I wasn't so sure. She didn't seem to have much time for me. I did have lunch most days with Sherlin, but she would be leaving for New York soon. I still wanted to hang out with Jeff and Hank, but they were now on the JV football squad, which didn't leave them much time for anything or anyone else, especially a girl. Now I was lucky if they just said hey to me in the hall.

Neither Maggie nor Samantha saw me. I grabbed my books quickly, hoping to catch up with them, but they were already out of the building. I vaguely remembered something about having to catch the bus on my own. Dad and Mom had lifted the after school activity ban on Maggie, and she told me she was getting together with Sam. It would have been nice for them to invite me occasionally to wherever it was that they were going. Not that I much cared for shopping, but once in a while it was okay. Maybe we could get a soda together. A half-block from the bus station, I saw Samantha. She was standing at the bus stop, waiting for the 3:15 to East Side. Where was Maggie? Then I saw her. She was a few feet away, getting into Jimmy's green Chevy. He leaned over to kiss her, and not a quick peck like that last time. My breath stopped. I couldn't believe it! She had lied to me, and to Mom and Dad! I ducked behind the nearest building and waited for Sam to catch her bus before catching mine.

The advertisement across from my bus seat showed two faces, a young woman and a young man, smiling at each other, teeth glistening, the words *Use Listerine for kissable minty fresh breath*. Then Father Gunther's face came to me. "It all starts with impure thoughts, then kissing and unclean touching. Remember the Sixth Commandment, *Thou shalt not commit adultery*, and the words in the Gospel from Jesus, 'anyone who lusts has already committed adultery!' And to break any of the Ten Commandments is a mortal sin — a *mortal* sin, which, without repentance, will bring you to the fires of Hell!"

I shivered, as the bus lurched. Was Father Gunther right? It is true that I had never been a tattletale. But how could I possibly do nothing when my own sister could be going to Hell? Telling Dad would mean betraying Maggie, and then Dad would be *so* totally angry that everyone would be miserable, just like before. I guess what I had is what you call a dilemma. I couldn't decide what was best, so I did nothing, and just kept worrying.

— ⌒ —

I sat at the dinner table, pushing the peas from one side of the plate to another.

"Petey, you haven't touched your food. I thought you liked meat loaf." Mom passed the ketchup to Genny.

"Just not hungry."

"That's not like you. Did you have something to eat when you got home?" I shook my head. "Well, eat your dinner then. Your father's been telling me to fatten you up some. You're too thin."

"I ate all my peas, Mommy." Mary beamed proudly.

"That's a good girl."

"Where is Daddy, Mommy?" Clare asked.

"He had to work late. Don't you remember that with the layoff now over he has to work a lot of overtime? Mom turned to Maggie. "I was planning on going to Novena on Saturday and was hoping you would come with me."

"Sorry, Mom. Samantha and I have to study for midterms on Saturday."

"But Maggie, you always go with me. What about confession? It's First Saturday."

I took a bite of peas and looked over at Maggie. She usually did go to Novena with Mom. I hated going. Just a lot of long, boring prayers that made me sleepy. When I asked Maggie why she liked Novenas, she said she loved the incense, that it made her feel light-headed but kind of wonderful at the same time. I told her that sounded freaky to me and she had laughed. Now she was turning down a chance to go.

"I know, Mom, but that's not until four o'clock, and I'm staying for supper at Sam's. I can always go next time."

"I suppose. You'll miss Father Gunther's talk." Mom was clearly disappointed that Maggie turned her down.

"We heard him speak at school."

"Oh, that's right. Is he as good a speaker as I've heard?"

Maggie and I exchanged a long look, remembering our conversation yesterday on the bus about Father Gunther's talk.

"Maggie, I, ah . . . was wondering, I mean, Whadyya think of that talk?"

She shot me an icy stare. "I don't want to talk about it."

"He gave me the willies. I mean I guess he's right about going to hell if you do that stuff, right? But he was kind of creepy."

"Yeah, he was creepy." She turned away and stared out the window. I had to say something, something about Jimmy and the kissing. Maybe if she thought about Hell and all that stuff Father Gunther said, then she'd call it quits with Jimmy.

"But do you feel like . . . I mean . . . I know you said you aren't seeing Jimmy anymore, but that kissing and stuff. He said it was against the Commandments. Aren't you worried?"

The vinyl seat squeaked as Maggie turned abruptly, her eyes pooled with tears. "Petey. I said I don't want to talk about it. Just shut up, all right?" Maggie had never told me to shut up before. I shut up just like she told me. We didn't talk at all that night. She didn't even brush my hair before going to bed.

Now I looked at Maggie across the dining room table, wondering how she'd reply to Mom. "He had everyone's attention." She pushed her chair away from the table. "Can I be excused?"

"But the Novena?"

"Mom, I'd like to go with you, but I have a lot of studying to do." I didn't blame her for not wanting to go. The thought of even looking at Father Gunther again gave me chills.

"Well, I suppose I can go by myself. Actually, Petey, you can stay home and watch your sisters. They would just get fidgety, and your father will be home late."

Dad had been working a lot of overtime lately. We rarely saw him on the weekends, and when we did he was too exhausted to talk and joke with us like usual. Last night there was arguing late into the night. Maggie was sound asleep, but I crept down the stairs and listened. It was about money again. Mom didn't want Dad going to work on Sunday, but he told her that if they were ever going to get back on their feet, he had to take all the overtime offered. He reminded her of the stack of bills that still had to be paid.

"Isn't there any way you can cut back on expenses, Rose?"

Mom's voice rose. "You don't know how much I've cut back already. I'm ordering half as many bottles of milk and mixing them with powdered milk. I'm making jelly sandwiches without peanut butter for the kids' lunches. And if you remember, we had macaroni and cheese twice last week, and the only meat we had all week was Spam."

"Yeah, I noticed. Look, I'm not blaming you for our money problems, but we eventually want to get out of this dump and buy a house, right? We can't seem to even pay the bills, let alone save money. I know you don't want to hear this, but tuition went up again this year at Holy Redeemer Academy. Maggie and Petey could be going to school for free at Gravor High."

"We've talked about this before, John, and I thought we agreed that the sacrifice was worth it. Academics are strong there and they have the positive role models of the sisters and brothers, grounding them in their Catholic religion."

"I know. I'm just saying that we have to cut back somewhere. Even with the overtime I'm getting, we're still in the hole."

I crept closer to their door. I heard the bed creak and the sound of bureau drawers opening and shutting. I could picture Mom getting her nightgown out of the drawer and starting her nightly ritual. The smell of Ponds night cream came first and then her rose-scented hand cream, as she rubbed her hands together. Again, the bureau drawer slammed and the bed creaked as my mother slipped under the covers. "The girls' education is too important. I want them to stay at Holy Redeemer."

"I don't see that it's done a whole hell of a lot of good for Maggie. It didn't keep her from sneaking around with that guy."

"John, that's over. You need to stop being so angry and forgive her."

"Do we *know* it's over? She could still be seeing him after school. I think we should have continued to insist that she come straight home."

"She's sixteen years old. We can't treat her like a child."

"Well, if she doesn't have enough sense to stay out of trouble, which we both know an older guy is, than we've got to protect her."

"Maggie's a good girl. I'm sure she wouldn't do anything she shouldn't. She just used poor judgment that one time."

"I hope you're right. But youthful passion and lust have a way of overriding good judgment."

"Well, as far as I can tell she is just busy with school, the Sodality Club, and getting together with Samantha. Petey's with her every day, and she hasn't mentioned anything to me about seeing her with Jimmy."

"Who?"

"The lifeguard she liked. His name is Jimmy."

"I don't want to have any reason to remember that name."

The light switched off as my mother sighed. "Tomorrow's another day. We'll manage the bills somehow. We always do."

My body pressed against the staircase wall, arms wrapped tightly around my knees. I sat there for a long time, and even when I did return to bed, I couldn't sleep. Maggie's secret burned in my chest. Words flooded my brain.

"Maggie's a good girl."

"And to break any of the Ten Commandments is a mortal sin, and will bring you to the fires of Hell!"

"I'm not a tattle-tale, Maggie."

"If she doesn't have enough sense to stay out of trouble, then we've got to protect her."

"Petey's with her every day, and she hasn't mentioned anything to me about seeing her with Jimmy."

If I told, would I be protecting Maggie? Would she be mad at me forever? Was Dad right? And what about all those things Father Gunter said? Warm tears trickled down my cheeks, but I held the sobs back, not letting go. My throat ached with the effort. It wasn't until morning when the alarm went off way too early that I remembered that I had an algebra exam.

Maggie

I lay on my bed, staring up at the ceiling. I was excited about meeting up with Jimmy today, but it wasn't the only thing on my mind. Petey kept glaring at me at the dinner table. Did she know somehow? I wanted to tell her about Jimmy. I'd never kept secrets from her or my parents before. That's what bothers me the most. It isn't the kissing. Father Gunther can rant all he wants, but Jimmy and I haven't committed a mortal sin. We're in love. I know at some point I'll have to come clean, but I can't do anything that will chance losing Jimmy. My parents are being totally irrational.

The guilt persisted. Like static on the radio, it was always there in the background. I didn't want to disobey or keep secrets, but why couldn't I have a boyfriend? Lots of girls my age were dating. When I told Mom some of my friends were even going steady, she said the subject was closed and it wasn't the same because Jimmy was older. So what if he was older? What's the big deal? I had to stop brooding. Somehow we'd convince them, get them to come around. Right now I needed to find something to wear. Samantha would be here any minute. Pushing the hangars aside in my closet, I chose a madras skirt and blue pullover. Jimmy liked me in blue.

"Maggie, Samantha's here!" Genny yelled.

I flew down the stairs, almost knocking Genny over.

"Where ya going, Maggie? You promised to play jump rope with me."

"Later, Genny. Going out with Samantha." I gave my sister a quick squeeze. She pouted, "But you promised."

I blew back a kiss. "Love you, Genny-bug. Maybe tomorrow."

Samantha leaned against her car. My mouth dropped open.

"Wow, Sam! I didn't think you'd really do it!"

"You like it?" She flipped her newly dyed red hair from side to side. I wasn't sure it suited her but told her it looked great. We hopped into the car and made the ten minute drive downtown. She pulled into a parking spot and reached into her purse. "You got a nickel for the meter?"

"Yeah sure." I fumbled through the sticky gum, comb, and hairbands at the bottom of my purse until I found a nickel. Slamming the car door, Sam stepped onto the curb and put the nickel in the meter. I unwrapped a stick of Juicy Fruit and put it in my mouth. "Where'd you want to shop?" I asked.

Sam pointed across the street at Kresge's Five and Dime. "The usual. I saw a new shade of lipstick in *Teen* magazine." She found Revlon's new Pink Temptation lipstick and I bought two satin baby blue hair ribbons, one for me and one for Petey. It was a luxury using up my babysitting money from last weekend, but I couldn't resist. We walked the two blocks to Gino's and slid into the only empty booth.

"What did your parents say about your hair?"

"My parents? Not much. Mom just laughed. Said I looked like my Aunt Eileen now. Dad didn't even notice."

"He didn't even notice! Are you kidding?"

"He's never home, works two jobs now, remember? I brought him a bowl of ice cream last night. He didn't even look up from watching Johnny Carson."

"My folks would kill me if I ever dyed my hair!"

"Jeez, Maggie. I would too. Why would you ever want to change from that gorgeous blond bombshell look you've got going?"

"I'm not a bombshell." Picking up the menu, my eyes drifted to the bright pink strawberry milkshake on the cover, wishing I had money to splurge.

Sam pulled the menu down from in front of my face. "Maggie Donovan. You have no idea, do you? Every boy in school is crazy over you. You could have any one you wanted. Take a look around. Don't you see?"

We sat in one of the three booths by the wall, across from the counter area. A few guys sat on stools facing the kitchen. The wallpaper was faded and peeling. A poster of a woman holding a steaming cherry pie was pinned next to the Mickey Mouse clock.

"What's to see? There's crud under the diner stools and the wallpaper is peeling. Same old cheap place."

"Not that, silly. The boys."

"What about the boys?"

"Every one of them has turned around to look over here."

"Pff- what are you talking about? Maybe it's your red hair."

"Naw, it's not me they're looking at. It's you."

I squirmed in the booth. "I think you're exaggerating. 'Sides, I'm only interested in one boy, anyway."

"Yeah, I know. What time is lover boy going to meet us, anyway?"

"I told him two o'clock, but he said he might be late."

A gum chewing waitress stood next to us, her pancake make-up plastered over visible wrinkles, limp gray hair pushed behind her ears.

"Whad'll it be?"

We ordered two cherry Cokes. I twirled the music wallbox on our table looking for something by the Beach Boys. "I sure hope I'm not slinging pizzas and taking orders for a living when I'm that old."

"Why would you be? You'll be married to a doctor. Isn't that what you said Jimmy is going to be?

"Maybe."

Sam shook her head. "Cute *and* smart. Maybe he's got a friend who likes redheads."

I laughed as the waitress set the drinks in front of us. Sam took one sip, and then leaned over and whispered in a hushed tone, "So, have you and Jimmy done it yet?"

"Samantha!"

"You can tell me. I can keep a secret."

My face felt warm all over, and I was glad the place was so dark. I pressed against the booth. "Samantha, don't even think such a thing."

"But I've seen you two kissing. And besides, you already told me you're in love with him."

"Yeah, but that doesn't mean I'd go all the way. I thought you knew me better than that."

"I know. You're a good Catholic girl."

I rolled my eyes at Sam's sarcasm.

She crossed her arms and spoke in her know it all way. "There's religion and then there's sex, and from what I've heard sex wins every time, despite what Father Gunther says."

I winced as an image of Father Gunther's stern face flashed before me. Rubbing the condensation on the side of my glass, I replied, "Yeah, he was heavy stuff."

"So, you haven't?"

"Haven't what?"

"*Maggie*, you know!"

I shook my head. "No, I haven't done it with Jimmy but Father Gunther's talk *still* made me feel guilty."

Samantha's eyebrows rose. "He *was* creepy, if you ask me, with that fire and everything."

"I know." I leaned forward and whispered, "Do you think not telling my folks about Jimmy is a sin?"

"You're asking *me* about sin? According to the nuns, I'm already going to Hell because I miss Mass sometimes."

"You shouldn't do that, Sam."

Samantha shrugged. "Sleep seems more important. My folks don't go all the time either, not like yours. You try talking to your Mom about all this?"

"I tried, a little, but I think they're both afraid of. . . you know ..."

Samantha twirled the straw in her cherry Coke, leaned over, and whispered, "Did I tell you that my mother is on the new pill?"

"Birth control pills?"

"Yup, and I plan to go that route when the time comes. No worries for me about babies, not until I want one anyway."

"But the Pope says..."

"Pope? *He's* not the one getting pregnant."

I wasn't sure what to say or what to think. Samantha made it all sound so simple. I wondered if my mother would ever go on birth control pills. I wouldn't have thought so, but then I remembered that day almost four years ago when I went with her to confession. For some reason we had gone to St. Catherine's church instead of St. Peter's. Clare was only a year old and Dad was out of work again. I probably shouldn't have eavesdropped, but when I heard Mom crying in the confessional, I couldn't help it. There was no one else in church so I crept forward and leaned against the wall with my ear just inches away from the thick scarlet curtain.

"What is it, my child?"

My mother's voice trembled. *"I — I committed — I mean — it's not just venial sins this time."*

"You have committed a more grievous sin, a mortal sin?"

"Yes, Father." She choked back the tears. *"I knew it was wrong, but my doctor said I shouldn't get pregnant again, so he gave me one of those things, you know, to prevent pregnancy. I didn't even tell my husband."*

"And are you still using this device?"

"No, Father. I — I removed it after two times."

"You must use abstinence, my child."

"I know. We've tried that before, but sometimes, well. . ."

I didn't hear the penance given. I was too busy scurrying back to my pew. The curtain lifted, and Mom walked forward to the altar rail. She knelt a long time, lit one of the votive candles, crossed herself, genuflected, and walked down the side aisle. I went to confession, said my Hail Marys, and followed. She was sitting in the car, her face all blotchy. I kept glancing over at her, hoping she'd speak, but her eyes remained riveted to the road.

"Did you hear me, Maggie?"

"What?" I looked back at Samantha.

"I *said*, maybe I could get my folks to talk to yours. I mean, my dad is seven years older than my mom."

"Really? I mean, they'd talk to them?" I almost bounced in excitement.

Sam took a long gulp of her cherry coke before replying. "Maybe. They like your parents and everything. Remember when they sat next to each other at the church picnic, laughing the whole time?"

"Sam, you're a life saver! It might really work!" I wanted to jump up from my seat and hug her. My mind churned. How could I get the Donovans and the Griffins together? Mom and Dad didn't have company over much, unless it was a special occasion. It would probably go better at the Griffins' house anyway. Dad couldn't blow his stack there. Should I invite Jimmy too? Neutral ground and all? Would the Griffins go for that?

"Sam, do you think..."

A kiss on the cheek interrupted me. "Jimmy!" I swung my arms around his neck. This time I did see the boys on the diner stools staring at me. "I didn't even see you come in."

"Too busy talking to keep an eye out, huh? Hi Sam." He looked over at Sam and smiled. "You ready, Maggie?"

I slid out from the booth. "I'll be back at 3:30." I couldn't wait to tell Jimmy our plan.

Sam slurped the last bit of soda. "I'll be here. Don't do anything I wouldn't do." She winked at me, and I blushed.

Petey

$\mathcal{I}$ hadn't planned on telling Mom and Dad about Maggie. It kind of slipped out because of my algebra test. Math was easy for me, and even without studying I should have aced it. But I didn't. I finished the first two problems and then images of Maggie and Jimmy in the car, my parents' quarrels, and Father Gunther's warnings all swirled in my head in one big blur. There was no room for algebraic equations.

My parents called me into the living room. I sat next to my mother on the couch. She spoke first. "Mr. Richards called."

"Mr. Richards? My Algebra teacher? Called here?" She nodded. Not once in nine years of school had my parents received a call from a teacher about me.

Dad spoke next. "Evidently you did poorly on your last exam. He said you didn't even finish it." The latest exam counted for thirty percent of my grade. Even with my other tests and homework, my average would dip to a C. I had never received anything other than an "A" in my life. Tears rolled down my cheeks.

"I'm sorry. I'll do better on the next test. I promise."

Mom patted my knee. "I'm sure you will, Petey. That's not our concern. Mr. Richards told us that you seem preoccupied in class lately. He said you usually volunteer to do problems on the board, but when he called on you the other day, you didn't even know what problem was being done."

Dad sat in the chair across from us, tapping the floor with his foot. His brow furrowed. Was he angry with me? Or just worried? I couldn't stand having my father angry with me.

"So, Petey, we want to know what's troubling you. Your father and I have seen a change in you. Even Genny's noticed. She told us that you wouldn't play basketball with her when she asked. I've never known you to turn down a chance to play ball, even with your younger sister."

"Is it because Maggie's been ignoring you lately, going out with Samantha all the time? We can speak with her about that if you want," Dad offered.

I turned to look at my father. "No, Dad, please don't do that. That's not it. Really."

"Well, then what is it, Petey? Your mother and I want to know."

Mom was smiling at me, but she had that crease between her brows. Her voice was soft and warm, wrapping around me like a winter scarf. "Petey, you know we love you. You can tell us anything."

I chewed the inside of my lip, drew in a quick breath, and responded, "No, I'm fine. My mind just went blank on the test. That's all." I looked down and saw little half- moon indentations on my wrist from my fingernails.

Mom's fingers lifted up my chin; her eyes fixed on mine. "I think there's more to it than that, isn't there, Petey?" If she hadn't put her arm around me and pulled me close, the tears wouldn't have come and the words wouldn't have tumbled out.

"I'm just worried about Maggie. That's all. And I don't want you to be mad at her. He's a nice guy, really. He took me home when I was sick, you know, the day my period came and everything. And he likes Maggie a lot, and she likes him. But I don't want her to go to Hell. Father Gunther says she is, but I don't think so. Even if he is a priest. Maggie wouldn't ever do anything *really* bad." I began to sob, and hiccup. Mom pulled me closer, and I buried my face in her chest.

Eventually I told them everything, pleading with them not to be too angry with Maggie. But as I told them what I'd seen, Dad's face grew dark. He and Mom exchanged that kind of look that makes your stomach turn over because you know someone is in trouble. Mom's grip around my shoulder tightened.

Dad clenched his jaw and curled his fingers into fists before speaking. "Go upstairs and tell Maggie that we want to talk to her."

Mom looked up at Dad and said, "Are you sure this can't wait until morning, John?"

"I want to see her *now*."

I hesitated, already questioning what I'd done.

Mom's hand came off my shoulder and patted me on the knee. "It's all right, Petey. You did the right thing. Now do as your father says."

I looked from one parent to the other, hoping they'd change their minds. Finally, Mom nudged me to my feet.

There was so much yelling I was afraid the neighbors might hear. At first I tried to hear what my parents were saying, but stopped when Dad started shouting swear words. Maggie's crying made me cry too. I buried my face in the pillow. Then Genny, Mary, and Clare came in from playing and I heard my mother telling them to go up to their rooms. Instead they came into my room. Clare's lips were quivering. "Why is Daddy so mad?" I pulled her onto the bed and gave her a hug, unsure of what to say. Genny and Mary stood pressed together like a twin popsicle on a stick. Mary's glasses slid down her scrunched up nose. Genny twirled her hair. Together they climbed onto the bed on either side of me while Clare crawled into my lap.

"What happened?" Genny asked as she began to pull the loose threads off the bedspread.

I had to give some explanation. "Mommy and Daddy are mad at Maggie."

"But why?"

I sighed. "You wouldn't understand, Genny."

She scowled and pulled harder on the thread. "Yes I would."

"You're not old enough."

"Am too. I'm almost ten."

Mary pushed up her glasses and sat up straighter. "And I'm seven."

Clare looked up at me. "Are you crying, Petey?" I wiped my eyes.

"No. I'm okay. C'mon, let's go to your room and I'll read you some books."

I read one picture book after another, losing track of time. Finally I heard Maggie coming up the stairs. I went to our room. She was on her bed sobbing. I wanted to apologize. I had promised not to tattletale, and yet I had. How could she not be angry with me? When the crying stopped, I knelt by her bed and tried talking to her, but she rolled over on her side, faced the wall, and said nothing.

"Please talk to me, Maggie! Please! I didn't mean to tell, really I didn't! I'm sorry. Won't you forgive me?" I heard each tick of the clock on the wall as the minutes passed. A knot ached at the base of my neck as I stared at Maggie's back. As if in slow motion, she turned. Her face was blotchy, her eyes red. She spoke in a raspy whisper.

"Why didn't you talk to me, Petey? You don't know what you've done. I had it all worked out. Jimmy and I were going to tell Dad and Mom this week at the Griffins. They would have listened to them, seen what a wonderful guy Jimmy is, and relented. Now, now, I..." The tears rolled slowly down her cheeks.

"Can I do anything to make it right? I didn't mean to hurt you."

"No, you've done enough. Go to bed, Petey."

I was dismissed. The achiness spread to my throat. I gripped Maggie's bedspread tight, wanting to reach out to her, but afraid of how she would respond. So instead, I did what I was told.

Numbed, I went through my nightly ritual. I washed my face and dabbed on astringent to clear the emerging acne. After brushing my teeth, I knelt to say my prayers, but for the first time in my life I couldn't pray. I had betrayed my sister. Would she, or God, ever forgive me?

The sheets were cold and crisp when I crawled into bed. I looked over at Maggie one more time. She still had her back turned towards me. With a deep sigh, I rolled over and stared outside. Rain began to pelt the window and the back yard maple tree swayed in the wind. The branches seesawed up and down. It was our favorite climbing tree. There was that one time, when Maggie and I climbed higher and higher, daring each other to go further. Then my foot slipped and I fell backwards, only to have Maggie catch my hand and pull me up. We perched together on the highest limb; a good twenty feet above the earth as I caught my breath, and she held me close.

Maggie

I couldn't stay mad at Petey. Her hangdog expression and constant tearful hugs made me feel like I should be comforting her instead of the other way around. She'd bring me cookies and milk as I sat at my desk doing homework. Then she'd sit on the edge of her bed staring at me and chewing the inside of her lip.

My world was now turned upside down. There seemed to be this invisible wall between my parents and me. Dad rarely looked my way and when he did it was with suspicion. Mom continued to kiss and hug me when I left for school and came home, but she fumbled for things to say. Once, she actually tried to talk to me about sex, but it didn't go very well.

"I know you're feeling certain new things in your body right now Maggie, but you have to wait until the time is right, when you're married."

We were sitting on the edge of her bed. I looked over at the crisp cotton-cased pillows lying side by side against the headboard, with the crucifix hanging on the wall above it. I'd seen my mother on her knees saying her nightly prayers by this bed as long as I could remember. But I also had heard the sounds of my parents' lovemaking from this bed. Once, Petey heard noises from the bedroom and asked why Mom was moaning. I almost told her, but decided to lie and say that Mom wasn't feeling well. I didn't think she'd understand any more than she understood about Jimmy and me. I searched my mother's face, noting the emerging wrinkles around her eyes, hoping for empathy. Tentatively, I asked, "Wasn't it hard for you and Daddy, Mom, I mean to wait ..."

"Of course."

I squeezed my mother's hand, imploring her to understand. "Imagine if you couldn't even *see* him, let alone touch him! Why can't we go out? I'm in love with Jimmy, Mom!"

"This is the first time you've fallen for a boy, and you're very young." She pulled away, gave my hand a pat, and stood. "Your father knows how one thing can lead to another, and you're just not ready for that yet."

"How does he know? He doesn't even talk to me anymore."

She stroked my hair. "Give him time, Maggie. He loves you, but you disappointed him when you disobeyed. And he knows, like I do, that you need to wait until the Sacrament of Marriage with the right person before you are together in that way."

She started to stand but I tugged on her arm until she sat back down beside me. "Mom, I know I disobeyed. I didn't want to, but Dad wouldn't listen to me. I don't know what to do." There had to be some way to make her see how this was all so wrong. I needed to be with Jimmy! They couldn't force us to be apart. They just couldn't. She was my last hope of convincing Dad. Tears puddled in my eyes.

She cupped my chin and tilted my head to look up. "When you need help, Maggie, turn to Our Lord. Why don't you come with me to Novena tonight? It's already half way through and you haven't made any of the evenings so far. I've missed your company."

That is not the answer I wanted. The thought of seeing Father Gunther again turned my stomach. Mom was looking at me expectantly. I knew she was trying to reach out and I didn't want to disappoint her. I'd been trying to talk to God in prayer. He just didn't seem to be giving me any answers. Maybe going with Mom would be a good thing. It was better than staying home and getting the silent treatment from Dad when he got home from work and I did like Novenas, especially the incense.

"Okay, I'll go."

Mom kissed me lightly on the forehead before leaving the room and heading to the kitchen to start an early supper.

— ᴖ —

The church was almost full when we arrived a little before six. We sat in one of the back pews. I pulled the kneeler down, and Mom and I knelt side by side, our shoulders touching. Both Father Gunther and Monsignor Neelan strode past us in the aisle, with an altar boy on either side. Father Gunther came first, his head bowed, his hands folded in prayer. Monsignor Neelan swung the thurible, filling the air with a heavy perfume. His ironed robe brushed the top of polished black shoes. Father Gunther still wore the brown robe and sandals that I'd seen him in at school. They strode together and took their places behind the altar. I breathed in deeply, feeling slightly lightheaded from the incense. My mother nudged me with her elbow and pointed to a prayer in the Novena pamphlet. I joined in the recitation:

My God! Because Thou are Infinite Goodness, I am sorry with all my heart for having offended Thee. I promise to die rather than ever offend Thee more. Give me holy perseverance; have pity on me and have pity on those holy souls that burn in the cleansing fire and love Thee with all their hearts. O Mary, Mother of God, assist them by their powerful prayers. Mom's soft voice mingled with mine. Father Gunther spoke passionately about God's infinite power to forgive if we renounce sin and turn to Him for forgiveness. My eyes locked on the large wooden crucifix above the altar. The cast of Christ hung from nails, his knees buckled, his arms stretched taut and dripping with blood. He had sacrificed for our sins, my sins. Was I in the state of sin? Did my actions offend God, or was I acting in conscience? I asked God this in my prayers, but again there were no answers. Was He giving me the silent treatment too?

My mother and I stood for the final hymn. I knew the words by heart, but sang softly so that I might hear my mother's beautiful voice sing out

Faith of our Fathers, living still
In spite of dungeon, fire and sword.
O how our hearts beat high with joy
Whenever we hear that glorious word.
Faith of our fathers, holy faith.
We will be true to Thee till death.

We knelt for the final *Our Father* and *Hail Mary*. Lifting up the kneeler, I stepped out of the pew, made my final genuflection in the aisle, and waited for my mother before walking to the back of the church. The vestibule smelled of wet wool as parishioners shuffled out into the misty, cold autumn air.

As I dipped my fingers into the holy water, I heard Monsignor Neelan's voice:

"Margaret, how wonderful to see you. I missed you the other Novena nights." He leaned towards me, his eyes intently staring into mine. They were steel gray like the drill bits in my father's toolbox. He had a broad smooth-shaven face, and there was a twist to his nose as if it had once been broken. His mouth was full, his teeth perfect, but there was this slight twitch in his upper lip. I found myself counting each twitch.

Mom looped her arm through mine. "Hello, Monsignor. Maggie's been busy with school, but she was able to come tonight."

He reached out, closing his hands over mine like a snare trap, holding them tight, while smiling at us both. "Yes, I see that, Rose. You must be pleased."

She beamed. I gently tugged on my hands, trying to free them, but he held them firm and looked back at me.

"Maggie, dear child. Forgive me if I intrude, but you look troubled. You are usually so cheerful. I do hope Father Gunther's solemnity has not soured your bright disposition."

"Sorry, Monsignor. Just a lot on my mind, I guess."

"Margaret, as pastor of my flock, my door is always open. I know what a confusing time this is for young people."

I sighed audibly as he finally let go and turned to pat my mother's hand. "Come by any time, Rose, or have Margaret come for a chat."

Mom replied, "Thank you, Monsignor. Maybe I will."

We were quiet for the whole ride home. Mom looked over at me often, looking like she was about to say something, but never did. It was late when we got home, and everyone was in bed.

Dad called out, "Is that you Rose?"

"Yes, I'll be right in." Mom turned to me. "It was nice having you come with me tonight. That was good of Monsignor Neelan to speak to you, don't you think?" She clutched my elbow as if she wanted to say more.

"Yes." I yawned and took a step toward the stairs.

Mom reached over and gave me a kiss on the cheek. "Well, it's late. Good night. See you in the morning."

Petey was already asleep so I opened the dresser drawer slowly to pull out a fresh nightgown, slipped my robe and slippers on, and crept downstairs to get my bookbag. I had some reading to do for history class tomorrow. Through my parents' bedroom door, I heard my father's voice rise,

"Monsignor Neelan? What the hell is he going to do?"

"Shh, not so loud. He'll talk to her. You know he is very fond of Maggie. She's been coming with me to daily Mass ever since she was a little tyke. He's watched her grow up. I think she would listen to him. I read in *The Catholic Digest* that adolescents often need adults other than their parents to talk to."

"But Monsignor Neelan? He's a man, and a priest to boot. How is he going to help our Maggie?"

"Please, John. Let's give it a try. I know Maggie is troubled."

"All right. I'll trust your judgment on this. You know your daughter."

"I'll talk to Maggie first thing in the morning, and then give Monsignor Neelan a call."

"Fine. But I want her straight home from school for a while, until we know she's through with this guy."

None of the words in my history book seemed to register. I was thinking of Monsignor Neelan's words,

". . . *my door is always open.... come by for a chat.*"

Petey

We woke up to the first snow of the season. I stared out the window. The brown earth appeared dusted with confectioner's sugar. When Maggie and I walked to the bus stop, our shoes squeaked as little white flakes collected on their soles. My breath blew warm into the cold air. Stopping to zip my coat, I couldn't believe what Maggie was saying.

"They want you to do what! Talk to Monsignor Neelan?"

"That's what Mom said."

"But why? He's a priest. What does he know about love?"

She smiled with that Maggie kind of smile that says the world is full of rainbows and sunshine, something I'd not seen her do in days. "I know. That's what I thought at first too. But he might be just the person to help."

The bus pulled up five minutes late. Clutching my hefty stack of textbooks with my left arm, I grabbed the bar with my right. Maggie dropped in our coins and I looked for an open seat. I always took a window seat to see the scenery. A couple of the passengers greeted Maggie as we walked down the aisle. She knew all the regulars. I flipped open my Algebra book and pulled out my homework, still unsure of one of my equations.

"So, you see, Monsignor Neelan might be the perfect person to help."

"Huh?"

Maggie sighed. "Didn't you hear anything?"

"Yeah. Neelan can help. I don't see how."

"*Monsignor* Neelan. Don't you get it? He's a priest. How could Dad and Mom not listen to a priest? I mean, all I have to do is make him see what a good person Jimmy is, and that we are really in love. Then he'll tell Mom and Dad not to keep us apart. Just like the friar in *Romeo and Juliet*. He'll be on our side."

"What are you talking about, Maggie?"

She sighed again and flapped her hand in exasperation. "Oh, never mind. I forgot you haven't read it yet."

I sighed too, and wished we'd never gone to the beach that day. Then Maggie wouldn't have met Jimmy and changed so much. All she ever thinks about these days is *him*.

The bus jolted to a stop at Spring St., and the fat old woman that always smelled like stale mothballs lumbered up the steps. I hoped she didn't take a seat near us like she sometimes did. I guess because Maggie always smiled at her and gave her mints. At least then she didn't smell so bad. Fortunately she slumped on the seat just behind the driver, facing the aisle. The driver coughed, closed the door, and pulled the bus back out onto the street.

I turned to Maggie and asked, "So when are you supposed to talk to Monsignor Neelan?"

"Tomorrow. Mom already arranged it."

I couldn't imagine that Dad was thrilled about this. He wasn't a fan of Monsignor Neelan's, not that he ever said anything, but it was the way Dad's jaw clenched, the way he grunted a curt hello, and then said nothing more. With everyone else, Dad was so much fun. No, it had to be mostly Mom's idea. Maggie opened her history book, and we didn't talk again until it was time to get off the bus.

We walked in silence up the hill. I stopped Maggie in the entranceway. "I don't think you should do it."

"What?"

"See Monsignor Neelan. I don't think he can help you."

"But of course he can. Why do you say that?"

I didn't have a specific reason. Like Dad, I wasn't a fan of Monsignor Neelan's. His on-the-mouth kisses, his crooked smile. He creeped me out.

"I don't know — I just don't think it's a good idea." I grabbed her arm. "Maggie, I mean it. Tell Mom no."

"Oh, Petey. Don't be so dramatic. Gotta run. Bell's about to ring." She gave me a quick peck on the cheek.

Maggie bounced down the hallway, turning to smile at everyone who passed by. She did seem more like herself this morning. But somehow I couldn't imagine Monsignor Neelan was the answer to her problem.

First period Religion class with Sister Alfred was even more boring than usual. Today she was droning on about the books in the Old Testament, telling us that there would be a quiz tomorrow. Tommy snickered to Brian, "The old bat probably knew Moses personally." Brian sniggered and Sister Alfred turned from the chalkboard to glower at them both. My day began and ended with Sister Alfred, who taught my last period Latin class as well. At least with Latin there was some logic. I liked conjugating verbs. Even though it was a dead language, it was fun to put together sentences, kind of like a puzzle. Sometimes Sister would rail about Vatican II changing the Latin Mass to English. To listen to her you'd think it was the end of the world.

After Latin class, I was almost out the door before I heard her raspy voice whistling through her teeth. "Miss Donovan."

The students pushed against me as I tried to turn back into the classroom.

"Yes Sister?"

"I need to speak with you for a few minutes."

I still had to get the rest of my books out of my locker before meeting Maggie and catching the bus. Sister Alfred never asked to speak to me before. What did she want?

"Have a seat, Agnes."

I cringed. I could handle the "Ms. Donovan" stuff but hearing my given name still unsettled me. I sat in a front row desk, with Sister Alfred a few feet in front of me, behind her old oak teacher's desk.

"I'm doing okay in Latin, aren't I Sister?" Ever since the phone call to my parents from Mr. Richards about my math, I'd been nervous it would happen again with another teacher.

"Of course. Your Latin grade is top-notch. I do hope you'll continue on with Latin all through high school. I don't get too many students who take it all four years."

So that was it, a pep talk to take Latin. More years of Latin was okay, but I wasn't sure about four years of Sister Alfred. She pushed a long chubby finger under her wimple and stretched her neck. A few strands of gray protruded from the side. I often wondered how much hair these nuns had under there. Did they ever comb it, or maybe some were bald?

"Have you ever talked with her about this?"

"What?" Oh dear, I missed what she'd said.

"Your sister. She's been with me in Sodality now for three years, and I really thought she might have a vocation. She is so very devout. But I've not heard her talk about a calling. I thought she may have discussed it with you. She often speaks of you."

Of me? Maggie often speaks of me? "I don't know Sister. I mean she used to talk about being a nun when we were little, but I don't know if she thinks about it much now."

"She's a very popular young lady. But when the Lord is calling you, all else counts for naught." Her bug eyes bore into mine. "I thought you would join the Sodality Club too, Agnes."

I fidgeted in my chair. "Well, yeah, Maggie said that. But I help with my younger sisters a lot after school."

"Of course. Well, if you hear Margaret speak of the convent, please encourage her to come see me. She seems somewhat distracted lately, and has even missed a number of Sodality meetings. I hope everything is all right at home?"

"At home? Well, uh, yes. I mean my parents have a lot on their minds with stuff, but we're fine." I knew better than to tell anyone about family problems.

She slapped her robe and rose slowly. I could hear her knees creak. "Good, glad to hear it. Well, I may yet talk to Margaret directly, but thought I'd make a couple of inquiries with you first. Thank you, Agnes. Keep up the good work."

A sudden image of Maggie dressed as a nun flashed before me, and I shivered.

Maggie

I had never been to Monsignor Neelan's office before. Mom walked me in, exchanged pleasantries, and said she'd be back in an hour. One wall of the office was covered with overstuffed bookshelves. His massive desk sat at an angle in the opposite corner, surrounded by richly upholstered furniture. With only a small casement window behind the desk, the room was dark, even in the daytime.

"Come in, Margaret. Have a seat. Would you like some tea or lemonade?"

"Maybe some lemonade would be nice."

I sat on the couch watching him as he stepped behind his desk and opened a small refrigerator. He poured lemonade into two tumblers on a tray, dropping an ice cube into each. Mom once told me he was Gramps' age, which would make him sixty-two. But unlike Gramps, who still had a full head of hair, Monsignor Neelan's hair was thinning. I knew this because during one of his visits Clare sat on his lap and pulled his biretta off by the tuft. Mom had been mortified and quickly apologized. He had only smiled, dusted off his biretta, and then placed it back on his head. It was there now as he walked towards me and took a seat in a large leather wing-backed chair.

His broad shoulders leaned forward, and his hand gently touched my knee. I stared down at the large hand with polished nails and massive ruby ring, momentarily distracted. His deep, rich voice brought me back.

He handed me the lemonade. "There you go, my dear. Now tell me about your friend."

I hadn't expected it to be so easy, talking about Jimmy to him. Maybe it was because it was no longer a secret. I told him about Jimmy's high grades, his athleticism, his kindness, and that he was Catholic. Finally I was getting a chance to talk about Jimmy to someone who would listen!

"You obviously have grown quite fond of this new friend, Maggie."

I nodded, twirling my hair with my finger.

His eyebrows rose. "Your parents have forbidden you to see him?"

"It's *so* unfair. I know they'd like him if they would just give him a chance."

"And if you never saw Jimmy again, how would you feel?"

I pictured Jimmy's face, the way he looked at me and made me feel inside. How could I explain that? A tear rolled down my cheek. I lowered my head and whispered "I think I love him."

Monsignor Neelan drew closer then, raising my chin with his fingertips, staring intently into my eyes and spoke. "Love. . . it's ..."

My lip trembled. He touched it lightly with his thumb. "A strong emotion."

I slumped back into the couch and swallowed. "I know, but it's what I *feel*. It's so unfair that my parents are doing this. Why can't I see Jimmy? It makes no sense."

He stood up, walked to the window, then turned to face me. "Your parents have your best interests at heart, Maggie."

I sprang from the couch and rushed toward him. "Couldn't you talk to them — at least make them give Jimmy a chance?"

"Margaret, why do you think your parents wanted you to speak to me?"

"I don't know. I suppose to get me to give him up, to see their point of view. But now you know how I feel. You'll talk to them, won't you? Please?"

"Hmm. Well, perhaps something can be arranged regarding Jimmy. But in the meanwhile we need to have some more talks. I'll speak with your mother, and see when she can bring you for another visit."

He walked me to the door and opened it. I was lightheaded, thinking of his words "... something can be arranged regarding Jimmy." Then I remembered my driver's test was next week. "Next week I'll have my license. I can drive myself."

"Didn't your father restrict you, Margaret?"

"Oh, I forgot."

"Well, I'm sure your father would allow you to drive over for appointments to see me. Don't worry. Everything will work out." He hugged me and I could feel the heavy weight of his body pressed against me. Kissing me lightly on the forehead, he stepped back and said, "Now go. I'll be calling your parents."

I dashed out the door and skipped into the parking lot.

Monsignor Neelan

e'd noticed the similarities before but having her sitting right next to him had unnerved him. It was as if Eleanor's ghost had appeared in his study. It wasn't only her looks. Margaret's voice had that same soft melodic quality. She twirled the ends of her curls with her fingers just as Eleanor once did. How could he not want her?

He remembered holding Eleanor's hand on the porch swing that warm spring evening of 1920. A yellow chiffon dress fell softly over her shoulders and a blue ribbon tied her golden tresses. The rich perfume of honeysuckle clung to the air. Her parents had been called away to attend to Eleanor's ailing grandmother. Being alone with her emboldened him, and as she pushed the squeaking wooden slats of the porch with her feet, he kissed her. Her lips, warm and moist, dizzied him, as they gently rocked back and forth. How long they kissed before she took his hand and led him inside to the parlor he did not know. But what they did in the parlor he will never forget. Her words, just like Maggie's of Jimmy, were ones of passion.

"I love you Robert." She'd whispered it in his ear as his body wrapped around hers on the sofa. He'd responded by kissing her neck, her shoulder, and unbuttoning the yellow silk buttons of her dress. When they had finished making love, her voice rose. "You won't ever leave me, will you, Robert?"

"What?" He kissed her again, his excitement returning.

"Tell me you won't leave me, Robert."

He cupped her breast, licking it gently with his tongue. "Never." He rolled back on top of her and took her again. Two weeks later he was on his way to Rome.

One of the Donovan kids answered the phone. Waiting for Rose to pick up, he fidgeted with the cord. A lot was riding on this conversation. He could convince Rose, but John?

"Hello?"

"Hello, Rose. It's Monsignor Neelan. He heard her suck in her breath.

"Hello, Monsignor. I was hoping you'd call. How did it go? Maggie seemed cheery when she got home. Did she say much?"

"She had quite a bit to say. We had a very fruitful conversation."

"Really? Oh, I'm so pleased. And did she talk about this thing with that boy Jimmy? I mean did she see why it just isn't right for a girl of sixteen. . ."

"Rose, let me stop you for a minute. Of course I tried to explain your point of view, but you must keep in mind that she is a young woman now, a young woman who believes she's in love." There was silence at the other end. He had to choose his words carefully. "I think I can help her to understand, but I don't think it's wise to be too heavy-handed."

"You think we're being too heavy-handed?"

"I think she needs some gentle persuasion. I'd like to continue to counsel her but in the meanwhile I think it would help if she thought that her parents were meeting her half-way. If she sees me as her advocate on the front end of this, I'm sure that I can gain her trust and get her to end this relationship. I suggest that you allow weekly supervised visits with Jimmy at your house on the condition that she sees me every week for counseling. Shall we say Saturday afternoons?"

"It might work, but I'm not sure that John will agree."

"I've seen young girls like this before, Rose. Her feelings for this boy will dim over time, but forbidding her from seeing him will only make her more determined that he is Prince Charming. Please, take my advice on this."

In the end it wasn't as hard as he thought. Rose called back an hour later to say that they agreed with his plan.

Petey

$\mathcal{I}$ don't know how he did it, but somehow Monsignor Neelan talked my parents into letting Maggie see Jimmy. But it had to be at the house. No going out on dates, and Maggie had to go for counseling sessions every week at the rectory. The whole thing was really weird. Maggie acted like she was on cloud nine. You'd think she'd be angry. She got her license, but could only take the car when she was going over to see Monsignor Neelan. I don't know what was worse, the fact that all I ever heard from Maggie was Jimmy this and Jimmy that, or that Jimmy himself spent virtually all of Saturday afternoon at our house, until that is she had to go for counseling with the priest. Dad even stayed home from work that first Saturday to meet him.

Maggie finished her chores early and spent the rest of the morning primping. She sat on the edge of the couch in her black skirt, tights, and blue sweater that Mom and Dad had given her for her birthday. I was in the living room when there was a knock on the door.

"Good afternoon, sir. I'm James Makowski. Most people call me Jimmy." They shook hands in the hallway.

Dad saw me peeking around the corner and called out, "Petey, go get us some sodas."

"Yes, Dad." I scurried to the kitchen and fumbled through the cabinets to find three glasses that matched. All I could find were the jelly glasses; Fred Flintstone, Betty, and Barney Rubble. I pulled out the ice cube trays and popped out two cubes for each glass. Balancing the drinks on a tray, I eased back to the living room. Maggie and Jimmy sat on the couch next to each other across from Dad in his recliner. No one was talking. They each took a glass.

"Petey, tell your mother that Jimmy is here."

I found Mom upstairs putting fresh sheets on the beds. "Mom, Jimmy's here."

She tucked in the last corner and pulled up the top sheet. "Hand me those two pillowcases, would you, Petey?" She held the pillow in her teeth while sliding it into the pillowcase. Pulling up the bedspread, she turned to me. "How's it going down there?"

"Pretty quiet."

She sighed. "I told your father that we should at least meet the young man. Then leave them alone a bit. Where's Genny? She's supposed to be helping me make beds."

"I think she went over to Nancy's house again. Mary and Clare are out back jumping rope." I helped tuck the spread under the pillows. "How long is he going to stay, Mom?"

"I don't know. A while, I guess. I told your father I'd keep the girls out of the house and let the two of them have the dining room. Dad's games will be on TV soon anyway."

It was nice to have Dad home for a change. I watched the Notre Dame game with him, but it was hard to follow the plays with Maggie and Jimmy laughing in the dining room. I could see their heads huddled close together. Dad wasn't commenting on the game as usual either. He didn't even shout with joy when Notre Dame intercepted and scored for a second time. His eyes were on the doorway into the dining room as he muttered under his breath. All I heard was "Damn Polarc," and something about Monsignor Neelan.

Maggie

ighttime was the worst. I would hug my pillow and press it between my thighs, rocking back and forth, imagining Jimmy beside me, as tears rolled down my nose. The love I felt for Jimmy was real. How could something so wonderful cause me to hurt so much and make my parents so angry with me? Even now that Jimmy was coming to the house, my parents barely spoke to him. And we couldn't go anywhere. I felt imprisoned in my own home. We were together but hardly touched. Sometimes we held hands or I leaned against him to feel the warmth and firmness of his body. I didn't know how much longer we could go on like this. This morning, we chanced a kiss, a long and delicious kiss. Then Mary and Clare came running outside and we had to pull apart. I suspect Dad was watching us and sent them out to play.

I had completed the nine days of the All Souls Novena, hoping prayer would bring spiritual serenity. Father Gunther gave a final sermon on the last night. I left the church feeling confused and betrayed by my faith. The gentle God I knew could not possibly condemn me for what I was feeling, could He? How could the love and desire I had for Jimmy be wrong? I had asked this question of Monsignor Neelan on my second visit.

"Of course you want him, my dear. God has given you a beautiful gift, a warm and loving spirit, and youthful body." Finally, someone who understood. I was hesitant at first to tell him about what Jimmy and I had done, all the kissing and touching, but he coaxed it out of me. I was relieved when he didn't condemn me. Instead, he leaned towards me, patted my knee, and spoke gently.

"You must channel this passion into your love for God. Only He can be the receptacle of such Love."

So I had prayed the same prayer every night this week. "Please God, show me the Way. Show me how I might love You, how I might give myself to You, and keep my love for Jimmy pure." As I reluctantly said goodbye to Jimmy at the door, I resolved to seek the Monsignor's guidance this afternoon during our counseling session. Only he seemed to understand my anguish.

I sat in Monsignor Neelan's study. I didn't plan to, but as he asked about Jimmy, I totally broke down. He held me close as I wept, gently rocking me back and forth. "There, there, Margaret. Lie back and relax. I can help you, my child, but you must trust me." Rising from the sofa, he took a glass of water from a tray on his desk.

"Here, Margaret, take a drink of this to calm yourself." The leather couch sagged under his weight as he sat next to me and handed me the water. It felt cool with a strange bitter taste. The wall clock ticked louder and louder. He raised his hands to my hair. His fingers were thick, his nails polished. He loosened the blue satin ribbon in my hair. It slid from my neck. He wrapped it around his wrist and brushed it across his lips. I stared at the crucifix on the wall as he rose to leave the room.

He returned swinging a thurible wafting the sweet pungent aroma of incense. Mesmerized by the filigreed gold orb swinging back and forth, I inhaled deeply.

Monsignor had changed into his purple-trimmed black cassock. Its skirts rubbed against me as he drew closer. "God has sent me to you,

Margaret. I am his chosen Disciple, ready to receive you. God knows your anguish, your pain, and great desire. He has sent me to you to quench your thirst. God is ready to receive you. Only say the word, and you shall be healed."

My mouth was dry, my limbs limp. The walls were moving toward me.

Untying the purple sash from his cassock, he laid it over my eyes. The silk was cool to the touch. He then asked me to open my mouth and placed a thin communion wafer on my tongue. As the wafer clung to the roof of my mouth, his fingers grazed my lips. There was a warm breath in my ear, and a soft whisper of, "Jimmy, Jimmy, Jimmy."

A hand cupped my breast. "I am here for you, my beloved. Come to me."

My breast rose and fell, the nipples hardening. I began to see soft white circles with vivid bubbles of fuchsia, indigo blue, and emerald green fading in and out. A warm sensation, as if I'd swallowed liquid rays of sunshine, surged through me. My mouth opened and was engulfed. His thick tongue pressed inside. The collar of my opened blouse now tickled my ear. My skirt bunched up to my waist. I tried to breathe, to speak. But no words came, and my breathing became shallow and labored. I was hot everywhere. My legs opened. My head was spinning, going round and round, even as my hips rose.

"Oh, God, Oh Jimmy!" I pushed upward, as his fingers probed, his tongue explored.

Off in the distance, I heard a guttural moan, and the words, "Eleanor, Eleanor." Why did Jimmy use my middle name? The chime of a clock struck as I screamed with pain. Each thrust matched the striking of four o'clock. I lay still and quiet, as a cloth wiped the stickiness from between my legs. The purple sash now lay on my bare breast. He sat on the edge of the couch, pushing sweat-drenched curls off my forehead. I stared, transfixed by the damp, bloodied cloth at my feet, and drew my legs up into a tight ball against my chest.

"Here, drink this." A pillow propped me up, and I saw a small china cup put to my lips. I sipped sweetened tea. "You have given the greatest gift you have to God, Maggie, the Temple of your body. Now you can remain pure with your boyfriend, knowing that only God has known your gift."

The darkened room began to come into focus. I could see his flushed face close to mine. There were lines around his gray eyes. The pupils were large and black, like little oval mirrors that showed my reflection.

Petey

Why didn't Mom and Dad see? Something was wrong with Maggie. I knew it on Sunday when Maggie, Mary, and I went to church alone. Dad was working and Mom stayed home with Genny, who was running a fever. Maggie walked us to a pew way in the back, not in our usual place. When it was time to go to communion, she stayed behind. I wanted to ask why, but was afraid. Catholics who didn't go to communion were not in a state of grace. But how could that be with Maggie? On the drive home, Mary leaned over the front seat and asked, "Maggie, why didn't you go to communion?" At first Maggie ignored her. "Maggie, didn't you hear me? I said why didn't you. . .?"

"I heard you, Mary. I just didn't, okay?"

I had never heard Maggie snap at Mary before. She was usually so patient with our little sisters, much more than I. Mary looked as if she were going to cry. Maggie reached one arm over the seat and patted her. "I'm sorry. How about we stop and pick up some doughnuts, okay?" Mary immediately grinned. "Doughnuts, yeah! Can I pick some?"

Maggie smiled. "Sure." Five minutes later, we pulled into the doughnut shop's parking lot and Maggie handed me a few dollars. Mary and I jumped out of the car, went inside and made our selections. I chose two apple-cinnamons, Maggie's favorite, and let Mary choose the rest.

When we arrived home, I found Mom sitting on her bed pressing a cold cloth to Genny's forehead. Genny's fever had risen, and Mom had called Dr. Shepley's emergency number. He made a house call later in the afternoon, and said that Genny needed to go to the hospital for an emergency appendectomy. Dad was not home from work yet. Mom quickly put together an overnight bag for Genny, gave Maggie and me some last minute directions about dinner, and said she'd call from the hospital to talk to Dad when he got home.

I have the date in my diary, November 17, 1963. That was the day that I should have told them, should have tried to find out what was wrong with Maggie. But all our worries had turned to Genny. She was in the hospital for three days. Maggie and I took care of Mary and Clare each night while Mom and Dad went to visit her. By Thursday, Genny was propped up on the couch, a pair of crutches in the corner. We all gathered round to look at her stitches.

Mary stared at the incision. "Will you have a scar, Genny?"

"The doctor says it will be small."

I perched on the end of the couch. "When will you be going back to school?"

"Next week, but I have to use crutches for a while." We had tons of questions. But finally Mom made us all stop. She said that Genny needed her rest.

On Friday, I expected Maggie to look more animated. She'd see Jimmy tomorrow. But the bus ride to school was the same as it had been all week. She sat in stony silence, and I couldn't get anything more than one or two word responses to my questions or attempts at conversation. Even Samantha noticed it. Approaching my locker, she said, "Hey Petey, can I talk with you a minute?"

"Hi, Samantha."

"Maggie's been like a clam all week. Seems sad too. I mean, I know about Genny's operation, and all. But is that it?"

"Yeah, I guess so. I mean, I don't know, really."

"Well, I'm kind of worried about her. I think it's still this Jimmy thing. Your folks are nice and all, but they really need to stop messing with Maggie's mind. I've tried talking to her but she's not saying much."

I slammed my locker. I didn't like Samantha sticking her nose into our family business. "I'll talk to her." All morning I struggled to pay attention in class, thinking about what Samantha had said. What could I say to Maggie? Should I talk to Mom? My thoughts were interrupted by an intercom announcement from the principal. Everyone was to leave class and report to the auditorium for an all-school assembly. In the middle of the day?

We all filed into the auditorium, anxious to find out why we'd all been brought out of class. The principal's voice sounded so grave. When he told us that the President had been shot some of the girls shrieked, and lots of us cried, including me. I mean, this was John F. Kennedy. We all loved him. Our first Roman Catholic president. There were pictures of him everywhere in the corridors and classrooms of our school. Dad would be devastated. How could this happen?

When Kennedy was running for president, Dad told me about how Kennedy had saved his men on the PT 109 boat and then was rescued in the Solomon Islands in the Pacific. Dad said he served there too and knew that it was all true. He had talked to some Marines who had helped get Kennedy off Choiseul Island. That's the kind of courage you want in a man who's president, he said. When JFK was first running for president, only three years ago, I read everything I could about him in the newspapers. Sometimes I'd listen to Dad read parts of the paper aloud to me.

I couldn't understand why this had happened. On the bus ride home, Maggie held my hand and let me cry on her shoulder. I forgot all about my promise to Samantha. The whole world was glued to their television sets as we watched the horrible pictures and listened to Walter Cronkite who gave the news with a shaky voice. Instead of eating in the dining room, as usual, we ate sandwiches in front of the television. I didn't even notice that Jimmy didn't come over.

Nothing was as it should be. I poured myself into my studies. Working algebraic equations or translating French was an escape from the tension at home. I now frequently heard Mom and Dad arguing. Sometimes it was about money, and other times it was about Maggie. Mom was often working late, calling me to get supper started. I don't think she slept much as she always seemed so tired, and not her usual patient self. Dad no longer joked with us at supper, played games with Clare, or read the newspaper with me. One night I heard him telling Mom about an impending strike at work. I remembered how much Dad and Mom had fought the last time there was a strike.

I was surprised to see Dad smiling and tousling Mary's hair as we came to the dinner table. Macaroni and cheese and hot dogs again? Pouring myself a glass of milk, I reached for the ketchup but stopped when I heard Dad speak.

"Listen up everyone. I'll be going away for a while. I've been offered a temporary loading job out of state."

Everyone started asking questions at once. Dad would be gone for about a month but the pay would be double. He'd be living in a rooming house with a bunch of other guys. I couldn't imagine a whole month without my father. He'd never been away from home before.

"I want all you girls to be on your best behavior. It won't be easy for your mother without me here, and I will have the car, so you'll have to stay close to home." He looked directly at Maggie. She put her head down, and pushed the peas around with her fork.

"Do you have to go away, Daddy?" Mary implored.

Clare got up from her chair and crawled onto his lap. "I don't want you to leave, Daddy."

"It's okay, Sweetheart. I'll be home before you know it."

"Will you be home by Christmas, Daddy?"

"Yes, Genny, I'll be home just before Christmas. And it will be a good Christmas, I'm sure." He looked up at Mom, and they both smiled for the first time in weeks.

That night Maggie seemed happier than she'd been in a long time. I crossed my legs and leaned against the wall as she flipped through the pages of a history book. She was singing some song I didn't know.

"You don't seem upset about Dad leaving."

She turned around and stared at me for a moment. "You heard him, Petey. He'll get double pay. Haven't you heard him and Mom fighting constantly about money? Don't you remember the Christmas that there weren't presents at all? Dad made up that story for Mary and Clare about Santa being sick and not being able to make deliveries. It just about broke his heart. This trip will mean we'll have presents for Christmas."

"Is that the *only* reason you're so pleased?"

"What do you mean?"

"You know."

"What are you talking about?"

I scowled and pushed my back harder against the wall. "You know what. Jimmy. Without Dad here, you'll probably drive off to see more of your *precious Jimmy*."

Maggie slammed her book and stood up. "Petey, don't use that tone. And just how do you think that is going to happen? You heard him. We all have to stay close to home. We won't even have a car."

Suddenly, she let out a delighted shriek, startling me so much that I bumped my head against the wall.

Rubbing the back of my head, I said, "What? What is it?"

"We won't have a car! Mom can't take me to see Monsignor Neelan! I won't have to go on Saturday afternoons anymore!" She threw her arms around me, squeezed me tight, and kissed me on the cheek.

Stiffly I replied, "Yeah, and then Jimmy can stay later, right?"

"Oh, Petey, you don't know. It's just going to be *so* much better now!" A tear ran down her cheek even as she beamed. She wiped away the tear and ran out the door. I stared after her.

But Maggie was wrong. Mom set her straight the following morning.

﹌

"Remember young lady that your father and I agreed that seeing Jimmy was contingent upon continued counseling sessions with Monsignor Neelan. He will be coming to pick you up Saturday afternoon. I've already arranged it." Maggie begged and pleaded, but Mom wouldn't budge.

I didn't like it when he came. Mom got all gushy and kept talking. I tried to hide, but sometimes Mom made me come out to say hello, and he'd do that kiss on the mouth thing, and I wanted to spit. Maggie stalled coming out of her room. Couldn't Mom see how she hated to go? It didn't seem to me that these "sessions" were helping. When Maggie came home from the rectory on Saturday afternoons, she never spoke. She'd lock herself in the bathroom and take long baths. If it wasn't for my friend Sherlin perhaps nothing would have changed.

Maggie

I scrubbed and scrubbed, and made the water as hot as I could. But he was still on me and in me. I knew now what was happening, and what he did. I wanted it to stop, but didn't know how to make it stop. At least I no longer bled. That first time I came home and bathed, and saw the trickle of blood between my legs, I was terrified. I knew it was not time for my period. Would others see? Could they tell by looking at me what had happened? But I knew that no one must ever know. *No one!* What would Jimmy think of me? Or Dad or Mom? If I hadn't wanted Jimmy so bad, hadn't yearned to be with him, it wouldn't have happened.

Monsignor Neelan keeps telling me that it's not a sin, that I belong to God now. But I knew it was my fault. I slumped lower in the tub until my head submerged, and there in the soapy water I let myself cry. How could Jimmy ever want me now? I came up gulping air, tasting soap bubbles in my mouth. Stepping out of the tub, I wrapped a large towel around me, but my legs began to wobble. I braced myself against the wall and then slid to the floor, choking back more tears, murmuring to myself, "No one must know. No one."

When Daddy left, I cried. I thought somehow he would find out even though I didn't want him to. And then he would rescue me. Somehow my Daddy would make it all right. Like that time at the movie theater. Dad took Petey and me to see *Old Yeller*. We sat through three cartoons, the previews, and one newsreel before the movie started, and then I just had to go to the bathroom.

"Why did you have to wait until the movie started?" Daddy chided.

"It's okay, Daddy. I can go by myself."

"No. Petey will go with you. And come right back. Don't go out to the concession area, okay? You've already had enough soda and popcorn."

We groped our way in the dark, feeling the carpeted walls until we found the exit. At first we thought we were all alone in the restroom.

My skirt fell to the floor as I squatted over the bowl. Petey pounded on the door. "C'mon, Maggie, hurry up. I don't want to miss the beginning."

"Okay, okay. I'm not the one who ordered Dr. Pepper, remember? You know that always makes me have to go pee." I flushed the toilet, zipped my skirt, and stepped out. Petey had retreated to the sinks, her eyes saucer like.

"What? What is it?" I asked. Her mouth opened, but nothing came out. Slowly she raised her arm and pointed to the last stall. A fat man with a greasy shirt hanging over his belly gawked at me.

"Hey, little girl." I froze. He reached me before I could even breathe. His hand grabbed my wrist, and then he touched my hair. "Pretty blonde hair. I like blonde hair." I know there was a scream, but I'm not sure if it was Petey's or mine. She ran. Petey was faster than anyone at school. She had won every schoolyard race we'd ever run. The fat man kept stroking my hair. His belly rubbed up against me. I could smell sweat; putrid, dank, sweat. Then it was over. Daddy was there, knocking the fat man down, twisting his arm, and took him outside. Petey and I stood in the concession lobby, catching just a glimpse of the flashing red police car lights. Daddy wanted to take us home, but we begged him to let us go back and see the movie. I cried a lot that night, but I don't know if it was because of the fat man or because of Old Yeller.

I wanted Daddy to make this nightmare stop too. A little voice keeps saying to me, "Tell him. Go tell him what happens in Monsignor Neelan's study. Let him hold you as you cry, and then you'll never have to see that priest again." If only I could believe that. . But I also remember what Monsignor Neelan said, *"This is our secret, Maggie. Remember that. If you speak of this, I will deny it and no one will believe you."* I've done something unforgiveable. Daddy would be so angry. I picture him yelling at me and the hurt look in his eyes. I don't think he could ever love me like his daughter again. Could he?

And Jimmy? I wanted to tell him too. Wanted his arms around me holding me tight telling me that everything would be all right, that he'd love me forever no matter what had happened. Last Saturday we sat in the living room. He was talking about Kennedy's assassination and the new President. My head pounded. My throat constricted, as I tried to hold it all inside. But finally a tear slid down my cheek and dropped off my nose. It puddled on Jimmy's hand. He rubbed it away with his thumb, and tipped my face towards his.

"Hey, what's this? You crying? What's wrong?"

I shook my head. "Nothing." This was my chance. Let it all out. But I was afraid. If our eyes met, would he somehow see inside and know? I wasn't the same Maggie. He couldn't wipe away my shame as simply as my tear.

He spoke again. "It's me, isn't it, babbling on about the assassination. I'm sorry. Let's talk of something else. You haven't said a thing about these forced visits with that priest. What do you talk about?" He shifted on the couch, turning to look at me.

I swallowed hard and looked down, avoiding his eyes. What if I did tell him? No, impossible. I couldn't take that chance. I couldn't lose Jimmy. Straightening up, I answered, "Oh, you know, just God stuff." I forced a smile. "What were you saying about President Johnson?"

He brightened. "He's a Southerner, so, you know, we were worried. But I think he'll support the movement." That's what he called it — the movement. Lately that's all he talked about. I'd seen some of the protests on television, the horrible brutality of the cops on those poor children. Petey and I talked about it some. Wondered if we could be that brave. It was hard to think of the outside world when my own world was crumbling.

"Maggie, have you heard about the poll tax?"

I tried to refocus. "Poll tax?"

"Negroes down south are made to pay a poll tax when they vote. It's a way of keeping them from voting." He shook his head, and then raised his voice. "Can you believe that? Gabe is right. We have to act! I've decided to go with him."

"Gabe?"

"You remember — my roommate."

"But where? Where are you going?"

"Mississippi. To help them register to vote."

Where was Mississippi again? Very far away. Maybe that would be where he'd go if he ever found out about what I'd done. First Daddy abandoned me, now Jimmy.

◆ ━ ◆

Samantha cornered me today by my locker and said that she knew something was bothering me. I almost told her but I didn't. Whatever it was, she said, I'd better talk to someone. But who? Usually I told Petey almost everything. But she just didn't understand my feelings for Jimmy. How could I possibly tell her about Monsignor Neelan? She'd be horrified.

I tossed and turned in bed. My throat felt sore from choking back tears. The clock downstairs chimed twelve times and I threw the covers off. I needed a glass of water. Barefoot, I crept down the stairs and found myself standing just outside my parent's bedroom door. I heard them talking.

"I'm going to miss you John."

"You know I hate to leave you and the girls. But this will mean we'll have a Christmas."

"Christmas isn't about presents."

"Maybe, but I swore I'd never look at those sad faces on Christmas morning again. I may not be much, but I'm going to make damn sure that my family is provided for."

"You've always done that."

"Have I? Not enough, I'm afraid."

"You come straight home after work every night, always anxious to see me and the girls. For that I'm grateful. I know how a lot of the guys stop at the bars and drink. When I was growing up, I saw very little of my own father."

"But your father was Chief of Police, a man of responsibility."

"His responsibility was me, and he seemed to forget that."

"You never lacked for anything growing up, Rose. My father drank and gambled away his paycheck, while his wife and children went hungry, or worse yet, had to hide from his angry tirades."

"And yet your mother loved him."

The bed creaked, and there was a long sigh. "I suppose she did. God bless her soul. I guess she remembered the way he was before the bottle took him."

"It can be an awful demon. My grandmother told me that my father drank some after my mother died."

"I'd probably take to drink too if I ever lost you, Rose."

"I'm not going anywhere." My mother paused before speaking again. "But it will be a long month without you."

"You know I'd rather be here, especially now with this Maggie thing. I still don't see why we should let her see the guy."

"Maggie's not a child. Like Monsignor Neelan said forbidding her to see Jimmy will just turn her against us. Besides, he seems like a nice boy."

My father's voice rose. "He's *not* a boy! That's the problem."

My mother sighed before responding hesitantly. I was sure she was trying to choose the right words, say nothing that would provoke my father again. "Maggie's always been mature for her age. It's not surprising that she's attracted to someone older."

"She'd forget him in time."

"I don't think so. I know she won't forget our actions. She might never forgive us if we go back on our word now."

"Has she said that? You've talked to her about all this?" my father asked.

"I've tried talking with her, but she doesn't say much. Monsignor Neelan says that she's making progress in counseling."

"Progress? I don't see any progress. She mopes around here like a maimed dog. How do we know she's making progress, just 'cause *he* says so?"

Another of Mom's sighs. "You know I trust Monsignor Neelan. I'm sure he's helping Maggie. He even said they've discussed her possible vocation."

"Vocation! You mean to the convent? I thought she gave up that idea a long time ago. So that's what your Monsignor is up to. He's not counseling her. He's brainwashing her. Jesus Christ, Rose, can't you see that?" I cringed against the wall.

"Shh, keep your voice down. You'll wake the children."

The bed creaked again, and I heard the scruff of slippers. I ducked around the corner. My mother's voice again. "I know you're mad, but it's not like that. Monsignor Neelan is just trying to help.

"And just how is talking about being a nun helping?"

"By sorting out her feelings. She needs to find out if she wants a future with a man or the Church."

"Yeah, he's helping all right. Confusing the hell out of her is more like it. I want Maggie to stop seeing Neelan AND stop seeing Jimmy. Get some normalcy back to her life, and ours."

"Give it a little more time, John, please?"

There was no answer, just the sound of someone moving in the bed, a soft kiss, and a repeated plea, "Please, John?"

My father sighed. His voice lowered. "Against my better judgment, which I wish you would trust more than Neelan's. If things haven't improved by the time I come home, I'm putting an end to all of it."

I pressed against the wall, then skulked to bed. My mother's words were a constant refrain as I lay sleepless. "You know I trust Monsignor Neelan." She'd never believe me.

Monsignor Neelan

e walked the few steps from the rectory to the church without an umbrella or raincoat, despite an icy rain pulsing from the gray November sky. His once-a-month confessional duty was his least favorite priestly chore. Father Thomas covered all the other Saturday afternoons and actually seemed to like it. If the bishop would permit it, he would have given over the entire job years ago. And now because of it, he also missed seeing Maggie. He slid the door aside and waited. He recognized the soft, meek voice immediately. Colleen Williams had been confessing to him for fifteen years or more. She would recite how many times she had lost her temper with her children, how many times she had lied to her husband about sneaking cigarettes, and how many times she had unkind thoughts about her mother-in-law. He tuned out right after "Bless me Father, for I have sinned." He was about to give her the usual penance of ten Hail Marys, when he heard sniffling, "I know it's a mortal sin, Father, but I just don't know what we would do right now if I were to get pregnant. My husband's out of work, and there's little enough room in the house with seven children and my mother-in-law. But isn't it also a sin to deny my husband the pleasures of a wife?"

"Tell me why you feel you have committed a mortal sin, my child."
He couldn't imagine Colleen committing a mortal sin of any kind.

"Because the church says it's a sin. He used one of those things, you
know, from the drug store, and I let him. Three times we did it with
protection. Dan says, I-I mean, my husband," —did she still believe he
didn't know who she was?— "that it's *his* sin, not mine, and that we have
to use something. But each time, afterwards, I feel so guilty, and I don't
know how to make it right. I know to be absolved, I must not only repent
the sin, but vow never to do it again, but I don't know if I can. I mean
if I would just have my change, my worries would be over, but my own
mother, God bless her soul, didn't have her change until she was 55. I
can't keep having babies."

God, the woman could prattle on.

"I'm just so sorry, I don't know, I'm so sorry." She was crying now.

He sighed. "My child, God knows your heart is pure. You have confessed your sin, and I will absolve you. If you stray again, I am here
to listen to your confession. God understands that we are all sinners.
For your penance I want you to say three rosaries, one for each transgression. — And," he paused slightly, "perhaps, should you stray *again*,
a rosary the next morning. Now bow your head, and recite the Act of
Contrition."

The memorized words came haltingly as she sucked in the end of
her tears. "O my God, I am heartily sorry for having offended Thee,
and I detest all my sins because of Thy just punishments, but most of all
because they offend Thee my God, who art all good and deserving of all
my love. I firmly resolve, with the help of Thy grace, to sin no more and
to avoid the occasions of sin. Amen."

"I absolve you of all your sins, in the name of the Father, and of the
Son, and of the Holy Ghost. Amen. Go now and sin no more."

The rain had stopped by the time he left the confessional and
stepped back outside. He looked upward to the nighttime sky, so thick
with clouds that not even a single star blinked through. "God, you deny
me even a glimmer of light?" He understood sin. What he didn't understand was absolution. Not for him, anyway. Because he knew he had

never repented. He understood Colleen's conflict, her knowledge that she would sin again. He too would sin again. But no one would be there to give him absolution, or even a touch of tacit permission, as he had tried to give Colleen. Even in the secular world, what he was doing was wrong. He knew that. But it was a path he'd begun long ago.

The first time he had disrobed a girl in his study and seduced her with the power of his authority, his Cross, his sex, he knew he would not stop. After that girl, there would be another. He didn't persist with one for very long. The risks were too great. Each time he had been able to buy her silence. Each time his powers of persuasion and her sense of shame had overcome any temptation to reveal the act. Each time his excitement grew with the girl's look of fear and the thrill of conquest. What drove him to this he didn't know and no longer cared. The others he could leave behind. He did some penance, begged his God for forgiveness, and tried to fight the temptation. But with Maggie, he knew he could not. He had already risked more with her than with any other. He had been careless with protection. Colleen's confession reminded him of this fear. With others he had successfully used the withdrawal method, or condoms, but with Maggie, he just couldn't. He wanted her too completely and too passionately to do either. He had even begun to try to see her outside of the rectory. He used any excuse he could think of to drive over to Holy Redeemer Academy, hoping to get a glimpse of her walking by. Just the sight of Maggie made his heart beat faster and feel young again. His God may be a forgiving God, but not when the desire overruled the remorse.

He pushed open the heavy rectory door, shook out his umbrella, and placed it in the umbrella stand. The fire in the study was almost out. He scattered the embers with a poker, tossed in a log, and squatted down to blow into the fireplace. A wisp of smoke tickled his nose. He coughed and stood. Leaning his arms on the mantel, his eyes shifted to the one photo it held. A small stocky boy in knickers and cap holding a football, looking up admiringly at the tall well-dressed man beside him with his hand resting on the boy's shoulder. Receiving that football from his father was one of the first and last memories of his father. He did remember the funeral. It was in a huge cathedral. There were hundreds of people. He watched the priests in their long cassocks swing incense over the coffin. He could barely see his mother's face through her veil. Burying his face in his mother's lap, he started to cry. She pulled a handkerchief from the folds of her black dress and said in a harsh voice, "Sit up straight and stop crying. People are watching." Was that when he began to hate her?

The evening stretched out long before him. He could finish the budget reports on his desk but the Bishop didn't need them until next week. The fire had begun to catch. He tossed in another log before walking to his desk. He needed to shake this sour mood, put aside painful memories. What he needed was a drink. He walked to the liquor cabinet and lifted out the bourbon. Pouring a double, he sat and stared into space. He downed his drink quickly and poured another. Why couldn't he stop? There had been times in the past that he thought he would stop. Long periods in fact that he remained chaste, and began to think he could regain the rewards of Heaven. But not now. He would not, could not, give up Maggie and suppressed any rational thoughts of doing so. No doubt this was the cause of his nightmares. Satan had visited him. The dreams always started with Maggie, her round, soft body under his, her face, so exquisite it should be painted for eternity. He would begin to caress her, kiss her, and mount her, moaning in ecstasy, only to look up at a face, so evil in its grimace that he knew that in this act of possession, he had become possessed. The words "You're mine" curled from the devil's lips, and Robert Neelan knew his soul had surrendered.

Tomorrow's sermon lay on the corner of his desk. His eyes caught the words from Matthew in the first paragraph. "Rejoice and be glad because great is your reward in heaven." He laughed out loud.

Petey

$\mathcal{L}$ ittle things in life change everything. If the washing machine hadn't broken down that Saturday morning, would things have happened as they did? I don't know. But I think it was the last straw for Mom. She'd been uncharacteristically cranky all morning. Dad called last night to say that he wouldn't be coming home this weekend as promised. He had to work both Saturday and Sunday. When Clare spilled her cereal, Mom had yelled at her and wouldn't refill the bowl. "Just eat what's left, Clare. It's your own fault for spilling it." Even Clare's tears hadn't softened Mom's edge.

Now Mom was looking for quarters, and I was gathering up the dirty laundry. There was a knock at the door. Lifting the lace curtains to peek out the window, Mom exclaimed, "Oh my. I lost all track of time. Petey, go upstairs and tell your sister that Jimmy's here."

Maggie was sitting at the edge of the bed, brushing her hair.

"Jimmy's here, Mags."

She bounded down the stairs. Since Dad had left, Jimmy had been arriving earlier on Saturday mornings. I doubt Mom even noticed. And there was a lot more kissing. Mom was too busy to chaperone. When I walked into the front hallway I saw them kissing. I knew I shouldn't but I watched them. Jimmy no longer had his summer tan, but the muscles were still there. I could see them through his sweater as he held Maggie tight. His eyes opened then, and he saw me. I turned away and dashed into the bathroom to gather up the dirty towels. By the time I dragged the laundry bags out to the front hallway Mags and Jimmy were in the living room with Mom.

"It's nice to see you again, Jimmy. How's school going?" Mom asked.

"Fine, Mrs. Donovan. How have you been?"

"All right. Although the children do miss their father, as do I. We had hoped he'd get home this weekend." She sighed. "But he has to work."

"Maggie tells me that Mr. Donovan has the car. How've you been getting around?"

"I get a ride to work. The younger children walk to school, and Petey and Maggie, as you know, take the bus. I'm able to pick up a few things at the grocery store during my lunch hour if I need to. But it is a hassle when the unexpected comes up, like today."

"What happened?"

"The washing machine finally broke down. It was a second-hand one that we bought last year. I had hoped my Laundromat days were over but it looks like we'll be taking the bus over there this afternoon. Which reminds me, Maggie, I want you to call Monsignor Neelan. Tell him not to come for you today. I need you to baby-sit."

Maggie's face lit up. "That's fine, Mom. But would you call him please? I only have a couple of hours with Jimmy."

"Okay, I'll call him, but don't forget I have to catch the 11:15, so Jimmy will have to leave by then. Sorry, Jimmy."

"Mrs. Donovan, I'd be happy to drive you to the Laundromat. We could leave at noon when I was going back to school anyway. If that's okay with you?"

"That would be wonderful! Do you have room for Petey too? She usually helps me at the Laundromat."

"Sure, plenty of room." He turned then, saw me standing in the doorway, and flashed a grin. I blushed, and ducked back into the hall.

"Thanks Jimmy. This will give me more time to clean up the kitchen." Mom yelled out, "Petey, if you've finished gathering the laundry, you can start cleaning the bathroom." I scowled. I hated cleaning bathrooms. Mom was still talking. "Maggie, don't forget your Saturday chores this afternoon, and you'll have to fix lunch for your sisters."

"Yes, Mom."

"Okay, then. You want some coffee, Jimmy?"

"Coffee would be great. Thanks, Mrs. Donovan."

I hurried to the bathroom before Mom caught me eavesdropping. Shaking the Ajax into the tub, I began to scour, pressing as hard as I could. I was on my knees scrubbing for a long time before realizing that my knuckles were raw. Turning on the water, I sloshed the chalky substance down the drain. The sound of Daffy Duck and Elmer Fudd along with Mary's high-pitched laughter emanated from the living room television.

"Mom, Jimmy and I are going to take a walk, okay?" I heard the door slam. Dad wouldn't have let them go. Why did he have to work so much, anyway? I sighed, knowing the answer to that. Only two more weeks 'til Christmas and Dad would be home; done with his road trip. Clare kept asking when we were going to get a tree. Probably not until Christmas Eve. The only decoration in the house right now was the advent wreath on the kitchen table. Tomorrow we would light the pink candle for joy. Right now, scrubbing the outside of the toilet, I didn't feel very joyful.

At noon, I put on my coat and dragged the laundry bag into the hallway.

"Here, let me get that." Jimmy lifted the bag easily, swung it onto his shoulder, and opened the car door. The back seat was loaded with books and notepads. "Just push those books on the floor, Petey."

Mom had already made herself comfortable up front. Maggie came running out and handed something to Jimmy. He gave her a quick kiss before getting into the driver's seat. Mom looked straight ahead. Maggie stood at the curb, jacketless, rubbing her arms for warmth. As we pulled away I looked out the window and saw her blowing kisses. Jimmy smiled into the rearview mirror.

Mom dropped a few quarters into her purse and snapped it shut. "This is very kind of you to take us, Jimmy."

"Happy to do it, Mrs. Donovan."

"Do they have washing machines in your dormitory on campus?"

"Oh, no."

"So you must have to go to the Laundromat too?"

He laughed then, a deep, rich laugh. My skin prickled with goose bumps, even though the heat was pumping out of the vents. "That would surprise my mother. She tells me I'm spoiled rotten. No, I take it home on weekends, and it gets put in with the rest of the family laundry."

"Well, I'm sure your mother doesn't mind doing it. She knows how busy you are with your studies."

"Well, uh, actually Georgia usually does the laundry unless she has the weekend off."

"Georgia?"

"She helps out at the house."

"I see."

Mom had that look on her face. The one that told me that she was trying to be nice, but inside was thinking bad thoughts. I guess she was thinking, like I was, that Jimmy's family must have money if they had a maid. You'd think she'd be happy about that, but Mom and Dad were funny about rich people.

Mom's voice was abrupt. "Take the second right after the post office. The Laundromat is right on the corner."

As we pulled up to the curb, Jimmy jumped out of the car to open the door for my mother and me. "Let me get those." As he set the laundry bags in front of machine #4, he said, "I guess Maggie never told you about my mother."

"Your mother?"

"She has polio. Caught it fifteen years ago. Dad carried her up the stairs, bathed her, and did everything for her until he started having back trouble. That's when we hired Georgia. She moved up here from Atlanta, where some of her family still lives. I'm hoping to visit them on my way South during semester break."

My mother loaded the washing machine while I pulled out the slot for the quarters. She stopped for a moment and turned to look at Jimmy.

"I didn't know about your mother's illness, Jimmy. That must have been very hard on you as a boy."

"Not really. I mean yes, in a way, when it first happened. It was a real blow, but I only have a few memories of my mother before she was in her wheelchair. But it hasn't really changed who she is, if you know what I mean."

"And this employee of your parents, Georgia is her name?"

"Yes."

"She's a colored woman?"

He nodded. "I owe a lot to Georgia, not only for helping my mother, but for opening my eyes to what life is like for Negroes in this country.

"I really never knew any colored, ah . . . Negro people. Maggie tells me that you are going south to do some kind of work for them. I hope you're not going to be in any of those protests like I've seen on television. You might get arrested."

"I'm going to Hattiesburg, Mississippi to help with voter registration. Most black people have not been allowed to register to vote because of poll taxes and absurd literacy tests."

"Do your parents know about this?"

"Yes. My mother told me if she wasn't in a wheelchair she'd go with me."

Mom poured the soap detergent in, shaking her head. "I could never do such a thing." She pushed the coin slot and turned to look at Jimmy. "You be careful. I don't want Maggie getting some phone call from a jail in Mississippi."

"I'll remember that, Mrs. Donovan. Are you going to be all right getting home with all that laundry on the bus? I feel bad leaving you, but I have a big paper due on Monday, and still have lots to write."

"Go on. Don't worry about me. I've taken the bus with laundry bags before. And I've got Petey to help."

Again, Jimmy smiled at me, a warm smile that made his blue eyes crinkle. He gave my neck a quick squeeze. "Yeah, I'm sure Petey's a big help. So long, then. See you next weekend." I touched the back of my neck. It was still warm. I stared after him. What was it like for Maggie when he touched her?

"Did you bring something to read?" Mom sat down in one of the plastic orange chairs and pulled some knitting out of her big handbag.

"Huh?" I turned to my mother. "No. Forgot. Can I have a bubble gum?"

She handed me a penny for the bubble gum machine. A big blue one rolled out, and I dropped it in my mouth. After the third bubble popped, Mom said, "Why don't you walk down the street to Sherlin's place. It's only half a block away. The laundry won't be done for a long time. I remember the Wangs are moving soon. She'd probably like to see you."

Mom was always encouraging me to go do stuff with a girlfriend. Usually hanging out with Jeff and Hank was enough for me. But since high school they didn't come around much. Sherlin's family lived above their restaurant. Since it was Saturday afternoon, they'd probably be pretty busy. All the girls helped out.

"I don't think she'll have much time for me, Mom. You know she helps with the food preparation in the kitchen."

"That's okay. Maybe they'll put you to work. Go on. It will do you good. No fun sitting in a laundromat watching the clothes going around in circles. I've got my knitting to do. It will be awhile before they're washed and dried." She leaned over and gave me a kiss on the forehead. "Go on. Just be back by two o'clock. Okay?"

"Okay."

The restaurant was dark even on this bright sunny day. Red Chinese lanterns hung from the ceiling. There was an older couple sitting in the corner eating. Otherwise the place was empty. I walked through to the kitchen, cracked the door, and peeked inside. Mrs. Wang stood by the counter, chopping onions. Mr. Wang was bent over some books at a desk in the corner. Two of the Wang sisters were also chopping vegetables. But I didn't see Sherlin.

"Hello Mrs. Wang. Remember me? I'm a friend of Sherlin's."

"Yes, yes. Petey Donovan." Wiping her hands on her apron, Mrs. Wang pointed to the back door. "Sherlin upstairs, in house. Go upstairs. Knock on door."

"Thanks, Mrs. Wang." The two girls stared after me, but Mr. Wang never looked up from his books.

Sherlin heard me coming up the stairs, and opened the door before I reached the top step. "Petey, what a surprise!" She grinned broadly and took me by the hand. "I am so happy to have a visitor. Come, I'll introduce you to my grandmother." We walked through their tiny apartment kitchen into the living room. Unlike the restaurant, the room was airy and light, with a big front picture window. Sitting in a rocking chair was a woman older than any I'd ever seen. "Petey, this is my grandmother." The old woman turned to me. She was wearing a blue shawl laced with gold thread. Her gnarled hand reached out, pulling me toward her. She spoke in Chinese, her sharp black eyes looking into mine.

"What did she say?"

"She says you have beautiful thick hair. That she once had hair like that, the envy of all of her village. But now, it falls away like the days on the calendar."

"Is it okay to ask how old she is?"

Sherlin laughed, and then spoke to her grandmother, who answered back. "She is 92."

"Your grandmother is 92!"

"Nai nai is my father's mother. My father is the youngest of seven children. C'mon, I'll show you my bedroom." The old woman let go of my hand and Sherlin and I walked down the hall to a small bedroom. There were two beds with a black bureau in between. "This is my bed, and this is my grandmother's bed."

"She sleeps in your room?"

"Yes, but it is no problem. She sleeps very soundly. I can even play my records, and she doesn't wake up. It's better than having to share with my sisters, who are all in another room across the hall."

"I saw two of your sisters in the kitchen."

"Yes, that was Hua and Lin. Chan is visiting with my aunt, but will be home to serve tonight. She does most of the waitressing, and if we are busy, I help too."

"Really? But you're only thirteen, like me."

"I'm fourteen now. But I have been waitressing for two years."

"I wish I could do that."

Sherlin laughed, "No, you don't. Believe me, it's hard work, although sometimes I meet very nice people who give me big tips. My parents let me keep a quarter of my tips. That's how I bought my records." She reached over and lifted a few from the stack. "Do you like *The Four Seasons*?"

"I don't know. I never heard them."

"Never? You'll love them. I'll play their album for you." Strains of high-pitched voices rang out. Sherlin leaned back on the bed with her eyes closed, singing along to "Sherry, Sherry baby..." I had never seen Sherlin like this. She was so quiet in school.

"That's my favorite song. I'm trying to get my family to call me Sherry, instead of Sherlin. I mean it could be my nickname, right?"

"Yeah, it's almost the same. But Sherlin is pretty."

"Not as pretty as Sherry. And it's more American. My mother uses the name Connie, which isn't her real name. Her real name is Chang, but she changed it to Connie, which sounds more American. I don't know why I can't do the same."

"Maybe when you get older, you can officially change it." I liked the song. If we had a record player at home Mags and I could save up for the album. I sat on the floor next to Sherlin as she flipped through her record albums. "We have a radio, but my folks listen to old music, you know, the music you hear on *The Lawrence Welk Show*."

She looked up at me. "Yeah, my parents watch that all the time. They think me and my sisters could be Chinese Lennon Sisters." I laughed. I couldn't imagine seeing four Chinese girls singing on *The Lawrence Welk Show*.

"Really? My parents say that about my sisters and me too. Except of course not the Chinese part. But I'm not much of a singer. My sister Maggie has a beautiful voice and sings all the time." I hesitated before adding, "not much lately though."

"I think Chan knows Maggie. They had a class together."

"Do you know yet where you're going to school when you move?"

"No."

"My mom says she thought your restaurant was doing well. She's surprised your family's moving."

"The restaurant is doing well," she replied tersely.

"Then, why are you moving?"

Sherlin turned back to staring at one of her album covers. "My father says we cannot stay in this town any more after what happened."

"What happened?"

Sherlin frowned. "Something I can't really talk about."

"Oh." I didn't know what to say next.

Sherlin was very quiet, her body hunched over, still staring at the album.

"My mother is on the Ladies Guild at church and they are going to ask Monsignor Neelan about having a farewell luncheon for your mother."

Sherlin spun around. With reddening cheeks, she yelled, "NO! She mustn't do that!" She slammed the record album on the floor.

"But Sherlin. Everyone likes your mother. She does a lot for the church. My mother told me how she irons all the linens, and prepares special eggrolls for the Guild meetings."

She jumped up, shaking her head. "Not any more. She stopped doing all that."

"But I'm sure Monsignor Neelan would be happy to..."

She pounced at me. "I don't want to hear *his* name again, do you hear me!"

"Who? Monsignor Neelan?"

"*He's* the reason we have to move. I hate him! He's a very bad man. Don't talk about him!"

"But he's a priest."

"A bad one. Just ask my sister Chan. My father says we have all been shamed, and now we must leave." She walked to the door. "I have to fix tea for Nai nai now. You must go."

"I-I'm sorry. I didn't mean to upset you, Sherlin."

"I'm not upset. I just have to fix my grandmother's tea. You can go down the back stairs."

Tears welled up as I bounded down the stairs two at a time. What had I said? Why was Sherlin so angry? I thought about her words. "*He's a very bad man...just ask my sister, Chan.*" What did Chan have to do with it? And why did she think Monsignor Neelan was a bad man? I had just lost my only friend. And deep inside, I was thinking of Mags, and Monsignor Neelan, the bad man. I ran all the way back to the laundromat.

⁓

Mom and I sat in the last seat on the bus, so we would have room for the laundry bags. I kept thinking of what Sherlin had said. Should I tell Mom? But exactly what would I tell her? That Monsignor Neelan, the priest she adored, was a bad man? I didn't know why Sherlin said that. But I knew Sherlin didn't gossip. Something made her say that. I started to open my mouth, not sure what words would spill out, but stopped. Mom was staring out the window, frowning intensely. She sighed and rubbed her forehead.

"Mom?"

"What is it, Petey?" She snapped.

"Nothing. Just, you know, you seem upset." I thought maybe she was worrying about Maggie too.

"I don't know how I'm going to tell your father."

"Tell him what?"

Mom sighed. "I got a phone call last night from your grandfather. He and Kitty are going to be spending Christmas with us."

"Gramp's coming! Who's Kitty?"

"His fiancée."

"Gramps is getting married? But he's old."

Mom smiled. "Old people get married too, Petey."

"But Mom, won't you be glad to see your father?"

She turned back toward the window, her breath making fuzzy O's on the smudges. "It's complicated, Petey. Of course I want to see my father. But your Dad is under enough stress without having your grandfather and his fiancée at our house."

"Daddy likes Gramps, doesn't he?"

She looked back at me, patting my hand. "Of course, sweetie, but sometimes people remember things from long ago, and it gets in the way."

"Gets in the way?"

"It's kind of a long story."

The bus turned on Broad St. "We won't be home for another twenty minutes."

Mom sighed again. "Guess it won't hurt to tell you. You know about Dad being in the war?"

"Yeah."

"And how we got married after that?"

"Yeah, Dad said he knew right away you were the one for him."

Mom smiled. "And I wanted to marry him, but Gramps was against it."

"Why? Didn't he like Marines?"

Mom shook her head. "It wasn't that. My father respected him for his service, but he still didn't want me to marry him."

"But why not?"

"He wanted me to marry a man with more education, more money. When he realized that we were going to get married against his wishes, he offered your father a chance at police work if he went back to school. But I didn't want him to do that. I knew what marriage to a policeman would be. Your father might not make a lot of money Petey, but at least he's home every night, and I don't have to lie awake worrying where he is or if he's alive. Even when my father was home, he was thinking about work, or getting phone calls. I didn't want that. But my father didn't understand, and still doesn't. He just sees how we're struggling and thinks we could do better."

"But Daddy works hard, Mom, and so do you. Gramps hasn't been for a visit in a year. And now he's engaged. So, I don't think he's thinking about long ago. He's probably thinking about the future."

Mom looked at me kind of funny. "Petey, you're pretty special. You know that."

I blushed. "Me?"

"Yes, you."

The bus lurched and we both gripped the laundry bags. I turned to my mother and asked, "Where are Gramps and Kitty going to sleep?"

"That's a good question. I guess I'd better start thinking about that."

"Kitty can have my bed. I can sleep on the rollaway."

"And your grandfather can sleep on the pullout couch in the living room. He gets up early every morning anyway."

I leaned against my mother. "It will be nice to see Gramps again."

"Yes it will, Petey."

Maggie

elief overcame me, knowing that I didn't have to see him to-day. Was there a way to convince Mom that I didn't need any more "talks" with the Monsignor? There had been very little talk on the last visit. Just remembering his body on mine makes me be-gin to sweat. Not today, thank God, not today. After, he spoke again of my vocation, of the importance of following God's call. Did God really want me to join the convent? Perhaps that is the only way to escape and to repent. As a nun, I would remain chaste and serve only Christ. In time, perhaps forget the shame of what happened in Monsignor Neelan's study, and yes even forget Jimmy, and my yearnings for him.

When Jimmy is here I push those thoughts away. Walking outside we dipped under the sheets on the clothesline to steal a long kiss. I sighed, thinking about his upcoming absence. Why did he have to leave me and go to Mississippi? He took my hand and pried open my fingers. Reaching into his pocket, he placed a small box in my palm.

I looked down at it. "What's this?"

"Open it. You'll see."

Carefully, I lifted the top of the box. Inside was a gold heart-shaped locket. With the tip of my fingernail, I opened it and saw a small photo of Jimmy and me.

"Remember that day we stopped at the photo booth and took our picture? I cut it down so our faces just fit." I stared at the smiling faces. Already it seemed like a lifetime ago. "You like it, don't you?"

"Of...of course I do. But I have nothing for you."

"That's okay." He took the heart pendant from me. "Turn around. I'll put it on you."

He lifted my hair. His warm breath tickled my neck as he fumbled with the clasp. "There, got it." I clutched the locket. Today, I would wear it. After that, I'd keep it under my shirt. Dad and Mom would not approve.

He spun me around, his arms encircling my waist. "I'm going to miss you so much, Maggie."

My head rested on his chest. "I wish you didn't have to go."

"It's only a few weeks. I'll call whenever I can."

We walked slowly, hand in hand, back to the house. Our time was up. Petey was dragging the laundry bag into the hallway as we entered. "Here, let me get that." Jimmy lifted the bag onto his shoulder. I started to follow them out to the car, but suddenly thought of something. I ran into the kitchen. Pulling a pair of scissors from the junk drawer, I cut an end piece of my hair. There was a string of blue ribbon in the drawer also. Perfect. I tied the bow on the hair and ran outside.

Jimmy came towards me and I held out my gift. "Here, a locket for a locket." He smiled broadly. I gave him a quick kiss, not even caring if Mom saw, and then stepped back onto the curb.

I blew kisses as he drove off, missing him already. I wanted to beg him to stay but didn't. This trip meant so much to him. At least talking about it filled our conversation. No more questions about my sessions with Monsignor Neelan. Thank God! He did ask why I was so quiet. I told him I was just tired, that's all, which wasn't really a lie. I wasn't sleeping very well.

The noon whistle went off. Better get started on lunch for the girls. The door slammed behind me as I walked back into the kitchen. Spreading peanut butter on white bread, I looked out the window to see Genny, Mary, and Clare playing on the swing set. Their laughter was so carefree. It made me want to go back in time. Maybe after lunch I could show them how to make little houses for the leprechauns with the twigs and leaves under the trees. My mind began to weave together a new story to tell.

I dropped the knife at the sound of knocking. Before I could even answer the door, he was there, in the front foyer, pinning me against the wall, breathing hard. The force of his body was suffocating. I tried to push him away, but couldn't. I tried to scream, but his hand closed over my mouth.

"Margaret, please. It's me. Hush, now. It will be okay. I couldn't wait. Don't you see? Hush, child. I'll be quick this time. Just relax." He reached under my skirt. Just then the phone rang.

"Don't answer that." His face pressed into mine, our noses touching.

My mouth wrestled free of his hand. "My mother said she'd call," I lied. "She'll worry if I don't answer." His steel gray eyes locked on mine. The pressure lifted, and I slipped from under him. Running to the kitchen, I rapped hard on the window and picked up the phone.

"Maggie? It's Dad."

"Daddy!" I started to cry.

"Maggie, are you okay? What's wrong?"

"Nothing, nothing, Daddy. I'm, ah, . . ." I breathed deeply and gulped in my tears. "Just so happy to hear your voice. That's all."

"It's good to hear your voice too, Sunshine. Is your mother there? I only have a couple of minutes to talk before my time runs out on this phone."

"No. She's at the Laundromat." My whole body was shaking. I could barely hold the phone.

"Oh. Tell her that I can't call tonight, but will be home next Saturday for good. I miss everyone. You helping your mother out with everything?"

"Yes." My breath released in short spurts. Why didn't I tell him? I half fell into the kitchen chair, trying to control the quivering in my legs.

"You sure you're okay, Maggie?" I could see my sisters running in from the back yard.

"Come home soon, Daddy." I squeezed the phone tight.

"I will. Give your mother a kiss for me."

"Daddy?"

"Yes? What is it?"

"Daddy, I just wanted to. . ., I mean, I love you."

"I love you too, Sunshine. See you soon."

I cradled the phone against my cheek, wishing my father back, wishing him here. I heard a car drive off, just as the girls came giggling into the kitchen looking for their lunch.

Monsignor Neelan

He drove faster and more recklessly than he'd ever driven before. What had come over him? He'd never in his life been so rash, so impulsive. Pulling into the rectory driveway, he slammed the car door and headed to his study. When Rose Donovan called to say that Maggie wasn't coming, he had stared at the couch and paced the floor, his mind tormented with images of her. He didn't even think it through. Just got into his car and drove.

He told himself it wasn't rape. That she wanted it too. But today, he knew better. The terror in her eyes told him that. It was all about him now, and his needs. He didn't like losing control of the situation, of himself. But thoughts of Margaret consumed him, his sweet, delicious Margaret, so like her grandmother. If he hadn't joined the priesthood. If she hadn't married, what might have been? Ridiculous to think of the past that could not be changed. But his mind drifted more and more in that direction.

So what now? If he couldn't let her go, then he had to find a way to keep her in his grasp. Everything else be damned. Margaret was to remain his at all costs. The convent was the only solution. Some girls were known to join the novitiate in high school, finishing out their studies in the convent. He would be her spiritual counselor, meet with her regularly. In the cloistered confines of the religious community, he knew she could be totally his. No more thoughts of Jimmy, or her parents. She would want it too. Sexual ardor and religious fervor were a potent combination; one he knew how to play to full advantage.

Then he remembered a phone call last year from Sister Alfred. At first he thought she was going to continue with her harangue about losing the Latin Mass. Sister Alfred taught Latin in the high school. Vatican II's recommended change of ending Latin Masses distressed her greatly. She gathered petitions and wrote letters to the Vatican. When no response came, she pleaded with him to keep at least one Latin Mass. With the bishop's approval, he said one Mass the first Sunday of each month in Latin. He was glad now that he did. She owed him one.

But her call wasn't about Latin Masses. She was distraught over the lack of vocations and thought he ought to be doing more to encourage them. Perhaps she was the perfect ally for his plan. He dialed the convent's number the next morning.

"Sister Alfred! Telephone! It's Monsignor Neelan."

He could hear slow clumping down the stairs and remembered that arthritis slowed her gait. He drummed his fingers on the table. She was out of breath when she picked up the phone.

"Hello."

"Sister Alfred, how good of you to take my call. I wonder if you could spare a few minutes of time to talk with me this evening regarding one of your students?"

"Of course, Monsignor. I'd be happy to talk with you. May I ask what student is of concern?"

"That can wait until our meeting, Sister. I'll be there at seven."

"Seven. Yes, certainly."

He hung up the phone, chuckling to himself. The old biddy would be in knots wondering what student could have possibly prompted a call from the Monsignor. He rarely visited the convent these days, not since Sister Francesca left. She had been a novice, still wearing the white veil. Soft brown curls edged her face, and doe-like eyes fluttered when he looked her way. As newly appointed Monsignor, he was the confessor for the nuns at the convent. Sister Francesca would cry softly as she confessed her sins. She shamefully confessed her thoughts of lust, and he listened intently. He suggested she allow him to counsel her in private. He took it slower then, still working out the steps, still honing his persuasive powers. But she opened up like all the others. She never did take her vows, leaving just before her two years as a novice were over. It was the first and only time that the Bishop got wind of his transgressions. He'd been called into his office.

"Monsignor, take a seat. I'd like a word with you." The Bishop directed him to a chair but remained standing, pacing back and forth with a pronounced limp.

He waited for him to speak.

"I'm afraid this visit is not for such joyful news as the first time I called you here. You remember that, no doubt?"

"Of course, Your Excellency. You informed me of His Holiness' approval of my nomination as Monsignor. I was humbled by the honor."

"As you know, you were awarded that honor because of your service to the Church. I have relied on your leadership on many of the diocesan committees as well as your reports back from the Vatican. There was no way I could possibly have traveled after my surgery."

"I was more than happy to help."

"And no one has had more success in raising funds for their parish than you. St. Peter's continues to thrive."

"Thank you, Your Excellency." The Bishop walked to the other side of the room, his hands clasped behind his back. He stared out the large stain-glassed framed picture window for some time before speaking again. "I now question that nomination."

"Question? But you just said, I mean, I have always worked..."

The Bishop abruptly turned, interrupting him. "I'm not questioning your service, Monsignor. Rather your faithfulness to your vows."

"My vows?"

"Your vow of celibacy to be more precise."

Despite the chill in the room, he was now sweating profusely. How much did the bishop know? Don't say any more than necessary. Maybe he had just heard a rumor. "Your Grace, please explain what you are referring to."

Bishop Feely slowly walked back and eased into the large chair across from him. With a deep sigh he fixed his eyes on Neelan and said, "I'm referring to Sister Francesca. Were you aware that she is in a mental hospital now?"

"I knew she left the order, but no, I didn't know that. I'm sorry to hear it. She did seem like a troubled young lady."

"Young is the operative word there, Monsignor . . . a teenager. You were her confessor, were you not?"

"Yes."

"Monsignor, I have reason to believe that you took advantage of Sister Francesca during those confessionals. What is your answer to that charge?"

He hesitated only a moment. "Who made this charge?"

"A reliable source. That is all you need to know."

Without knowing his accuser, he was unsure how to answer. If it were only Sister Francesca, he could win the she said/he said game easily. But what if it were another priest, nun, or doctor? Did he dare deny it and be found caught in a lie? Perhaps confessing was safer. He made his choice. He shook his head and forced the tears.

"I know I should have come to you sooner." *Dropping to his knees, he bowed his head and kissed the Bishop's ring.* "I tried to help her, told her to seek professional counseling. But she refused. Told me that she didn't want to reveal her sins to anyone but me."

"I know the confessional is private, but these sins... they were of a sexual nature?"

Monsignor Neelan looked up. "Your Excellency, she thought the convent would be a refuge from the desires she felt. But her libidinous thoughts only increased." *He shook his head.* "I don't know how it happened. One minute I was trying to talk to her, and the next, she was disrobing. I'd never seen a woman like that... I mean... somehow ..." *He looked up.* "I have sinned. Please, please, forgive me. ..."

Bishop Feeley placed his hand on the Neelan's head. "It is not my forgiveness that you must seek, Monsignor, but God's."

"Yes, yes, I know. I have prayed constantly, asking His forgiveness."

"And you are sorry for this sin, my son?"

"Extremely."

"I will hear your full confession, Monsignor. But first I must know — Is this the only time you broke your vow of celibacy?" He lied and answered yes. *"And you are fully repentant and resolved to sin no more?"*

"Yes."

He made his full confession and was given absolution. Bishop Feely then informed him that the convent confessional assignment would be given to another priest. His transgression was kept secret, as he knew it would be.

— —

He arrived promptly at seven. Sister Alfred answered the door. Her black veil dipped slightly as she bowed her head. "Monsignor, do come in. It is such an honor to have you here. May I fix you a cup of coffee or tea?"

"Tea, please. A little milk, no sugar."

She led him to the library. "Please, have a seat, Monsignor. I'll be right with you." She waddled to the kitchen, the rosary beads swinging over her wide hips. He took a seat on the high wing-backed chair, the only furniture that looked comfortable. She would sit on the low sofa next to him, the coffee table between them. Overstuffed bookshelves hugged the ceiling and circled the room. The one window was draped with a tawny print, faded enough to allow the glow of the rising full moon to shine behind him. He had rehearsed his words carefully, but still found his palms sweaty, even on this brisk December evening. Would the old nun find it curious that he had a personal interest in one of the students? He was about to make an unusual request.

She set the tray on the coffee table, poured his tea, and offered him the creamer.

"Thank you, Sister."

"Now, what can I do for you, Monsignor?"

"I understand that you still head the Sodality Club, Sister, as well as teach most of the Latin classes. You continue to impress me with your diligence and service to the students."

"All in the name of the Lord, Monsignor. His work continues to call us."

"Yes, that is true. And of course there continues to be good enrollment numbers at Holy Redeemer, I understand."

"We had the largest freshman class ever this year. My Latin I class has forty-two students. I would have liked to have two classes instead of one, but we do not have enough staff for that."

"Vocations are down, Sister. I know that. We've had few ordinations these past few years. It concerns the bishop. And what about the Novitiate? Do you have any new novices?"

She shook her head. "Unfortunately, no. Perhaps you remember our discussion some time ago about that very problem."

"I do, and I have been giving that some thought, which brings me to the reason for my visit. It has come to my attention that one of your students may have an interest in joining the order. I know the family well, and this young woman has spoken to me of her possible calling."

"Really? And who might that be?"

"Margaret Donovan. I believe she is in the Sodality Club, is she not?"

"Yes. I've known Margaret for three years now. She is a devout girl, there's no doubt about that. When did she speak with you about this, Monsignor?"

"Fairly recently, why?"

"It may explain her change of demeanor. There's been something bothering the child. I've known that for some time. She's a popular girl in school, but lately she has shown less interest in her friends, less interest in her studies too. It has concerned me."

He sipped his tea and sat back in the chair. The old woman leaned forward expectantly. He let her wait before speaking again. "Well, she is thinking seriously of this, Sister. I do believe she has a genuine vocation, but is troubled by her uncertainty. I think she would find peace once she makes the decision, the sooner the better. I was hoping you could talk with her about applying for admission to the Order."

"Now, Monsignor?"

"Yes."

"She is quite young. While the order does accept girls as young as sixteen, it is not common."

"The family is experiencing some hardship, Sister. Mr. Donovan had been laid off for a long time, and the family moved into low-income housing. I understand that he is back at work, but Margaret is a devoted daughter and is very concerned about her family."

"I wasn't aware that the Donovans were struggling."

"If the girl has a definite vocation, and enters the convent, the family would have one less mouth to feed."

"That's hardly a reason for entering the novitiate."

"No, of course not. But Margaret, I believe, is ready for such a step. I think that she is a most remarkable young woman with a strong spiritual core." He leaned forward, set his teacup on the table, and gazed intently into the old nun's eyes. "Guidance from someone like yourself, a wonderful mentor to young girls, would be most welcome."

Sister Alfred's eyes brightened. "Well, perhaps such a move would bring peace to Margaret. I am pleased that she has voiced this interest to you. Actually, I'd recently taken it upon myself to speak with her sister about this possibility."

"Her sister?'

"Agnes."

"Oh yes, Agnes. I wasn't aware that she had any interest in the convent."

"Oh no, she doesn't, but I was inquiring about her sister's possible vocation. I've seen Margaret's deep religious devotion. She is often at daily Mass, and lately she's been in chapel praying. I know she is very close to her sister, and thought it best to be discreet in my inquiries before talking to Margaret directly."

"I see. And did her sister reveal anything?" His pulse quickened. He hadn't thought of the sister, of what she might know.

"No, not really. I asked if all was well at home, knowing how distracted Margaret has been, but she didn't indicate there were problems. I knew the father worked at the loading docks, but I wasn't aware of the financial difficulties."

"You will speak to Margaret, then?"

"Of course. I will be only too happy to do so."

He smiled. "Thank you Sister."

One step closer. Now to convince Maggie's parents. That would take more effort.

Petey

I wasn't sure what to make of Kitty, Grandpa's fiancée. I wanted to like her. But she wasn't what I pictured when I thought of a grandmother. For one thing, her hair was not gray or white, but bright reddish-orange. It was teased in a bouffant style, and every morning she went around and around it with the hairspray can, until I started coughing from the smell. The bedroom was a bit crowded since they arrived a few days ago. Kitty took my bed, and I slept in a rollaway that was set up next to Maggie's bed.

Kitty told me that I should start wearing make-up to cover the dark circles under my eyes, and wondered why I had those anyway? I was far too young for that, she said. Well, between her smoker's cough, and Maggie tossing and turning next to me all night, I didn't sleep much. At least Kitty didn't smoke in our room. Mom told her that she could smoke in the living room or outside, but not in the kitchen or bedrooms. I think she smoked in the bathroom too because I could smell it there. It made my nose twitch. She also talked a lot, about all kinds of things. It was Kitty who introduced us to the new hit musical sensation, the Beatles. She listened to their songs on the radio, and said the new craze reminded her of Frank Sinatra's hey-day, when all the girls screamed and fainted every time he crooned a song. Now girls were doing the same crazy stuff when the Beatles sang. Gramps said he thought they looked ridiculous with their tight pants and long hair, but Kitty chided him, "Oh, Joe, don't be so old-fashioned. They're the new look." I was shocked that anyone would talk to Gramps that way. Most of us kids were a little afraid of him, but Kitty didn't seem afraid of anyone, not even my grandfather.

Unlike Kitty, Gramps didn't talk much, but you always knew what he was thinking. As my mother often said, "Gramps's steely glare can bore a hole right through you." Sometimes he looked at us kids with that look, and we knew we'd better not argue back. But he never looked that way at Kitty. When he looked at her, his eyes were soft and almost twinkled.

Dad came home the weekend before Christmas, just as he'd promised. Maggie hugged him so hard, he said he couldn't breathe. Mary and Genny wrapped around his middle like bookends while he tossed squealing Clare into the air. Stooping to put her down, he saw me standing in the corner. "Petey!" I ran into his open arms. He gave me a big hug, then stroked my hair and kissed me on the cheek. I could feel his whiskers.

"Do you have a beard now, Daddy?" I asked.

He laughed. "Been a bit lazy. Haven't shaved in a while. What do you think?"

"I'll be the judge." Mom stepped forward, kissed him, then rubbed his beard. "Think I'll get out the razor." He laughed and held her in a long embrace. When he looked up, Gramps and Kitty had joined us in the foyer. Dad stopped smiling, let go of Mom, and took Gramps outstretched hand.

"Good to see you John." Gramps said.

"You too, sir."

"John, I want you to meet Kitty, my fiancée."

Dad again stretched out his hand. "Nice to meet..."

Kitty pulled him towards her and gave him a quick hug and peck on the cheek. "Ooh, you sure you want to shave that off. Feels yummy to me!" Then she laughed, a deep throaty laugh that made me jump.

"You've got a wonderful family here, John. I hope you don't mind us barging in like this, but I've been dying to meet everyone."

We all sat down to lunch. Mom had done more than her usual bologna and cheese sandwiches. There was a big pot of beef-noodle soup with Italian bread. After saying Grace, Mom began ladling out the soup. Dad asked, "So, what's been going on? Clare, you first."

Clare jumped up from her chair and grabbed a piece of paper from a nearby desk. "I made you this picture, Daddy."

Dad pulled her onto his lap. "Let's see. Is that you there in pink?"

Clare nodded. "And Mommy's next to me and that's you right there." She pointed to the top of the picture.

"Very nice. You're quite an artist. I'll put that on the mirror in my bedroom to look at every morning." He gave her a quick squeeze as she slid off his knee and sat back next to Maggie. Genny and Mary each told him something about school. I wasn't listening. It would be my turn next. What could I tell him? Maybe this would be a good time to tell what Sherlin said about Monsignor Neelan being a bad man. I looked at Maggie. Mom said she wasn't seeing him today 'cause of Dad coming home, and Jimmy wasn't coming over either because of his upcoming trip south. Maybe the whole thing was going to go away. Yeah, maybe I was worrying about nothing.

"And you Petey?"

"We dissected a frog in Biology. It was neat. We used scalpels and cut the throat first, and then between the legs and down the belly. The teacher said to be really careful not to cut too deep, 'cause then the guts would spill out, but she said I did a great job. It smelled kind of bad from the formaldehyde. Some of the kids were sick, but..."

"Ooo- gross." Genny scrunched up her nose.

"I think that's enough about frog dissection talk at the dinner table." Mom said.

Dad turned to Maggie. "What did you do this week?"

Maggie shrugged and said "Not much. Why don't you tell us about your week, Daddy?" Within minutes we were all laughing as he told us a funny story about one of his coworkers. I leaned forward and put my elbows on the table (even though we weren't supposed to), and watched the family all smiling and laughing, just like it used to be. I wanted it to stay this way forever. Then Dad pushed back his chair. "So, who wants to go pick out a Christmas tree?"

Everyone jumped up in excitement, yelling "Me, me, me!"

"Well, grab your coats. We're leaving in five minutes.

Since it was so close to Christmas there weren't very many left on the lot. As usual, we all argued about which one to get, but in the end, Dad made the decision. It was smaller than I would have liked, but probably not a bad choice, given that Gramps was now sleeping in the living room.

Decorating the tree was always an all family activity. Gramps helped string the lights, and Kitty got into a tinsel throwing match with Mary. They ended up laughing, rolling on the floor in tinsel. Finally she sat up coughing, plucking bits of tinsel from her hair.

Once the tinsel was vacuumed and the ornament boxes put away, Gramps came into the living room with a big bag. Our eyes grew big as he lifted out gifts wrapped in gold with big red bows. What could they be? Gramps had never sent gifts before. There was a large one with a big bow labeled, *To Maggie and Petey. Love, Gramps and Kitty.* Also, separate ones for Genny, Mary, and Clare.

Kitty said, "Now, no peeking. Your Gramps and I picked these out special when we sent shopping in New York City."

Maggie suddenly perked up. "You were in New York City? Did you see the Christmas tree at Rockefeller Center?"

Kitty sat back on the couch next to Maggie. "Sure did. Went to Radio City Music Hall to see the Rockettes too. Now that's a show! Even rivals the best in Las Vegas, well, except for maybe Elvis Presley. No one can beat Elvis."

Gramps lifted Clare onto his lap. "Tell them about the time you met Elvis, Kitty."

Maggie edged closer to Kitty. "You met Elvis Presley?"

Another hearty laugh from Kitty. "I guess you could say that. He was shooting a movie called *Viva Las Vegas.* I was just coming out of the ladies room in the casino, and bumped right into him. Of course, I was blushing and apologizing like a country bumpkin, but he was ever so nice, saying, 'No, Ma'am. My fault. I wasn't watching where I was going.' He even gave me his autograph. I'll show it to you later."

Turns out Kitty had been to lots of places. Mom didn't seem to pay much attention to any of her stories until she told us about going to Rome and hearing Pope John XXIII speak.

"Nothing against this new guy Paul VI, but Pope John was the only Pope that seemed to really connect with people, you know. I mean I wasn't raised Catholic, so I have a hard time believing all this infallibility crap (she actually used that word), but at least John XXIII seemed like a real person, someone you could talk to."

My mother winced, then said, "Excuse me; I have to get dinner started."

Kitty yelled after her. "Do you need help out there, Rose? I'm not much of a cook, but I know how to peel potatoes."

"No thanks. The girls will help me when I need it." I started to get up to go to the kitchen but stopped when I heard Kitty ask Maggie if she had a boyfriend.

"Well, where is this Jimmy? When am I going to meet him?"

"He only can visit Friday nights and Saturdays. And we don't really go out. I don't know if you'll see him, 'cause he's leaving for Mississippi."

"Does he have family there?"

"No. He's going to be helping people register to vote."

Had Kitty seen all that was happening down south? It made me mad when I watched it on television. All those people hollering, spitting and throwing things at Negroes. Mom and Dad watched and shook their heads, and sometimes Dad said stuff about why was everyone causing so much trouble. He was thrilled that Jimmy was going away but not because he thought it was a cool thing to do. I was afraid to tell him that I'd like to do that someday too. It wasn't right that black people (that's what I heard Jimmy call them sometimes) were treated that way. I'd seen the water cannons and the dog attacks. Sometimes it seemed the world was awfully messed up. Why did people do stuff like that?

I didn't know many black people. There was a boy in my elementary school named Raymond. He was kind of quiet and skinny. Raymond kept to himself mostly, but one time on the playground some kid was picking on him, even called him the "N" word. I could've told the nuns about the name calling. They'd have rapped the kid with a ruler for that. But I didn't want to tattle-tale. Instead I kicked the kid in the shins. Raymond and I played together after that for a while, until he moved.

Maggie told Kitty more about Jimmy's work down South in what she called "The Movement."

Kitty nodded her head and said, "Well, good for him. Young people are the ones that need to change things. If he gets back while I'm still here, you be sure to let me meet him, okay sugar?"

"I will, ah…?"

"Call me Kitty. I told you it's okay to call me by my first name. I sure ain't your Grandma, and don't think I want that title anyway."

＿ ＿

I woke early Christmas morning, even before Mary and Clare. The sky was gray and soft snow was beginning to fall, the first of the winter. Kitty lay in my bed on the other side of the room, her orange hair rolled tight in curlers, her mouth open, expelling a raspy snore. I rolled over and looked at my sister. Despite my resolutions to talk to her after my conversation with Sherlin, I hadn't done so. And things weren't right with Maggie. I knew that. Yesterday I found two pieces of wood in her bed. What was that about? On her bedside table were books about saints and martyrs, and a booklet about the Sisters of St. Anne. Was she still thinking of becoming a nun? I'd thought she'd given up that idea a long time ago. I couldn't imagine it. Not Maggie. She used to laugh all the time. But not anymore. Sometimes I could hear her crying softly to herself into the pillow. When I asked her if she was okay, she'd just tell me to go to sleep. At least Kitty's stories made her smile.

"Maggie, Maggie, wake up. It's Christmas." I shook her shoulder. Her arm swung from the bed, and a set of crystal rosary beads dropped to the floor. She opened one eye.

"What?"

"It's Christmas, Mags. Let's get up before the others do."

"What time is it?"

"Five-thirty." She moaned, and rolled away from me. Usually Maggie was the early bird, but not lately. I couldn't wait for her. Throwing off the covers and grabbing my robe, I peeked into my sisters' room. No sign of life yet. I crept down the stairs and over to the tree. Crystal icicles reflected the multi-colored lights. Little clumps of tinsel dappled the branches, evidence of little Clare's hand in decorating. Gramps lay huddled under a quilt, his large feet protruding at the foot of the sofa bed. I sat on the floor, hugging my knees for warmth. Santa had arrived. Mary would get the Easy-Bake-Oven she'd put in capital letters on her Christmas list. There was also a silver sled propped up in the corner. A hand gently touched my shoulder.

"Merry Christmas, Petey." Mom stood in her white robe, the one Dad had given her last Christmas. She sat down next to me, pulling me close. Her soft breath warmed my neck. I leaned back against her full bosom. It was special, having her all to myself. Should I tell her about Maggie crying in bed? No, that would ruin the moment. I breathed in the combined scent of the vanilla extract that Mom dabbed behind her ears and Christmas pine tree.

"You've always been the first one up on Christmas, Agnes Mary." For once, I didn't mind hearing my given name. Gramps began to snore loudly, and my mother laughed. "Of course it might have been your grandfather's snoring that woke you. I'd almost forgotten how raucous his snore can be."

"So he snored when you were little?"

"Oh yes, that's usually how I knew he was finally home and in bed."

"Didn't you see him come home?"

"No. I often waited up for him, or at least whenever Nana let me, but usually it was for naught, as he came home past my bedtime, and was often out the door before I got up."

"Every day?"

"Except Sundays. He sometimes worked on Sunday, but not until after church. That was my favorite time of the whole week. He would brush my hair and select a ribbon to put in it. Then polish my patent leather shoes and put on my hat. We'd walk to church hand in hand. Sometimes on the way home we'd stop for doughnuts, just like your Daddy does now. I'd lick the glaze on my doughnut as he stirred cream into his coffee. People would stop by our booth to talk. Everyone knew my Dad."

"Because he was a Police Chief?"

"Yes, and a very good one. But as a child I didn't think much about that. I just wanted my father home with me. I realize now how hard it must have been for him without my mother, even with Nana's help."

"I don't remember Nana."

"I know. Your great grandmother died when you were just two. I think Maggie remembers her some. She was a hard task-master, but loving too."

"What's a task-master?"

"Someone who makes sure that you do everything you're supposed to."

"Like you do."

My mother squeezed me gently. "Well, I guess I am more than I mean to be. But today, there won't be any chores for you, Agnes Mary. How does that sound?"

I smiled up at her and we continued to gaze at the Christmas tree until more feet came padding down the stairs, and the dawn's quiet broke into children's squeals. If only the day could have ended with such joy.

Maggie

The first present I opened was the red and gold wrapped box from Gramps and Kitty. It was a record player! Finally I could play records like so many of my friends. Petey seemed pleased too, though not as much as I. Kitty told us that she was going to take us shopping to buy ten records of our choosing as part of our Christmas gift. I couldn't imagine Petey selecting any records, as she'd never shown any interest. To my surprise, however, she said she wanted some songs by *The Four Seasons*. By mid-morning I'd made my list: *Blue Velvet* by Bobby Vinton (my all-time favorite), the new Beatles song *I Want to Hold Your Hand*, *Surfin' USA* by The Beach Boys, and *Stand by Me* by The Drifters.

Mary was thrilled with her Easy Bake Oven. After church and breakfast, I read the directions and helped her make her first cake, which we served as part of dessert after our big dinner. The best part of the day was having Dad back home. By midday, the snow had accumulated to three inches, and he announced that he was going to take us all sledding. Petey and I put on two layers of pants, thick socks, and boots, while Genny, Mary, and Clare were bundled up in snowsuits. We wore our new hats and mittens from Dad and Mom, each set a different color. The best sledding hill was at the town park, only four blocks away. Dad led the way, as we caught snowflakes on our tongues. Clare stood at the top of the hill, clutching the reins of her new sled, jumping up and down in excited anticipation. Dad insisted that she ride with him the first couple of runs until he was sure that she could handle the sled by herself. We took turns or paired up with the other sled and saucer.

I wrapped my body around Petey as we positioned ourselves on the sled, my feet against the steering rods, and my hands holding the ropes. Dad gave us a push, and we sailed down the hill. Our breath burned warm in our throats; then emitted vaporous mini-clouds into the air when we exhaled. Sledders dotted the hillside. As we cruised to the bottom a small child jumped out in front of us. I pulled the rope, and pushed the right side of the sled's rudder, steering us to the left. We swerved suddenly and tumbled into the wet snow. I rolled off Petey and asked if she was okay. She answered with a snowball to my head! I ran from her, scooped up some snow, and threw one back. We were laughing and out of breath by the time we got back up the hill.

Mom had some warm cocoa waiting for us when we returned. I helped Clare take off her snowsuit and boots. She sat on my lap at the kitchen table as we sipped our cocoa. In between sips, I read her nursery rhymes, and together we made up some silly ones of our own. Clare giggled, her soft curls pressed against my cheek as I held her tight.

That night, I didn't lay in bed, hungering for the briny smell of Jimmy's sweat or the taste of his warm mouth. Nor did I wake in terror, dreaming of Monsignor Neelan's study. Instead, I smelled baby powder, tasted snowflakes, and drifted up into cool white clouds. Weightless, everything in miniature below, I looked upward and saw the sun, a thick yellow orb warming my face. Then the air turned hot, the sun broke like a pierced egg yolk, coating me in heavy goo, and I began to fall. The earth rose before me, and I screamed as pain gripped my insides. I woke to see Kitty and Petey standing over me. My hands clutched my stomach.

"What's wrong, child?"

"I don't know. Something's happening to me. A terrible pain . . ."

"Where? Where does it hurt?"

"Down low, here." I touched my lower abdomen.

"Is it your period, Maggie? Do you get cramps?"

"A little like that, but it's worse than cramps."

Kitty pulled back my covers. There was blood on the sheet. I sat up and started to get out of bed, but fell back. "I feel faint." I mumbled.

"Petey, go get a towel from the bathroom. Maggie, just lie down."

There was a gushing from my groin, as if my insides were being sucked from me, and I whimpered, "What's wrong with me?"

Kitty bent over me, her lips pressed together, her brow furrowed. Tenderly, she touched my cheek.

"Maggie, it would appear you've just had a miscarriage."

"A... a miscarriage? That can't be! Are you sure?"

"Honey, I've had one myself, and I know."

"You mean I. . . I lost a baby? I was pregnant?"

"I'm afraid so. You didn't know?"

"No." My body trembled.

"You want me to go downstairs and get your mother now?" Kitty started to turn away. I reached for her hand.

"No! I mean, no. I can't have her know, I mean..." I began to cry and couldn't stop. Petey stood behind Kitty, her mouth agape, her eyes transfixed like she was in some kind of hypnotic trance. Then she drew closer and I reached for her. "Oh, Petey, what have I done?" My sister's arms enveloped me.

Kitty gently lifted me from the bed. I leaned against her as she half-dragged me to the hall bathroom. She had me sit on the toilet and spread my legs. The warmth of the washcloth on my thighs calmed my tremors as my head rested on Kitty's shoulder. Petey stood in the doorway chewing her lip.

"Petey, get your sister a fresh nightgown and underpants."

I dressed slowly as Kitty stripped the sheets off the bed. My legs wobbled like spaghetti. I slumped down onto Petey's bed.

"Well, I don't know how I'm going to get fresh sheets out of the downstairs closet without your mother waking up. The closet door always squeaks so." Kitty said.

"That's okay, Kitty. Maggie can sleep with me." Petey pulled me gently into her bed. She held me close and kissed my cheek. I nestled into her neck, and let my tears fall on her shoulder.

— ◦ —

It was Kitty who told them. I thought Daddy might hit me at first, something he'd never done, but Mom yelled, "John, no!" and he turned away. We sat on the edge of the bed, Mom and I.

"How, Maggie? How did this happen?"

Dad turned away from the wall and glared at Mom. "I think we know how, Rose. I was afraid something like this would happen when I left. You were supposed to be keeping an eye on things."

"John. I swear. They weren't alone much. Really."

"They were alone enough. Where did you two sneak off to this time, Maggie?"

"We didn't Daddy, honest."

He stepped toward me. I was shaking all over. "More lies, Maggie? How can you deny this?"

"We didn't do anything. Daddy. Please, please. You have to believe me." I reached for my father's hand, but he slapped it away.

"I don't even *know* you anymore, Maggie." He stomped to the other side of the room and pounded the window sash.

I was crying hard now.

Mom stood up and walked to my father. She touched his elbow. "John? Listen to me. I'll make an appointment with the doctor. If he confirms what Kitty said, we'll talk some more. And I think I should tell Monsignor Neelan too."

I cringed at his name, holding in the upswell of vomit. *He* was the one who did this. I wanted to tell them, but I was ashamed and frightened.

They wouldn't believe it anyway. I longed to jump from the bed and throw my arms around my father, to feel a forgiving embrace, to hear him call me by name, and tell me that everything would be all right. Instead, I shrank into myself, and watched him walk out the door.

— —

Sleep wouldn't come. Tomorrow I had an appointment with Mom's gynecologist. He would be asking questions. What should I say? Despite my resolve to keep everything secret, deep down I wanted to tell, wanted someone to know the truth. I rolled over for the umpteenth time and drew my knees up toward my chest. Petey slept peacefully across from me. I tried to time my breaths to hers to calm my racing thoughts. I longed to crawl into her bed, wrap my body around hers, and absorb my lost innocence.

On the way to the doctor's office I would be alone with Mom. Maybe then I could tell her. Maybe it would be the beginning of making it all right. Yes, tomorrow in the car, I'd tell. The knot in my stomach began to ease and finally I fell asleep.

— —

"Hurry up, Maggie. Our appointment is at 9." Mom called through the bathroom door.

Pinching my cheeks in an attempt to retrieve lost color, I yelled back, "Be right there."

Mom was already in the car. As I opened the passenger door, she said, "Mary wants you to sit in the back with her."

"Mary?"

"I'm taking her to the eye doctor after your appointment. She needs new glasses. I can't afford to take two days off of work, so booked her appointment after yours." Her tone was curt. I'd heard some arguing this morning between her and Dad. It was probably about me. I'd become a major source of stress and worry for both of them. Guiltily, I slammed the front door and climbed into the back seat. I would not be talking to Mom today.

Mary leaned against me, her thick taped-up glasses perched on the end of her nose. She thrust *Sleeping Beauty* into my lap. "Read to me, Maggie."

"*Once upon a time there was a beautiful princess. . .*"When the spinning wheel pricked the princess' finger and the wicked witch's spell of deep sleep had been cast, I stopped reading and turned my face toward the car window.

"Finish the story, Maggie."

The book lay on my lap. Raindrops rolled down the pane, matching the tears on my cheek. If only I could go into a deep sleep, and then wake up, this nightmare over.

Mom parked the car. "You'll have to finish the book later. We're here at Dr. Pratt's office."

I quickly wiped my cheeks with the back of my hand and got out.

As we entered the office, Mary immediately ran over to a large fish tank. "Ooh, cool. Look at the fish!" I didn't follow. Instead I sat nervously next to my mother waiting for my name to be called.

A tall unsmiling nurse came into the room. "Margaret Donovan?"

I turned to my mother. "Aren't you coming with me?"

"No. They said I could come in after the exam. You'll be fine, Maggie. Dr. Pratt is very nice." She patted my hand. "Go on, now. The nurse is waiting for you."

The examining room was small, with a chair, a sink, and some kind of table or bed with a sheet on it. Metal cup looking things protruded from each side. "Take off your skirt and underpants, and drape this cloth over you on the examining table. The doctor will be in to see you shortly." The expressionless nurse handed me a white cloth and directed me how to drape it over my legs.

My fingers kept slipping as I tried to unzip my skirt. Where should I put my underwear? I looked around but there was no cubicle. Finally I bunched them up on the chair with my skirt and stepped up to the table.

I wrapped the white cloth tightly around me. Still, my legs were cold. The door opened.

"Hello, Margaret. I'm Dr. Pratt. I'll be examining you today. Do you have any questions before I begin?"

I shook my head. What questions should I ask? I had no idea what was going to happen. Robotically I followed his instructions. Unbind the sheet so it hangs loosely over my abdomen. Put my feet up in those metal things he called stirrups. Lie back on the table. Relax? How could I? What was he going to do? The cold metal against the soles of my feet sent shivers all through me.

"Spread your legs further apart, Margaret." Gently he pushed against my shaking knees with gloved hands. "Just relax now, dear. This will only take a couple of minutes."

I looked down, and saw his bald head bend below the sheet. A rush of cool air, and then ...

"*Oww...!*" I gasped. What was that inside me? He was probing. I sucked in my breath and told myself not to cry. My hands dropped to the side of the table. I felt faint.

"Almost done." He stood up, snapped off the gloves, dropped them in the wastebasket, and began washing at the sink. "You can get dressed now. I'll have the nurse bring in your mother."

He stepped back into the room, followed by Mom. I sat with my arms crossed at the edge of the examining table, my skirt slightly askew, my underpants spotted and wet, my head bowed.

"Mrs. Donovan, your daughter has indeed had a miscarriage. The fetal tissue has been entirely expelled so she shouldn't need any further treatment. There may be some residual bleeding, and I'm going to write a prescription for iron pills. She should probably have some blood work done later but I think that might be too much for her today. She was somewhat woozy on the table."

Mom wrapped her arm around me, and I rested my head on her shoulder. "She'll be all right then, Doctor?"

"Yes, but there is the issue of prevention. I can write a prescription for birth control pills."

"That won't be necessary. This won't happen again, Doctor. Margaret is a good girl."

Dr. Pratt shook his head. "Mrs. Donovan. I'm sure she is, but it's been my experience that once girls become sexually active, it continues. Let me write Margaret the prescription. As long as she follows the directions, she will be protected."

"Doctor, I told you, that won't be necessary. Margaret is a good *Catholic* girl."

"And the boyfriend?"

"He won't be seeing Maggie anymore."

I lifted my head and stared at my mother. Her lips were tight. She was already grabbing her purse. "Thank you again, Doctor. Come on Maggie. I need to get Mary to her appointment."

We rode back in silence. I ignored Mary's pleas to finish the book. They wouldn't let me see Jimmy again. They were ashamed of me. Nothing I said would make a difference.

Monsignor Neelan

He lifted the wheelchair into the trunk and slammed the door shut. The last thing he wanted to be doing today was taking his mother to an art auction. But given how rarely she got out and that he'd promised this outing some time ago, he had no other choice. Rose's phone call, however, had put him into a state. When she told him of Maggie's miscarriage, he gripped the phone, waiting for the accusation. It didn't come. The boyfriend was the accused. Now he just had to make sure it stayed that way.

He jumped at the snap of his mother's clutch purse, followed by her raspy voice. "I heard there will be some Gordon Grant originals there. You know since he died last year, the value of his paintings has doubled. You remember the one I purchased last year?"

She was twisting her rings back into place. Her fingers were bone thin, laden with heavy jewelry. She was dressed impeccably in a navy blue ensemble of wool coat and skirt. A ruffled white silk blouse encased her neck. What did she say? Something about a painting. He nodded.

His mother rambled on. "I put it in the study. But I'd love another. Perhaps another of his ship paintings."

What must John be thinking about all this? They would be coming to see him tomorrow. He had to be prepared. So far, Maggie had kept her mouth shut. Would she stay quiet?

"Don't you think you better turn the wipers on, Robert? How can you possibly see out the windshield?" The intermittent drops had turned into a drizzle. He hadn't noticed.

"I hope you had enough sense to bring an umbrella."

"Of course, Mother."

"I don't think you've heard one word I've said, have you?"

"Yes, I have."

"Pff. I finally agree to an outing with you, and you're about as entertaining as a stiff. Did you make reservations at Hemingway's for dinner?"

Damn. He knew he forgot something. He'd make some excuse to bow out at the auction and find a phone to call. Hopefully they'd still have seating.

They were only two blocks from the cemetery. "We've got plenty of time, Mother. Are you sure you don't want to stop at the cemetery to see Father?"

"Not in this rain. You took me there last week, remember?"

Once a month he drove her to the cemetery. She left fresh flowers, said a quick prayer, and complained about the declining upkeep. He used to ask if she wanted to visit Betsy's grave too, but she always refused, so he had given up. The only tears he ever saw his mother shed were at Betsy's funeral Mass. He gave her his handkerchief and she dabbed her eyes with it as the Bishop offered his condolences. After that Betsy's name was never spoken. All her pictures were put away. Her boyfriend left town and was never seen again. How many people knew of the baby?

When his mother told him that she had purchased a separate burial plot for Betsy, away from his father's, he became very angry. It was one of the few times that he had raised his voice at his mother. But as usual, she didn't listen. The last time he visited Betsy's gravesite, it had become overgrown. The small rose granite marker read

ELIZABETH NEELAN and Infant Son
1900 — 1921

He brushed clumps of dirt and pine needles from the granite slab. Now he routinely slipped Bertha some extra money to bring flowers to the grave and keep it tidy. The tears he used to shed at her gravesite had long dried up, replaced with anger and bitterness. Why did she have to do what she did? And then die, leaving him alone with Mother, and with his own demons. They had been inseparable in their youth. Betsy was constantly getting them into scrapes, raising the ire of Mother. To get away from her they would sneak off to the widow's walk at the top of the house until she cooled down. In adolescence he was so busy with football, studying, and the Debate team that he didn't spend as much time with his sister. But she continued to be the rebel, defying Mother at every turn. She often chastised him for his compliance, once asking, "How is it you are so persuasive on the Debate team and with all your friends, yet never stand up to Mother?" He had no answer for that. He did her bidding when he left Eleanor and went to Rome. Her money and influence had opened doors for him, and he followed. But she did not know, nor would she ever know, of his secret life. At least Betsy had been open in her rebellion.

He drove up to the museum's entrance, grabbed the umbrella from the backseat, and lifted the wheelchair from the trunk. After handing the keys to the valet, he wheeled his mother inside. The auction was in an upstairs hall. He pushed the elevator button repeatedly and stared at the lit arrow, tapping his foot.

"Stop that tapping. I swear, you're still as impatient as ever. Always want what you want when you want it, right Robert?"

"Mother, let's not get testy."

"Testy? Just stating the obvious. For someone so impatient you're sure dragging your feet with your career. You know I talked to your Uncle Ned. He doesn't understand why you haven't been made Bishop yet. You're still living in a parish rectory for God's sakes."

"I'm perfectly comfortable, Mother."

"You know why I'm putting my money into art, don't you?"

"What?"

"The art. It will all be yours someday." She'd told him all this before. As her only heir, she had made sure that despite his vow of poverty, he would be a rich man. She invested in things that he could keep, and the accounts were in a trust, one that he could borrow from discreetly if needed.

He wheeled her up to the front of the room. "Are you settled for the moment, Mother? I need to use the restroom." She shooed him away and began chatting with the gentleman beside her. He looked for a pay phone. Flipping through the yellow pages, he found the number for Hemingways. He wished they were already there. He desperately needed a drink. What was he going to say tomorrow? If Maggie spills the beans it will just be her word against his. And if the Bishop got wind of it? He'd probably be transferred like Father Kirkland had been after he was accused of molesting altar boys. How could he make sure Maggie kept quiet? Then he remembered Sister Alfred's words. "I know she is very close to her sister." He smiled. He knew what to say.

Petey

aggie didn't eat much of anything for the next few days. Mom took her to the doctor, who confirmed that it had been a miscarriage and told Maggie to rest. I tried talking to Maggie about it but she turned away from me and didn't speak. How could Jimmy do such a thing? Just when I'd begun to think he was a nice guy. I wanted him to go away, out of our lives, and get Maggie back, get our family back.

If it hadn't been for Kitty and Gramps the whole house would have turned into a tomb. On Saturday, Kitty told Mom that she and Gramps were going to take us to the new roller skating rink in town. I wanted to stay home with Maggie but Mom insisted that I go with them.

The rink was large and somewhat dark inside. There were lights flashing from the ceiling. We all lined up at the rental desk to pick out our roller skates. Gramps laced up Clare's skates, and I helped Mary with hers. Genny and I had roller skated once before, but were still pretty shaky on our feet. We clung to each other and stepped onto the rink. I could see Gramps holding Clare by one hand as she gripped the side railing with the other. Kitty was doing the same with Mary. I marveled at the people gliding along so gracefully. Genny and I decided to let go of each other and try on our own. I swung my arms back and forth for balance and propulsion. In time, I was moving along and keeping up with some of the other skaters. Genny waved at me as I skated past her, but then she fell on her bottom. I skated to the railing and offered my hand to help her up.

"I'm okay. Go." She motioned me away. So I skated on, picking up pace, pushing my feet and gliding to the rhythm of the piped-in music. As I passed Gramps, he yelled over "Doing great, Petey!" I grinned. I felt so free! I started to lean forward and swing my arms more, like I saw other skaters doing. I was going faster and faster. As I approached the curve, swinging my right leg over my left, I felt a little wobble, but managed to stay on my feet. All my concentration was now on keeping upright and moving forward. No thoughts of Maggie or Jimmy. Suddenly I saw Gramps coming along beside me. Clare was now with Kitty and Mary. He turned his body to face me.

"Gramps, you're skating backwards! How do you do that?"

He grinned at me. "It's not hard, once you get the knack of it. You're picking this up so fast. I think you could do it." After an hour of Gramps's patient tutelage, I was ready to try it on my own. It was slow going at first, but finally I was gliding backwards with some ease, that is until I knocked some poor little boy over.

"Oh, I'm sorry. Are you all right?"

The kid got up on his knees. "I'm okay."

Gramps came up next to him, and gave him a hand up. "You were doing great, Petey. Just got to keep an eye out, that's all."

"I don't have eyes in the back of my head like Mom does."

"You ready for a break? I think Kitty is taking the other girls over for a soda."

"Sure." We stepped carefully off of the rink, our skates clunking on the wooden flooring. We sat on the benches to unlace our skates and put on our shoes.

The concession area was crowded. Kitty and the other girls were already sipping their sodas. We found a booth nearby. "What will you have, Petey?" Gramps asked.

"I guess a soda."

"You want an ice cream soda?"

"Really? I can order one of those? That costs more."

"Sure, go ahead. I may have one myself."

"Okay, then, I'll have a root beer float."

The waitress came over, pulled the pencil from behind her ears. "What will it be?"

"Two root beer floats."

"Did you say that you've skated before, Petey?"

"Once. But it was a long time ago. I was invited to a friend's birthday party, and she had it at the rink in the next town over. We didn't have a rink in town then."

"Well, you learn fast."

I smiled. "It was fun. But I'm not as good as you Gramps. When did you learn to skate?"

"I've been skating since I was a little tike. Went every Saturday. I took Kitty roller skating on our first date."

"Did she like it?"

"Kitty loves everything. That's what I like about her."

It was fun talking to Gramps. Just him and me. "How did you meet her?"

"At my retirement party. It was in one of those big halls, and the room was packed with people, but I spotted this redhead over at the bar. She was looking my way. Trust me Petey, you can tell when a woman is interested." His lips curled up in a mischievous smile. I tried to picture Gramps talking to Kitty for the first time. It seemed strange to think of old people dating. I'd seen pictures of my grandmother and knew that she didn't look anything like Kitty. I wanted to ask about my grandmother but didn't know how.

"How did you know you wanted to marry Kitty? Was it like when you met Grandma?"

Gramps tucked his head down and didn't answer. The waitress set down our floats. "Thanks Miss." He tore the paper stripping off of his straw, dunked it into the foaming white froth, and took a long sip. "Good choice, Petey. Haven't had one of these in ages."

"I'm sorry Gramps. I shouldn't have asked you about Grandma."

"No, it's okay, Petey." He patted my hand. "When your grandmother died, I tried not to think about her, about anything really. I just did my job, worked day and night. It wasn't fair to your mother. I know that now. And she probably hates me for it. But sometimes a man gets a chance to make things right, start over. Kitty helped me to see that. It may be too late with your Mom, but maybe I can start getting to know my grandchildren."

"It's not too late with Mom, Gramps."

"I'm not much for talking. Don't know why I'm talking now, but just can't seem to find the right words with your mother."

"She'd like to talk with you. I know she would. She's just got a lot on her mind right now, you know?"

"Yeah, I know, and she probably didn't need company right now, but I sold my house, and we're waiting for our new house in Florida to be finished. Did your mother tell you that?"

"No. Wow! Florida, where it's sunny all the time?"

Gramps laughed. "Almost. Once we're settled, maybe you and Maggie could come for a visit."

"Really? That'd be great! I love the beach."

"Be good for Maggie to have a change of scenery. Get away for a bit after all this."

I frowned. I'd managed to forget about Maggie all morning. "I don't know if Maggie would go."

"But why?"

I shrugged my shoulders, and took a long sip of my root beer float. I didn't want to talk about how she wanted to be near Jimmy, or how it was all Monsignor Neelan's fault for convincing Dad and Mom to let her see him. None of this would have happened if it wasn't for that priest. Maybe Mom and Dad would make her go with me to Florida. But she wouldn't be fun like she used to be.

I looked up from my float to see Gramps twirling his straw in the foam at the bottom of his glass. I saw him in his uniform once, with his holstered gun, badge, etc. All those years of police work. I'd never

thought about his life much, what it must have been like as a police of-
ficer, or what it was like to raise a daughter alone.

"Do you miss being a policeman, Gramps?"

He smiled at me. "Sometimes. Guess I still think of myself as one,
somehow. I check in at the station a lot, keep up on what's happening".

"Did they let you keep your gun?"

"It's in my name, so yes, it's mine, and I always have it."

"You mean you have it on you now?"

Gramps laughed. "No, of course not. It's in my suitcase at home.
Don't tell your mother though. She'd have a fit."

"Did you ever shoot anyone?"

"You're asking a lot of questions, girl."

"Did you?"

"There were times I had to draw my weapon, but no, thank goodness, I never shot anyone."

"I asked Dad once the same question, but he wouldn't tell me. Do you
think he shot anyone in the war?"

"Most men don't want to talk about what they did in the war, Petey. I
expect your father did what he had to do. It's ugly business, nothing like
what they show in the movies." He looked me straight in the eye. "You
remember that, you hear?"

"Yes, Gramps."

"Now, let's give that roller skating another go, shall we?"

Monsignor Neelan

They arrived promptly at 2 o'clock. He almost didn't recognize John. With deep circles under his eyes and a haggard expression, the man appeared to have aged years in a few short weeks. He shook his hand and led the family into his study. All three sat on the couch. Mother and daughter pressed together while the father perched tensely on the edge, his clasped hands hanging between his knees. The priest watched Maggie closely to see if her ashen face revealed anything, but she remained silent. Rose was the first to speak.

"It's so good of you to agree to see us on such short notice, Monsignor. We're hoping you can be of help."

He saw her glance at her husband tentatively. John pulled the knot on his tie, and coughed.

"I'm happy to help in any way I can. First, can I get you something to drink?"

"We don't want to be any bother."

"It's no bother, Rose. I know how you like your coffee. I've made a fresh pot. Sit back and relax. Let me pour."

He poured two cups from the silver pot on the tray. "There's cream and sugar here if you like it. Maggie, would you like some too, or perhaps a soda?" She shook her head. Sitting across from them, Neelan chose his words carefully.

"Rose has filled me in on the situation, so I know what has happened. Have you spoken with Jimmy yet about this Maggie?" Again, she shook her head.

"You think I'm going to let my daughter speak with that bastard after what he's done?"

"John, please."

John ignored Rose's plea. "If you know what's happened then you know that my daughter should never see that guy again. She should never have been seeing him at all. And *you*, Monsignor, shouldn't have encouraged it. Should have let me do what I thought was right from the beginning. Put a stop to it."

He was expecting this, but it still unnerved him. He stared at the father's temple, where a protruding vein pulsed with each angry word. He waited for it to subside before responding. "Of course you're right John. I see that now." John exhaled deeply for the first time, and sat back on the couch. Rose glared at her husband, before speaking again.

"Monsignor, I hope you understand that our daughter's situation has upset my husband greatly."

"Of course, my dear. I'm greatly disturbed also. You know how much I think of Maggie. We all want the best for her, but these things happen."

"It's not going to happen again, not if I can help it." Again, the vein popped out like a meat gauge of the man's anger.

Validate and support. Simmer the anger, then persuade. "I agree. We have to do everything we can to avoid that. I've been thinking a lot about it since Rose called the other day. Maggie has spoken with me about Jimmy, and I believe she is a young girl of tremendous passion and capacity to love, which perhaps has led her to the present situation, but she is also a very good and religious girl. Certainly you see that in your daughter. I think this would be an ideal time to discuss her possible vocation."

He looked John in the eye, knowing that the father would be the tough sell. Rose would be thrilled to have a nun for a daughter. As he expected, John did not look pleased.

"And just how is this supposed to help Maggie?"

"Maggie is confused right now. She has feelings for this boy, but it's her youth and her passion. I believe her deep-set faith is powerful and long lasting. In the convent, she'll be away from temptation, in a contemplative setting, where she will be listening to the Lord and His Will." He took a deep breath and went on. "I've taken the liberty of talking with Sister Alfred. She has guided Maggie three years through the Sodality Club, and believes strongly that she does indeed have a vocation. Sister told me recently that she has rarely seen a young girl with such devotion to Our Lord. Were you aware that Maggie visits the chapel at school daily? Sister Alfred sees Maggie there praying on her knees every noon time, when she goes in to change the altar linens."

Rose smiled and put an arm around her daughter. "Do you feel you have a vocation, Maggie?"

"Maybe. I've been praying a lot about it. Sometimes I think so, but then I think of Jimmy..."

"I told you, Maggie. I don't want to hear that boy's name!"

He saw the red-faced father lurch forward, the daughter shrink into her mother's arms. Push the father now; help him to see that the convent is the answer to getting Maggie away from Jimmy, removing her from temptation.

"The novitiate sometimes accepts girls into the convent in high school. I think under the circumstances, it might be good for Maggie to consider early entry into the novitiate. I'm sure that you see that this is a crucial time for Maggie, and that given certain temptations, her vocation could be lost, which would be a waste. This is also the time that she needs to be in a prayerful, contemplative environment. The sisters could give her that."

Rose responded with alarm. "You mean have her go away from us now, before she even finishes high school?"

"The novitiate is only two hours away. You could visit on weekends."

John stood up, rubbed the back of his neck, and began to pace. Stopping abruptly, he asked, "But what if she doesn't have a vocation? And what about her education?"

"It needn't be permanent. If she and the Mother Superior find that the convent is not the place for her, that her calling is elsewhere, than she could leave the novitiate. While there, she would continue her education under the tutelage of the nuns. They would conference with her teachers to ensure that her studies are continued properly." He stopped, looked directly into the father's eyes and added, "And of course, only *approved* visitors would be allowed." He rose and put a hand on John's shoulder. "I know this is a lot to think about. Perhaps you and Rose would like to step into my library to discuss this proposal, while I hear Maggie's confession." Reaching into his pocket, he draped a stole around his neck and led the parents to the door. "The library is the second door on your left."

He watched them walk down the hall, waiting until he saw them enter and close the door before turning to look at Maggie. She was curled up on the corner of the couch like a cornered rabbit. Pressing his large frame next to her, he took her hand. It was limp and cold. A small tear rolled down her cheek, moistening her upper lip.

"Maggie?" Gently he rubbed his thumb over her hand. "Maggie? Talk to me." She stared blankly at the wall. "Maggie, I'm here for you." He kissed her on the cheek, now salty with tears. He wanted to do more. But he knew enough to wait; knew that she would be his again in time — *if* all went as planned.

Her shoulders dropped, and the sobs came, softly at first, and then louder. She hiccupped as she spoke. "What shall I do? My parents hate me. Jimmy is gone."

"God will take care of you, my child. Don't worry. I will make all the arrangements for the convent. He is calling you to be with Him, and you will be surrounded with fellow Brides of Christ, engaged in prayer and service to the Lord." He watched her intently. Everything depended on this moment of acquiescence.

Finally she looked at him, her eyes pooled with tears, like liquid blue gemstones. "I have been in chapel every day praying, and I did talk to

Sister Alfred. She said I must be sure. But I'm *not* sure. So I don't think I have a vocation. I haven't stopped loving Jimmy. If I enter the convent, I'll never see him again. Don't you see? I can't. I just can't do it." She straightened and pulled her hand away.

He hadn't expected this. He thought the parents would be the hard sell, but he needn't have worried. John and Rose Donovan's anger was directed at the absent boyfriend and their daughter. Even after the miscarriage, she had kept their secret. He would be more careful in the future. What he said now *had* to convince her or there would be no future with Maggie.

"I think you should reconsider. God does want you, and as I told you, I am His instrument."

"No, he doesn't, and you. . . you aren't" She pushed away from him and stood, backing towards the door. Abruptly, he grabbed her arm and yanked her back. His heart was racing, his thoughts jumbled. He wouldn't let her get away, couldn't let her ruin this.

He pushed her against the door. "Maggie, you *must* say yes. If you don't ...I"

She glared at him. Suddenly the color was back in her cheeks. "You what?"

"I've been watching your sister Agnes. She's blossoming into a pretty little thing, isn't she?

She raised her eyebrows. "Petey? My sister Petey?"

"Yes, with that lustrous long hair."

Her whole body stiffened. Her pupils dilated. "She'd never go near you."

He gripped her arms. "There's talk at the Vatican II Council of allowing altar girls. I'm sure your mother would have Agnes be one of the first girls to sign up. I would take special pains to train her, just as I've taken time with you, Maggie." His eyes held hers for a long time, and finally, when he saw it, that look of defeat, he released her. She collapsed on the couch, burying her head in her arms.

He took a deep breath. "So, I've taken the liberty of speaking to Reverend Mother at the Convent of St. Anne. I'll talk to your parents about arranging a visit?" He couldn't see her face, but saw her head slowly nod. Gently lifting her hair, he kissed the back of her neck and whispered, "Soon, Maggie, my love, soon."

Petey

This can't be happening. When Maggie told me that she was going to a convent, I didn't believe her at first. But Mom and Dad said it was true, and that she would be leaving within the next couple of weeks.

The house was stone quiet. I was surprised that everyone was still sleeping, even Clare. Maggie, especially, had been sleeping late, sometimes missing the bus and staying home. She'd become a hermit. She never joined the family in the living room to watch television and ate most meals in the bedroom, if she ate at all. When I went downstairs to the bathroom, I heard Dad and Mom talking in the kitchen.

"Give it more time, John. Be patient with her."

"My patience is running thin, Rose, and not just with Maggie. When the hell are your father and Kitty leaving, anyway?"

"Sshh, keep your voice down."

"Why should I keep my voice down? It's about time they got up. We sure could use some help around here."

"They help out. Their new house should be ready soon and then things will go back to normal."

"Normal? Nothing has been normal around here for weeks, Rose."

The door slammed as he left for work. I crept back up the stairs and crawled back into bed. Maggie was sound asleep. Her face was pale, almost translucent. I thought back to the time we found a fish on the beach, gray and almost lifeless. I had picked it up gently and tossed it into the sea, but it had been too late. Not enough life left to recover. If Maggie became a nun, she'd never recover. She couldn't go into the convent. She just couldn't. If she became a nun, I'd never get my sister back. She'd be locked away, sad and lonely. Maybe next Sunday after church I should talk to Monsignor Neelan and make him change everything. The thought made me shudder. What was I thinking? I could never talk to that man, and he'd never listen, anyway. What did Sherlin mean that he was a bad man? Why did she get so angry that day? I had to talk to Mom, get her to see this plan wasn't right for Maggie. I got up, put on my terrycloth bathrobe, and walked into the kitchen. Mom was packing her lunch for work.

"Morning, Petey. I'm glad you got up before I left for work. I wish I didn't have to work on a Saturday, but I do. I left a list of groceries on the refrigerator for your grandfather to pick up, and oh, don't forget to give Clare her cough medicine. I sure hope I don't have to call Dr. Shepley. We can't afford another doctor bill and..."

"Mom, you *can't* send Maggie off to a convent. You just can't!"

Mom spread mustard on the bread while speaking. "You should be happy for your sister, Petey. She has a true vocation, and will make a wonderful nun."

"But she's only sixteen!"

"We are quite aware of that, but we feel that this will be best for her at this time."

"But Mom, I don't think she really wants to go at all." I leaned against the counter, trying to get my mother to look at me.

She wrapped her sandwich in wax paper before answering. "I'm sure you think you know what your sister wants, Petey, but she's already told us that she wants to be a nun."

"That's because Monsignor Neelan told her so. This is all *his* idea, isn't it?"

"You know better than that. Maggie's often talked about joining the convent."

"Mom, please, please, don't let her go. You know you wouldn't have agreed to it except for what happened. Don't punish her for that. Please, Mom?" I was pleading like a small child begging for candy or a toy at the store. I didn't know how else to reach her.

She slipped the sandwich into a brown paper bag along with an apple. "She's not being punished. It's just best for her to join now, before Jimmy comes back."

"I know what Jimmy did, but you can't send Maggie away. You just can't!"

"Petey, you're too young to know what you're talking about."

"Mom. I don't think you should listen to Monsignor Neelan. I think he's a bad man."

She whirled around, lunchbag in hand. "Petey! You're talking about a priest, a monsignor, no less! This discussion is over. I know you love your sister, but this is her decision, and ours, not yours. You will be able to visit her on weekends."

"Mom, please, *don't* let her go."

"That's enough, Petey. I've got to leave for work now. I left some hamburger out to thaw. Maybe you could make some meatballs for dinner. Don't worry about Maggie. Everything will work out. You'll see." A car horn honked. "Oh, there's my ride." She pecked my cheek and went out the kitchen door.

I stood, my arms hanging limply by my side. What more could I do? I shivered. The house was cold. Dad insisted we keep the heat register low to keep the bill down. I went into the bedroom to get my slippers. Kitty was just waking up. Her red hair stuck out like corkscrews, almost turning my welled up tears into laughter.

"You suppose you could get me a cup of black coffee, Petey? I sure need something to get me moving this morning."

"Okay." I put on my slippers and headed back into the kitchen, plucked the yellow cup and saucer that Kitty liked from the cupboard, and poured coffee from the still percolating pot on the stove. Turning around, I almost bumped into her.

She reached for the cup. "Sorry. Didn't mean to scare you." She sat at the kitchen table, and took her first sip. "You're an early riser, aren't you, sweetie."

"Sometimes, but Maggie's usually up before me."

"Hmm. Not lately though, huh? I couldn't help but overhear some of your conversation with your mother this morning. I don't very often hear your mother raise her voice. Care to share why she was so upset?"

I looked up at this woman I hardly knew, who only a few days before had been by Maggie's side washing blood off her thighs. I didn't know if she knew about the convent plan.

"I just wanted her to keep Maggie home, not send her away."

"Send her away?"

I told her then about Maggie entering the convent soon. Her eyes squinted tight, spreading folds of wrinkles across her face. "And you say this was Monsignor Neelan's idea?"

"Yes. I think so. I mean Maggie agrees and all, but I think he's the one pushing it. It's not fair. Can't they see that Maggie is confused? I don't want her to go away. She needs to be here."

"And your parents support this?"

"Yes, but I think it's only because of what happened, you know, that night."

"This Monsignor Neelan, is he the one who said Mass on Christmas?"

"Yes. Do you remember him?"

"Yeah, I remember him. Your mother introduced us. Smooth talker. Kind of full of himself, if you ask me. And you say that Maggie has been seeing him for counseling? How long has that been going on?"

"It's been a couple of months or so, I think."

"I see."

I watched her gulp more coffee. "Kitty, can I tell you something else?"

"What is it, Petey?"

"Well, I have this friend. Her name is Sherlin. Her family owns the Dragon Palace restaurant downtown. Have you seen it?"

"Sure. Your grandfather and I had lunch there one afternoon. Good Chinese food."

"I visited Sherlin one day and I mentioned Monsignor Neelan, and Sherlin got really upset. She said he was a very bad man and that he was the reason that their family had to move out of town. But she never said why, and wouldn't talk about it with me after that."

Kitty lit up her first cigarette of the day. She took a long drag, blew out the smoke, and sipped her coffee. "Did she say anything else?"

"Something about how they were shamed. She said just ask her older sister, Chan."

Kitty crushed out her cigarette on her saucer. "Honey, when you get dressed this morning, put on something nice. You and I are going out to lunch."

"We are?"

"Yup. I'm in the mood for Chinese food."

"You mean at the Wang's restaurant?"

"We'll pick up those groceries your Mom wants, maybe even stop at the five and ten, and then go on over to Dragon Palace. So you better get moving."

"But Mom left me a list of chores, and I've got to check on Clare, and make sure she doesn't have a fever."

"Maggie and your grandfather can do that. You and I are stepping out today."

I opened the dresser drawers, and found the yellow sweater from last Christmas. Should I wear a skirt? Kitty said to look nice. Reluctantly, I grabbed the brown one from the closet, and fished for brown knee socks to match. Maggie stirred in her sleep, but didn't wake up.

I helped Kitty find everything at the grocery store, and she then treated me to some hair ribbons, barrettes, and crossword puzzle book from the five and dime. We arrived at the Dragon Palace at 11:30, just as they opened. Sherlin looked up from folding napkins at the corner table. I hoped she wasn't still angry. She came over to us and smiled.

"Hi Petey!"

Good. She seemed happy to see me. "Hi, Sherlin. This is Kitty, my grandfather's fiancée. We're going to have lunch together."

"Hi, Sherlin. It's nice to meet you. Petey has told me what a good friend you are."

Sherlin looked over at me and smiled. "Do you want to sit anyplace special?"

"How about here by this beautiful painting?" Kitty walked towards a corner booth under a large watercolor print of lotus blossoms.

Sherlin gave us our menus, poured our water, and headed to the kitchen. I stared at the menu with all the strange names.

Kitty looked up from her menu. "So, what do you recommend?"

"Me? I've never eaten here before."

"But I thought you come here to see your friend?

"Yeah, sometimes. Mrs. Wang gives me egg rolls to take home, or dumplings, and of course fortune cookies, but not a meal."

"Did you like the eggrolls?"

"Oh, yes. They're delicious."

"Well, I know just the thing. We'll have the PuPu platter, which has a combination of things, including eggrolls. How's that sound?"

"What's a PuPu platter?"

"You'll see."

After giving our order to Sherlin, Kitty excused herself to go to the ladies room. Already I could smell rich aromas coming from the kitchen. Two chopsticks sat next to a Chinese zodiac placemat. I picked them up and tried to remember how Sherlin held them, but they kept falling from my hand. My eyes wandered around the dining room. Red fringed tassels hung in the window. Gold platters with Chinese symbols perched on wall shelving. What would it be like to go someplace like China? Just sitting in this restaurant was foreign to me. I'd never gone out to eat before except for the dime store soda fountain. Scrolling through the zodiac signs on the placemat, I found mine. Born the year of the tiger, which said I was strong and intelligent, but had a short temper. I guess Mom would agree to that. I kept on reading. ... "can be over confident and traitorous." Traitorous? I gulped. Did Maggie think I was a traitor? My lip trembled. A tear dropped on the placemat. I quickly wiped it away as Kitty approached.

"Here comes our PuPu platter. Doesn't it smell delicious?"

Blue flames licked the sides of the hibachi grill; ringed with egg-rolls, chicken wings, spare ribs, and other fried foods that I'd never seen before. I was mesmerized. Kitty encouraged me to try each food item, and I wasn't disappointed. I was still munching on the final spare-rib and licking my fingers, when Sherlin came by to clear our plates.

Kitty handed Sherlin her plate. "Everything was delicious, Sherlin. My compliments to the chef. Does your father do the cooking?"

"Both my father and mother cook, but my mother is in the kitchen today."

"Would it be possible to thank her personally?"

"I'll go ask her. Would you like some tea?"

"That would be lovely. Thank you."

A few minutes later, Mrs. Wang came out of the kitchen carrying a tray. On it was an ivory teapot etched with blue-green bamboo leaves. She poured us each a cup of tea. "Hello, Petey. It is good to see you again. Is this your grandmother?"

"No. I mean not yet. She is my grandfather's fiancée, Kitty."

"It's nice to meet you, Kitty. I am Sherlin's mother, Connie. Did you enjoy your lunch?"

"Very much. I know Petey did also, but I think she would also enjoy spending some time with your daughter. And perhaps you would join me for tea?"

"Well, I don't know."

"If they can spare you in the kitchen, there is something important I wish to speak with you about. It concerns your daughter, your older daughter, Chan."

Mrs. Wang set down the teapot and looked intently at Kitty. She motioned for Sherlin to come to our table.

"Sherlin, why don't you take Petey into the kitchen and have some of that coconut tapioca custard I made this morning?"

"Oh, Petey, wait 'till you taste it. It's yummy!"

I followed Sherlin out to the kitchen, glancing over my shoulder briefly to see Mrs. Wang sitting in my chair across from Kitty, already pouring tea.

Maggie

I look over at the clock. 11:00 a.m. How did I sleep so late, and why do I still feel so tired? As I push the covers off, one of the wooden boards falls to the floor. My feet must have shoved them to the bottom of the bed again during the night. My self-selected penance without the necessary discipline. *The Lives of the Saints* lie open by my bedside. Which saint was it that had used wooden boards? How can I be a nun when I can't even commit to one act of penance?

The house is strangely quiet. Not even the sound of Saturday morning cartoons from the living room. I pull the shade and squint at the bright sun. Petey's worn sneakers sit next to her crisply made bed. Kitty's make-up is strewn across the bureau. Shuffling to the kitchen, I find the house deserted. Where is everyone? I remember that Dad and Mom both had to work today. As I open the refrigerator for the orange juice, I see the note.

> *I've taken Mary and Clare to the park since it's such a nice day. Genny is over at her friend's house. Kitty took Petey out to lunch and shopping. See you later this afternoon, Sleeping Beauty.*
> *Love, Gramps*

I curl my legs up under me while nibbling on some dry toast. The day stretch-es out before me, empty and solemn, to be filled, I know, with the persis-tence of doubt and fear. Tomorrow I will be introduced to Sister Martha, the Reverend Mother Superior at the Convent of St. Anne. Mom and Dad will drive me there after church. There have been phone conversations, but this will be our first meeting. If all goes well, I will begin as a postulant in a few weeks. I haven't told any of my friends yet, nor Jimmy, who will be home soon. He called from Mississippi yesterday before Mom or Dad got home. He's all excited about the work he has done down South. I was scared when he told me about the police in riot gear, but he said there had been no violence. He thought it was in part because of all the white clergymen who came to help. Hundreds of colored people stood in line waiting to register but only twelve managed to register to vote. Even so, Jimmy said it was a huge victory. He was so animated and enthusiastic about it all. In so many ways he seems to be worlds away, and I have trouble remembering his touch and the way he looks at me. Perhaps, he'll become so involved in this new work of his that he will forget all about me, although he said he missed me.

I want so desperately to see him, to be in his arms again. But how can I tell him about what has happened? How can he possibly love me or forgive me after what I've done? First, I thought maybe there was a chance; we could put it behind us and I would still be able to go to col-lege near him. But now, after what Monsignor Neelan said about Petey? Sweet, innocent Petey with *him*! I shudder. I *have* to protect Petey, no mat-ter what! Even if it means going to the convent.

I walk back to my room, and pull out a black tee shirt. I place it on my head, pressing the sleeves against my ears and staring at myself in the mirror. As a little girl, I had pranced around with black shawls and a cloth draped over my head, pretending to be a nun. It had all seemed rather glamorous then. I imagined myself to be Sister Benedict in "The Bells of St. Mary's." Ingrid Bergman was so beautiful and always smil-ing. But the girl in the mirror wasn't smiling. I throw myself back on the bed. With no one home, I could cry as loud as I wanted. My tears flood the pillow, and the bawling makes me hiccup.

I don't know how much time has passed. Finally I sit up, totally exhausted. Oh, God, what am I to do? Prayer had brought no answers. Sometimes He did seem to be telling me that He wanted me to be a nun, was calling me to serve Him, especially when I sat in the chapel at school and watched the altar candles flicker on either side of the sanctuary. Would the nuns be kind and good like Sister Benedict, or would they be like Sister Paula Marie, always ready to torture me? Would they let Monsignor Neelan come, or protect me from him? And how could I leave my family? When they came to visit, could I play with my sisters? And Jimmy, oh God, forgive me, I do still love him. I've tried to forget him, but I can't. Will he react like Daddy? Get angry and stop loving me. I know I've shamed my father. He refuses to believe that Jimmy is innocent. But I can never tell him the truth; I don't really understand what happened myself. I mean I knew what was going on at some point. Could I have stopped it? But how?

Dad wants me out of his sight. At least entering the convent will accomplish that. And it has been my mother's dream for years to have a daughter become a nun. It would make her happy. But would I be happy? I always believed that somehow everything would work out. Now, it all seems hopeless.

Gramps and my sisters will be home soon, or maybe Kitty and Petey. I can't face them. Petey will know immediately that I've been crying. Lately, she is always watching me. I have to get away, escape everything. Grabbing my winter coat from the closet, I slip on my shoes, and head downstairs. I push open the front door and step outside, surprised at the warmth. Mom calls it a January thaw, when spring seems to erupt in the middle of winter, teasing us with the hope of better days to come. But I know better days aren't coming, that I will still be trapped.

The phone rings as I leave the house but don't stay to answer it. I hear Genny slam the back door, pick up the receiver and call out.

"Hello. Maggie! Telephone! I don't respond.

"I don't think she's home. Who's this?"

"Oh, hi, Jimmy. It's Genny. I don't know where she is. I just got home from my friend's house."

There is a long pause before Genny says, "They're both working today. Sure, I'll tell her."

I carefully close the front door and creep down the front steps.

Petey

Kitty and I drove up just as Gramps, Mary, and Clare walked into the yard.

"Hi Gramps!" I jumped out of the car. "Kitty and I had a Pu-Pu platter!"

"Is that so?"

"Yup. Everything was delicious. I still liked the egg rolls best, but it was so cool to see the flames and everything. And I got to see my friend Sherlin, who played some of the records that she got for Christmas, while Mrs. Wang and Kitty had tea and talked."

"Do the Chinese celebrate Christmas?"

"Oh, Gramps, the Wangs are Catholic, remember? Mrs. Wang gave us some coconut custard for dessert that was scrumptious! And Kitty took me to the five and dime where we shopped for a while. She bought me some hair ribbons and barrettes."

Gramps leaned over me to give Kitty a kiss, patted my head, and asked, "Who wound her up?"

Kitty laughed. "Petey and I had a fun day together, didn't we? Looks like you took advantage of the nice weather to get out. Where did you go?"

"There's a park a few blocks from here with a playground and pond."

Mary was hopping up and down excitedly. "And we fed the ducks too. One of them almost bit Clare's hand off!"

I rolled my eyes, knowing Mary was prone to exaggerate.

"Really, it did! If you don't believe me you can ask Gramps."

Gramps put his arm on Mary's shoulder. "Well, let's just say, I had to do a little bit of duck-shooing and grandchild comforting for a moment there. But no injuries."

"Is Maggie still sleeping?" Kitty asked.

"I don't know. She was when I left. Genny went to a friend's house."

Just then the back door slammed and Genny stepped outside. Kitty reached into her shopping bag and took out a bag of chocolate chip cookies. "Hi, Genny. Why don't you take these cookies and share them with your sisters. I have to talk with your grandfather for a bit. Petey, make sure nobody has more than three cookies each."

"Three! Wow! Mom never lets us have that much!"

"Well, grandmothers are more generous. Stay outside and play until I call you to come in, okay?"

"Sure." I started to walk into the back yard, but then ran back to give Kitty a quick hug. "Thanks, Kitty, for today; you know, lunch and everything."

"You're welcome, Petey." She hugged me back and stepped into the house. When everyone finished their cookies, we played tag, and then grabbed our hula-hoops leaning against the house. I tried to show Mary and Clare how to do it, but they couldn't get the hang of it and gave up.

"Can't we go in now, Petey?"

"Kitty said we had to stay out until she called."

Clare squeezed her legs together and wiggled. "But I have to go to the bathroom."

"Okay, go on."

"But you have to come with me 'cause I can't do these snaps on my jumper."

"All right." I walked Clare to the bathroom, undid the snaps at the shoulders of her green corduroy jumper. She perched on the edge of the toilet, her pink panties dangling around her ankles.

"I have to poop too, and sometimes it takes a long time for my poop to come. Will you wait for me?"

"Yeah. Don't forget to flush the toilet and wash your hands."

The bathroom door was ajar and I could hear Gramps' voice rise from the living room.

"Are you sure about this, Kitty?"

"Connie Wang doesn't seem to be a woman to spin tales, Joe. I doubt her daughter is either. Don't you see? It explains everything."

"But why didn't she *tell* anyone?"

"C'mon Joe. Think about it. This is a priest, a very powerful, persuasive priest. Who knows what he's told her? She's scared shitless." I tiptoed closer to the living room, my body pressed against the hallway wall so that I couldn't be seen.

"The *bastard*! I can't believe he would do this! He hasn't changed a bit."

"But I thought he was your friend in high school?"

"Yeah, before he stole Eleanor." I heard him sigh, and then there was a long pause before his voice spoke again in a hushed tone. "I was in love with her the first moment we met."

"And then Bob Neelan came along?"

"Yeah. She fell for him big time. Probably didn't hurt that he had become quarterback of the football team. A lot of girls were drooling over him. What they didn't know was that he should never have been quarterback. Should have been Will Morrison."

"Will Morrison?"

"Will had the best arm I've ever seen. Coach Nunes knew it too. But Will was no match for Bob Neelan."

"Bob beat him out in tryouts?"

"No. Bob beat him out in being a first rate scoundrel. He blackmailed the coach."

"Blackmailed him?"

"Bob caught the coach drinking whiskey in the locker room one day. Threatened to report him unless he made him first string quarterback. I overheard the conversation, tried to dissuade Bob, but he just sneered and told me that I needed to grow up. Not long after that he took Eleanor from me, and then left her for the seminary."

There was a long silence before I heard my grandfather again. His voice was choking. "Jesus Christ, how could he? Maggie. Poor sweet Maggie."

For a moment I thought I heard crying. I squatted down on the floor and ventured a peek around the doorjamb. Gramps was sitting on the couch, his head in his hands. Kitty had her arm around his shoulder. I could just barely hear her.

"It's okay Joe. Any man would cry."

He lifted his head then, his hands clasped over his knees, his face red, his teeth clenched. "The rat bastard doesn't deserve to live!" He jumped up and slapped his knees. "I'll kill him! God, help me. I'll kill him!" Kitty put her hand on his shoulder, her voice too soft for me to hear.

His anger scared me. Who did he want to kill, and why? Suddenly I remembered what he told me at the bowling alley. The gun — in his suitcase. Would he use it to kill someone? They were still talking in the living room. I tiptoed to my parents' bedroom. Kneeling on the floor, I tugged at the suitcase in the closet and unsnapped the latch. Frantically I shoved the clothes aside. It wasn't there. Then I saw a small black pouch at the bottom of the suitcase. Slowly, I unzipped it. With trembling fingers, I lifted out the gun and placed it on my lap. It laid cold and heavy against my thighs. I stroked the barrel and lightly touched the trigger. With both hands, I raised the gun, surprised at its heft. I pointed it toward the wall, picturing Maggie and Jimmy kissing in the car. I saw Maggie lying in bed, blood seeping between her legs. I saw Jimmy laughing, calling me "Squirt." Hatred seethed up like vomit. My finger encircled the trigger ... I dropped the gun and whimpered. I heard footsteps in the hall and the toilet flushing.

"Petey, I need help with my jumper!"

I scampered back to the bathroom, just as Gramps stormed down the hall towards the bedroom.

Fumbling with the jumper snaps, I saw Gramps walking briskly back to the living room. I strained to hear the conversation.

"You know where I have to go, Kitty."

"Can't you wait? We haven't even talked to Maggie yet."

"No need. We know what he did."

I heard a door slamming and car tires pealing out of the driveway as Clare and I stepped into the kitchen. With a pensive frown, Kitty stood holding the edge of the curtains, staring out the window. Clare let go of my hand and ran to her. She touched Kitty's arm and asked, "Are you okay?"

Kitty looked down with a forced smile. "I'm okay, honey." She looked at me and asked "Where's your sisters?"

"They're still out in the back yard."

Kitty opened the back door and called for my sisters. They came in, stamping their muddy shoes on the doormat. "You kids can all go watch TV for a while. I'll be upstairs talking to Maggie."

Two minutes later, Kitty peeked out from around the stairwell. "Genny, when you came home from your friend's house, was Maggie still in her room?"

"I think so. Her bedroom door was shut. I didn't really look 'cause I was watching television."

I knew what that meant. A bomb could go off and Genny wouldn't hear it if she was watching TV. Mom keeps saying that Genny needs to have her hearing checked.

Kitty came down the stairs and sat next to me on the couch. "She's not in her room. Do you know where she might be, Petey?"

"Maybe she went for a walk. It's such a nice day."

"I hope so, although she shouldn't have left Genny here alone."

I watched her as she picked at the threads of the couch, stood, walked to the window and stared. The *Lone Ranger* theme song blared from the TV set.

Just a short time ago she was comforting Gramps as he cried here on the couch. I'd never seen a man cry before. What upset him so much, and where did he go? Did he see the gun? What was Kitty talking about when she said it explained everything? And where was Maggie? I wanted to ask what was going on, but the look on Kitty's face when she turned around stopped me. Her lips were pressed tightly together and her eyes were puffy. This morning's laughter seemed worlds away.

Clare had fallen asleep leaning against me. Gently, I lifted her head and eased it onto the couch. Mary and Genny were lying down on the rug, elbows propped under their chins, glued to the television set. I followed Kitty into the kitchen. She was drinking another cup of coffee, and crushing out a cigarette.

"Where'd Gramps go?"

"He went to see someone." I sat in the chair across from her as she tapped another cigarette from her pack. "I wish I knew where Maggie was."

"She might have gone to Samantha's."

"Do you have her phone number?"

"No. Maggie told me it was unlisted. But she lives just three blocks over, at 93 Smith St."

"Well, I can't just sit here. I'll walk over there. It shouldn't take long. Watch your sisters until your parents come home."

Kitty stuck the cigarette back and took a final sip of coffee. Lifting her coat off the wall peg and pulling on her boots, she glanced back at me. "Don't worry Petey. She's probably with Samantha or out for a walk."

I sat chewing the inside of my mouth, hoping she was right, but my sickening stomach said that Maggie was not just out for a walk.

Monsignor Neelan

He had just finished the final touches for tomorrow's sermon when the doorbell rang. Saturday was Mrs. McNair's day off, and Father Thomas was away for the day. He'd have to answer the door. Could it be Maggie? He didn't think so. Her parents had said that with the prospective entrance to the convent, she needed to spend weekends with family. He reluctantly agreed. It would be safer for him not to be near her now. He would have to wait.

He looked through the peephole. Joe Kelley was standing on the rectory doorstep.

His hand hesitated on the doorknob. Did Joe know about Maggie? Would she have told someone now, after so much time had passed? The doorbell rang again. He opened the heavy oak door slowly.

Forty years had passed since they last spoke. The years showed on Joe. His face was drawn; his frame shrunk from the once six-foot brawny friend of old. His hair was snow-white, but his eyes were still sharp and now glared at him. Neelan's chest tightened.

"Hello, Joe. I was hoping you'd come by for a visit. Rose told me that you were in town. How nice to see you. Come in. It will be great to talk about old times."

"I'm not here to reminisce."

Monsignor Neelan saw the jaw muscles clench. His stomach turned. He *must* know. Surely he could persuade his old friend that Maggie was confused and telling tales to protect the boyfriend.

Joe shoved past him, his muddy shoes leaving footprints on the Persian carpet.

He directed him to the study and then quickly poured two glasses of whisky from the decanter, offering one to Joe.

Joe shook his head. "I'm not here to drink either."

"Really? Never knew you to turn one down before. This is Maker's Mark bourbon, the best. But suit yourself. I could use one. Been working all afternoon on my sermon. I hope you'll be at Mass tomorrow. I heard that you were visiting. Thought you might stop by for a chat. We could have caught up, y'know, talked about our old football days." He set the decanter down slowly. "I understand you're engaged. Rose introduced me to your fiancée. I believe she said her name is Katy?"

"Kitty."

"Oh yes, that's right. Congratulations. About time you got yourself a good woman."

"I had a good woman. You know that." Joe remained standing, his eyes fixed on Neelan.

"Of course. Of course. But that was a long time ago."

"For you maybe. Not for me. I don't forget the people I love as easily as you."

Maybe his visit was not about Maggie. Just here to vent about Eleanor. They'd never spoken about her death. Neelan stepped over to the window, drew the blinds slightly to avert the late day sun. The parking lot was empty except for his old friend's battered Chevy. He kept his back to Joe and took his first sip. "I haven't forgotten Eleanor, Joe. It was a tremendous shock and loss to me when she died. I'm sorry that I wasn't able to get to her funeral."

Joe scoffed, "Prr — You? At her funeral? I don't think so."

Neelan turned around, twirled the ice in his glass with one finger, and spoke.

"Joe, I'm sorry for your loss. I sent a Mass card, kept her in my prayers. I know it was hard for you, but you've done yourself proud with Rose. She's grown into a wonderful woman with a good husband and beautiful daughters."

He saw Joe stiffen. "I'm here about Maggie."

"Maggie? Rose must have told you about how I've tried to help her ... you know, with the boyfriend? The poor girl is quite confused, sometimes to the point of being delusional. But her strong faith is helping her get through all this. I'm sure you see that."

"I see a sixteen-year-old granddaughter whose innocence has been robbed by an old *pervert*."

Monsignor Neelan took another sip of bourbon, set it on the end table, and looked at Joe. "What exactly has Maggie said to you, Joe?"

"Nothing. But I *know*. You hear that, you filthy bastard! I *know* what you did. Joe charged forward, his voice becoming a low growl. "The game is up, Bob. I want to hear it from you directly, how you *defiled* my granddaughter."

Neelan backtracked behind the desk, almost tripping on the edge of the carpet.

Joe was yelling now, slamming his fist on the desk. "You're no priest! You never were. I knew that from the very beginning. From the day you left Eleanor when she needed you most."

"I don't know what you're talking about. I left Eleanor because of my vocation. I left to become a priest. She knew that. She understood."

Joe stopped, his knuckles pressed on the corner of the desk. Dropping his head slowly, he breathed deeply before lifting it and glowering at Neelan. "She *loved* you. God help her for that, but she did."

At first Neelan couldn't move with those dark eyes boring into him, but finally he edged from behind the desk. He shrugged his shoulders, as if to throw off some pestilence, and looked at Joe. "Love comes and goes. She flew into your arms quickly enough. I'd think you'd be happy I left." He circled around the room.

Joe followed, his voice rising again. "Happy? I wanted nothing more in the world than to be happy and make her happy. She tried to be, pretended to be, but it was *you* she loved." He drew closer, shoving Neelan in the chest. His voice lowered. "Maybe in time she would have loved me, if she had lived, and we had raised Rose together, but we didn't *have* that time." He turned around and muttered, "Your precious God took her from me."

The room seemed to be closing in on him. Retreating from Joe, Neelan retrieved the bourbon, his hand shaking as he gripped the glass. The melting ice cubes had watered his drink from a deep brown to light amber. Was it true? Eleanor had loved him, even after he'd abandoned her? Lifting the drink to his lips, he swallowed, savoring the rich burn of alcohol steadying his voice as he spoke. "I'm sorry that grief has made you so bitter."

Joe stood across from him. "Don't feel sorry for *me*, Bob. I never gave up on love, like you did. You lost not only Eleanor, but so much more. I've made my share of mistakes, but they were honest mistakes. What you did to Eleanor is in the past, but *Maggie* . . . dear sweet Maggie, how *could* you?" His words spewed between clenched teeth. His fist exploded in his palm.

Neelan gulped to quell his rising fear. He knew that he must choose his words carefully. He put his palm up. "Joe, I've told you. I was counseling Maggie. That's all. Whatever you heard, whether from Maggie or someone else that implies anything more than that, is a lie." His left eye began to twitch.

Joe stepped forward, his eyes blazing, seeing his spit spray the priest's face. "You might be able to fool others, but you can't fool me. You forget how long I've known you, how you use people, and toss them aside. YOU ARE NEVER TO SEE MAGGIE AGAIN! You hear me, you sick bastard. No more! Don't you *ever* lay a hand on her again!" An adrenaline rush poured through him as he grabbed his old friend's shirt and shook him up against the wall. For a full minute they stared into each other's eyes, before Joe's clenched fists let go and dropped to his sides. "You disgust me."

Neelan tried to keep his voice from shaking. "You forget, Joe. Maggie will be entering St. Anne's Convent. I'll continue to be her spiritual counselor."

"You won't use Maggie again after you see *this*."

Joe reached into the inside pocket of his jacket. Neelan flinched, and instinctively stepped back.

Petey

$\mathcal{I}$ heard the girls squabbling in the living room, but for once chose to ignore it. Staring at the imprinted swirls of ivy on the kitchen wallpaper, I couldn't move or think. The stale odor of cigarettes permeated the room. A lone cigarette protruded from the Lucky Strike carton. I picked it up, edging it between my two fingers as I'd seen Kitty do, and put it to my lips.

Mary came running into the kitchen, crying "Petey, Genny hit me!" Quickly, I shoved the cigarette in my pocket. "Petey?" She touched my arm. "Did you hear me? Genny hit me."

I turned and said sharply, "Go watch TV, Mary."

"But Genny changed the channel. I told her I wanted to finish watching *Make Room for Daddy,* but she said she already saw it, so she changed the channel to *American Bandstand*."

"I said, go watch TV!"

Mary stomped her foot and sulked from the room. "It's not fair. Genny always gets to watch what she wants." I sighed. I should probably sort it out. I also needed to check on Clare since Mom had said she wasn't feeling well this morning. Instead, I sat, rolling the cigarette in my pocket.

Mom was the first one to get home. She opened the door, and started unbuttoning her coat. "Hi Sweetie. Is your father home yet?" I shook my head. "Is that Mary squalling in the living room? What's going on now? Just once I'd like to come home to a peaceful household. Did you make those meatballs for supper like I asked?"

A slow tear rolled down my cheek, and again I shook my head. Mom's heavy brown purse clunked on the table as she sat in the kitchen chair next to me. "What's wrong, Petey?"

"Maggie's gone."

"What do you mean, she's gone?"

"Kitty took me to lunch and Mary and Clare were at the park with Gramps, and Maggie stayed home in bed, but when we got home, she wasn't here."

"And Genny?"

"She went over to Nancy's, remember?"

"So, where is your grandfather now?"

"He went to see someone. He seemed really upset about something."

"And Kitty?"

"She went over to Samantha's house to see if Maggie's there."

"How long ago was that?"

"I don't know. I didn't look at the time."

Mom gave me a quick kiss on the forehead. "Go wash your face Petey. Maggie will probably come walking through the door any minute." But her smile was forced, and she had those worry lines between her eyebrows.

Cupping the cold water in my hands, I splashed my face and stared at myself in the mirror. Did I look as changed as I felt? Loose strands of hair fell forward. Unlooping the rubber band, I pushed them back into the ponytail. I took a deep breath and tried to exhale the worry, anger, and frustration. The sound of a car pulling into the driveway spurred me back to the kitchen. *Please God, let it be Sam bringing Maggie home.* But it was the Plymouth station wagon. Dad was home from work.

Mom was already outside, running into Dad's arms, "John, she's gone!"

"Who's gone?"

"Maggie."

Together they came into the house. Dad put his lunch pail on the table, and they both sat down. He leaned forward, inches from my mother. "Tell me exactly what you know."

"Not much. I just got home myself and Petey told me that when she and Kitty came home from lunch that Maggie was missing."

"Who saw her last? Did you talk to all the girls?" He saw me then, standing in the doorway. "Petey. What do you know about this?"

"Like Mom said, Gramps took Mary and Clare to the park and I went out with Kitty. Maggie was home in bed when we left."

"Where was Genny?"

"She was at Nancy's house." Dad stood up and Mom and I followed him into the living room. Mary and Genny ran to him, but instead of scooping them into his arms as usual, he turned off the television set and told the girls to sit down.

"We aren't fighting any more Daddy. Honest. Please don't be mad."

"I'm not mad at you Genny. I just want to talk to you both, that's all."

"About Maggie?"

"Yes, Genny, about Maggie. When you came home from your friend's house, was Maggie here?"

"Well, I didn't see her. But maybe she was still in her bedroom. I didn't really look 'cause the phone rang when I walked in, and then after that I went to watch some cartoons on TV. But I told him that I didn't know if Maggie was home."

"You told *who* that you didn't know if Maggie was home?"

"Jimmy. He called here and said he was coming over."

"He said he was coming here? When?"

"I don't know. He just said he was coming over, and to tell Maggie. But I didn't see Maggie, so I didn't tell her."

"Did you go to her room and look to see if she was there?"

"No. I turned on the television."

"So, maybe she was still in her room?"

"Maybe. I thought I did hear something later, like maybe someone was in the house, but I didn't get up to look 'cause my favorite cartoon was on, and I just didn't."

"This is very important Genny. You say, you thought you heard a noise, and maybe someone was in the house. Was the noise coming from Maggie's room?"

"I don't know. Maybe. I think I heard a door slam, and voices. But maybe it was from next door. I don't know."

"Voices? You mean more than one voice?"

"I think. I mean, I don't remember for sure. It was just for a minute. Like I said, I wasn't really listening, and the television was loud."

"Was one of those voices a man's voice?

Genny shrugged, "I don't know, Daddy." She started to cry. "I'm sorry, Daddy. I should have looked for Maggie, but I didn't. I'm sorry."

Dad patted her shoulder. "That's okay, Genny. We'll find her. It's not your fault. You can finish watching your show now."

I followed my parents into the kitchen and jumped a mile when Dad's fist hit the table, upending the sugar bowl. "Sneaky bastard! Waits until we're not here before coming for her! Son of a bitch!"

"John, what are you talking about?"

"Maggie's so-called boyfriend. He called and said he was coming over. Don't you see what happened? He came over like he said, and left with Maggie without anyone knowing."

"You think Jimmy was here? That Maggie's with him?"

"It's the only thing that makes sense. Where did Kitty go to look for her?"

"I don't know. Petey said Kitty was checking her friend's house."

They turned toward me then. "Petey, do you have any idea where Jimmy and your sister might have gone?" I leaned against the door-frame, put my head down, and twisted one foot around my leg.

My mother came toward me and bent low, "Petey, if you know where Maggie is, you need to tell us. She's not thinking clearly right now and needs our help. Did she ever talk about places she and Jimmy went?"

I looked into my mother's distraught face. "She told me once about meeting him at the beach."

Dad reached for the doorknob. "The beach, huh? I'll find her."

"Can I come too, Daddy?"

"No. Stay here with your mother."

"But I want to help find Maggie."

"You've already helped."

Mom let out a deep breath as Dad slammed the door behind him. Turning toward me, she said, "Petey, would you get those meatballs made? I need to check on Clare."

Pressing the breadcrumbs into the hamburger, I cracked an egg and sprinkled salt and pepper into the mixture. I blinked, trying to keep the welled up tears from dripping into the bowl. I wished Dad had let me go with him. Jimmy had finally done it. First the pregnancy, and now this! He'd taken Maggie away from us, and I hated him! Hated him!

I called Genny from the living room, to come clear off the dining room table before setting it. Surprisingly she came right away, with Mary helping out too. I glanced at the clock. How long had they all been gone? I remembered Maggie's anxious plea not to tell of her rendezvous with Jimmy at the beach. I was angry at her and I told her she'd better stop seeing him. But I never told Mom and Dad, until now. Then that awful night with the miscarriage, the stupid convent talk, and Gramps so mad about something. Maggie now missing and having to tattletale on her. My mind was like those abstract paintings with all the colors mixed up.

Kitty's red hair poked through the door as she stamped her feet on the mat. "Kind of muddy out there. I don't see your grandfather's car. Isn't he home yet?"

"No. Did you see Samantha? Has she seen Maggie?"

"I saw her, and no, she hasn't seen Maggie." My shoulders slumped as I kept rolling the meatballs, plopping them one by one into the fry pan. "Are your parents home yet? I need to talk to them."

"Dad's out looking for Maggie and Mom's in the bedroom with Clare. She's sick."

"Would you go get your mother for me? Tell her I need to talk to her — right away."

I quickly washed my hands in the sink and went to the bedroom. Mom was taking Clare's temperature. "Mom, Kitty's home and wants to talk with you."

"Did she find Maggie?"

"No, but she wants you to come right away."

"Oh, all right." She pushed Clare's curls from her forehead and gave her a quick kiss. "Be back in a few minutes, sweetie."

I followed her to the kitchen. Kitty was hanging up her coat. "Rose, there's something I need to tell you about Maggie."

"But Petey said you didn't find her."

"No, but I have some information that you need to hear."

"What is it?"

"You better sit down."

They both sat at the kitchen table, forgetting I was even there. I continued rolling the meatballs. Kitty spoke first. "It wasn't Jimmy."

"What? You mean Jimmy didn't take Maggie away?"

"No, I mean the pregnancy. Jimmy didn't do it."

"What are you talking about?"

"Look, Rose. I spoke with Connie Wang today."

"Connie Wang? What does she have to do with Maggie?"

"You knew the Wangs were leaving town, right?"

"Yes, but . . . "

"They're leaving town because of Monsignor Neelan and what he did to their daughter. He had sex with her, Rose. Connie told me everything. He did the same to Maggie. Don't you see? It wasn't Jimmy. Monsignor Neelan is the one, all those "counseling sessions." She made quotation marks in the air.

Now I knew. *That's* why Sherlin called him a bad man. Monsignor Neelan had sex with my sister? For a minute, I thought I might throw up. Then I thought of Jimmy. It wasn't him after all. I was ashamed, ashamed of all those ugly, hateful thoughts I'd had of him when it was the Monsignor who had hurt her. *He* was the reason Maggie cried in her bed at night, the reason she locked herself in the bathroom, soaking in the tub. I smashed the last meatball, watching the red beef slide through my fingers.

Mom's tears were quiet ones, but her voice trembled. "Monsignor Neelan did it? But he's a priest. How could he do this? Are you sure?"

"I haven't talked to Maggie yet, but I'd say yes, after talking to Connie Wang, I don't have any doubt."

My mother's face blanched, as if bleach had been poured on it. I could barely hear her whisper, "My baby. Oh God. This is all my fault."

Kitty leaned forward, putting her arms around my mother. "You couldn't know, Rose."

"But I *should* have known. She's my daughter. Why didn't she tell me?" Her head dropped forward into Kitty's chest and I saw her shoulders shake.

"Mommy!" Clare called out from the bedroom.

Mom slowly lifted her head, pulled a handkerchief from her pocket, and blew her nose. "I better go check on Clare."

"Give yourself a minute. I need to take off these muddy boots, and change into some slippers. I'll check in on her and see what she wants."

My mother nodded and collapsed back into the chair.

The scream made me bump the fry pan handle. Grease splattered my arm, but I ignored it, and ran to the bedroom. Mom stood next to me, as we both stared at Kitty. The suitcase lay open on the floor. She was on her knees pawing through it.

"Jesus Christ. It's gone. He took it with him."

"What's gone?"

"His gun. Joe's gun."

"My father had a gun in there, in my house?"

"Yes, but it's gone."

"He had no right bringing a gun into our home. Where is my father, anyway?"

"He went to the rectory to see Monsignor Neelan."

"Rose, I need to go to the rectory. I'm worried about what Joe might do."

"Do?"

"He has a gun Rose. I'll need to call a taxi to get over there. Where's the phonebook?"

My mother sat on the edge of the bed with her head in her hands, mumbling, "Maggie, my baby Maggie."

I answered Kitty. "It's on top of the refrigerator."

"Thanks Petey. I'm not much of a praying person, but say a couple of quick Hail Mary's that your grandfather hasn't done anything foolish, . . . and stay with your mother." I nodded. Had he really seen the gun? Even after . . .

I did pray. Hail Mary's poured silently from my lips as I held my mother. I had no words to comfort her. We sat in silence until we heard a car engine in the driveway.

"Please God, let that be Maggie come home to us." Mom jumped from the bed and ran to the kitchen.

It was Jimmy.

Monsignor Neelan

The massive grandfather clock struck four, the onset of confessions. He sat immobilized, his body bent over on the leather couch. His reflection stared back at him from the shine of his wing-tipped black shoes. An old man, a man without redemption. He clutched the paper Joe had given him and reread the words, words that scorched his soul.

> Dear Joe,
>
> I think you may already know, or at least suspect. I saw it in the way you looked at me sometimes. Is that why when I asked you to feel the baby moving inside of me, you always refused?
>
> You are a good and dear man Joe, and will be a good father to our Rose, won't you? Perhaps I should not tell you at all, but you have loved me, and are entitled to know that yes, I married you with the child already in my womb. Please don't hate me for it. I was a woman very much in love. But Robert loved his God more than me, or at least that is what he said. And I never told him about the baby. Forgive me for loving him, when I should have loved you. I am a coward, I know, but I couldn't bear to tell you and see the hatred in your eyes for me. In time, I hope you will forgive me, as I hope God will. I will be with Him soon. The Doctor has told me

that too much damage was done, too much blood lost. Thank God that
Rose is healthy.

Remember dear Joe that Rose is your child in name and needs your
love. Kiss her every day for me. Tell her that her mother loves her.

Your loving wife, Eleanor

He kept staring at her words, stunned by their revelation. Rose was his daughter. That meant Maggie was... his granddaughter. Joe was right. He was a pervert, an unredeemable pervert. His hands dropped to his sides. Joe had kept the letter a secret all these years, had known that Rose was not his daughter and yet had raised her as his own. If Eleanor had told him, would he have stayed? No. He would have abandoned her. That fact sickened him, but it was true. He had never put the needs of others above his own ambition. And now? What could he do that would make things right? He did not have the courage to face Maggie again, or Rose. He could ask for a transfer, but if Joe reports this, as he threatened to, the Bishop may not overlook this transgression. He might be able to convince him that it was all a ruse, a trumped up story made up by a wayward girl and a naïve, trusting family. But then there's the letter. Would Joe go so far as to share the letter with the Bishop, reveal his paternity? Would he go to the police?

Deliberately, he stood up, tottered slightly, his knees weakening. He walked to the smoldering fireplace on the other side of the room and poked the embers with the andiron. Two logs left in the bin. He lifted one and tossed it into the fireplace. A slice of wood caught his middle finger, and a drop of blood fell on the letter. He squeezed his finger and let the blood dribble on the words.

A small blue flame cradled the log. He tossed in the letter, watched the flame erupt, then simmer, leaving charred parchment in its wake. Despite the fire, he shivered and crossed the room to his desk as if his legs were frozen ice blocks. He poured and gulped another whiskey, then another. The purplish red pom of his biretta caught his eye. It sat perched on top of the corner coat rack. Deliberately he unclasped the hook of his mantelletta, lifted it from his shoulders, and draped it over the back of his valet. Next he untied his purple sash, draped it on the hook under the biretta, and began unbuttoning his cassock. Lifting a wooden hangar from his wardrobe, he hung up the cassock. His thick fingers reached under his clerical collar, clawing at the studs that held it in place. With practiced ritual, he pulled it from his neck and set the starched circle on his desk, caressing it lightly with his fingertip. He turned to the wardrobe again, bending to open the bottom drawer. He lifted out the white silk stole purchased in Rome and blessed by the Pope. On it were elaborately embroidered the fourteen Stations of the Cross. He fingered the smooth silk, his thumb crossing over the image of Christ on his knees and bent under the weight of the Cross.

The rectory had been built to his specifications, with broad oak beams above. Stepping up from his chair to the desk, he edged the stole's end through the slim crack above the beam. Once the double knot was secure, he kissed the stole, made the Sign of the Cross, twisted it into a loop, and slipped it over his neck. No one heard the raspy gaggle after he took his last step into the air, or Kitty's scream when she walked through his office door.

Petey

I answered the door and was surprisingly pleased to see Jimmy, my hatred dispersed like shooed shore birds. Dressed in faded jeans and college sweatshirt, he looked fatigued.

"Jimmy!"

"Hi Squirt. It's nice to see you too!" His eyes seemed bluer than ever. "Is Maggie home?"

Mom stepped in front of me. "We thought she was with *you*."

"Mrs. Donovan. Hi. What do you mean you thought she was with me? I've been on the road all day. Called from a pay phone. Didn't Genny tell you I called?"

"Yes, but we thought you'd already come and left with Maggie, because Maggie is gone."

"Gone? Gone where?"

"We don't know. Her father is out looking for her right now."

"But why would she go anywhere? She knew I was coming over, didn't she?"

"It would appear now that she never got the message."

"Oh." His eyes darted around the room. "Can I just wait here for her then? You think she went over to Samantha's?"

"Kitty already checked there."

"How long has she been gone?"

"We're not sure. Mr. Donovan and I both worked today, and Maggie's grandparents were both out for a good portion of the day as well."

"But Genny was here when I called. Doesn't she know when Maggie left?"

"No. She said that when you called she had just come home from a friend's house and thought Maggie was in her room. When we heard about your phone call, we assumed that you had since come here and that the two of you had left together. As I said, Mr. Donovan is out looking for you both."

Jimmy squinted and took a step back. "Wait a minute. Are you saying that Maggie's father thinks I took her *away* . . . that we ran off together?"

My mother nodded, "I'm afraid so. My husband was quite upset."

"Mrs. Donovan, I would never do that. I know you and Mr. Donovan have never liked me seeing your daughter, but I would never do a thing like that."

"We had reason to believe you already had."

"Why? What do you mean?"

"You better sit down to hear this."

I didn't want to hear the whole story again, but I listened anyway. I was surprised that Mom could say the words, could talk about the miscarriage and Monsignor Neelan and the awful thing he did to her. Now it was me who was crying quietly as I watched Jimmy's face turn red, his teeth clench, and knuckles whiten as he gripped the table.

"I'm sorry to have to tell you this Jimmy, but I want to spare Maggie. She's been through so much already. Please don't be angry with her. She's only just a child, don't you see. It wasn't her fault."

There was a long pause before he spoke. "I'm not angry at Maggie. Don't you understand? I love her. I would never hurt her." He shot out of the chair, already reaching for the doorknob. "I need to find her, to talk with her. Where is your husband looking?"

I was surprised to hear my own voice. "I told them about the beach, about how you and Maggie used to go there sometimes. Maggie told me not to tell, but I had to. I'm sorry." My voice broke. "I'm worried about her." I blinked repeatedly as his eyes penetrated mine.

"That's okay, Petey. I'm worried too, but I'll find her and bring her back. I promise."

I moved towards Jimmy. "I'll go with you."

Mom pulled me back. "I don't want you going anywhere."

"But Mom, the beach is a big place, and . . ."

She glanced at Jimmy and said in a clipped tone. "I'm sure Jimmy knows where to look."

"But Dad, what about Dad? He doesn't know about ... everything."

Mom fell into the chair and put her hand up to her face. "Your father." She rubbed her forehead, took a deep breath, and looked up at Jimmy. "If he sees you there, if you find Maggie first, and he sees you with her . . . I don't know."

Jimmy turned back towards Mom. "You don't know what?"

"I've never seen him so angry. Don't know what he'll...."

Genny raced into the kitchen. "Mom, Clare's throwing up!" Mom jumped up and followed Genny back into the living room.

"Grab the bucket from under the bathroom sink, Genny!" Mom squatted in front of Clare, and held her head, as she wretched onto the floor. "Mary, go get some towels!"

Jimmy and I stood in the doorway. I watched as Genny returned with the bucket, and Clare vomited once more. "Mom?"

"What? What is it?"

"What about Maggie?"

"Go, go with Jimmy, and bring her home."

I turned to leave but stopped when I heard my mother's voice again.

"And Petey, if you see your father tell him what you know. Bring her back, do you hear me?"

"Yes, Mom."

I slammed the car door shut as Jimmy peeled out of the driveway.

Maggie

I don't know how long I've been walking. Long enough that I need a rest. I stop and sit on the bus stop bench. When the bus pulls up, I reach into my pocket and find a quarter and a nickel. Just enough. I take the first empty seat, press my cheek against the window, and watch my tears smear the dust. Hunching my shoulders, I raise the collar of my coat and curl up against the window, avoiding other passengers. The bus is empty by the time it reaches the beach. Standing to pull the cord, I stagger to the door. Diesel exhaust fills the air as the bus pulls away, replaced by the pungent smell of sea salt. I stand at the edge of the parking lot and take a deep breath before heading towards the beach.

The unseasonably warm temperatures have attracted other beach strollers. Three children run up and down the boardwalk. A young mother pushes a baby stroller, stopping at a bench where an old couple sits. They smile and coo at the baby. I duck under the railing and jump onto the sand. It's a long, expansive beach. Taking off my shoes and socks, I dig my toes into the cool dampness. A couple lie stretched out on a beach blanket wrapped in each other's arms. They kiss, oblivious to my presence. Even so, I give them a wide berth and walk closer to the shoreline. The sea is calm. I walk slowly past the sandpipers skittering along the high water mark.

Just a few short months ago I was here with Jimmy, holding hands as we ran barefoot in the sand. A distant memory now.

The tide is at its highest. To reach our spot I have to wade through the inlet, climb over some rocks, and ascend the dune into the knoll. It takes only seconds for the icy water to numb my feet. Sitting on the sand, I hug my knees. Tears roll down my cheeks and trickle onto my lips. I stare at the shoreline and see myself at three running with my father, splashing in the water. Closing my eyes, I picture myself at six, stretched out in my mother's arms as she gently tells me to relax and let the water hold me up. Then Petey is by my side as we swim together. She grins back at me as she pulls ahead. And then there's Jimmy. I press my hands onto the sand and feel resilient warmth, like the memory of the passion that was ours. All that I had once known was lost to me now — Jimmy's love, my father's love, my mother's love. And Petey? My dear sister whose love I so cherished, who always bragged about having me as her big sister. Would she too abandon me if she knew?

The ice cold water laps onto my toes. My feet begin to tingle. I want the numbness again, but not just for my feet. I want to end the hurting. I can't go back and face them all. I can never tell them what he did in that room. Nothing will be the same as it once was.

Calm waters stretch endlessly before me, a beckoning refuge. Slowly, I get up. The sun sits on the purpled horizon, a magnetic golden Deity. I follow His call. Each step into the frigid waters deadens another part of my body, but I inch forward. How long will it take? How long before I don't feel anymore?

The water swallows my neck, and I watch my hair float in a circle. My toes barely touch. I take another step and look upward to see the first star appear. Is God there? Is He waiting for me? Or has He abandoned me? Suddenly a seagull appears. He dives lower, hovering only inches from my head. I can see its black eyes and long beak. He caws repeatedly, his white underbelly undulating with each call. His wings flap, yet he remains constant against the breeze. I try to call out to him, but my voice is gone. Panic sets in. Am I already dead? I stretch my arms but cannot feel them. My companion caws again. I want to grab hold of him and be lifted high into the air, carried to shore. I want life. My voice returns and I cry out.

"God, help me!" I am crying and thrashing with my arms. My legs kick but are tangled in kelp, my body heavy with clothing. Despite my efforts the shoreline seems no closer. A wave washes over me, and I sputter, trying to breathe but gulping water instead. My arms flail, but I can no longer feel them. The water seems to be rising, and I can no longer see the shore. "Please, help!" I cry out into the darkness.

Petey

I am alone in the car with Jimmy, clutching the sides of the passenger seat as the car careens around corners. Once, my hand slips, and my body leans into his, brushing against his muscled arm. I blush and force my body to right itself. Familiar downtown sights rush past me like faded postcards. Judson's Bar and Grille, with its' usual milieu of characters milling in front, the Beach Street Soap and Suds Laundromat, the antiquated Grand Cinema with its protruding glass box office window. I think of the many Saturday matinees that Maggie and I saw there and expel a wistful sigh. Jimmy glances at me, but I am too ashamed to speak.

Again, we make a hard turn, and I grip the seat cushion even tighter. Hudson Boulevard is a wide street lined with large ornate homes, each meticulously landscaped. Most are three stories, topped with widow's walks or spires thrusting into the sky and expansive porches in front. Maggie and I had chosen 263 Hudson as our favorite. The yellow clapboard mansion has a wrap-around porch with Doric style white columns. A widow's walk stands like an ornate cage at the top of the roof. Over the front door is a curvaceous fanlight with amber glass. Maggie once said we could buy the house and live there together when she became a famous movie star and I was a world-renowned scientist.

We pictured ourselves sitting on the wicker chairs petting our cats. I push these faded dreams aside, and focus on the remaining mile before arriving at the beach.

I glance over at Jimmy. His white knuckles grip the steering wheel. I open my mouth to say "Slow down," but don't speak. Instead I stare at his face, the one that has filled me with hatred before. I see the square jaw and slight ridge on the nose, the face that Maggie kissed. But now his face seems contorted. Is he also confused, angry, and worried? Perhaps Dad has already found Maggie.

We pull into the parking lot dotted with cars. Jimmy turns towards me. "If she came here, she'll go to our spot on the south end over the rocks and into the dunes." Jimmy parks in the first row of the lot. Getting out of the car, I hear footsteps running on the nearby boardwalk. My father is there before I can even get to the other side of the car. He looks like a raging bull about to charge.

"Daddy, no!" I am jumping on his back, pulling on his arm. But it is too late. His punch has already landed. I scream, "Jimmy!" and watch the body slump against the car and fall to the pavement. Dad stares down at his victim, his fists still clenched. On my knees, I look at Jimmy and then up at my father. "Daddy, what did you *do*?"

He appears to see me for the first time. His eyes dart from me to Jimmy. "Don't look at me like that. Not after what *he's* done."

"But, Daddy. It wasn't Jimmy who hurt Maggie. It never was."

"*Of course it was!*"

I tug on his arm. "Daddy, listen to me. After you left, Kitty told us she found out who hurt Maggie. It was Monsignor Neelan."

His head cocks to one side, looking at me mystified, as if snow were falling in August.

I bend over Jimmy. "Is he all right, Daddy?" He doesn't answer. "Daddy? Jimmy, is he ..."

My father squats down, examines Jimmy's head, and replies, "Concussion, maybe. Might need to go to the hospital but let's give it a minute. He may come around. I only hit him once." I remember Mom talking about Dad's boxing days in the Marines and how he'd won most fights from knockouts. It might take more than a minute.

"Daddy, we still need to find Maggie."

He nods.

I stand. "You stay with Jimmy. I think I know where she might be." Before he can answer, I begin running. Once the boardwalk ends, I jump onto the beach, my sneakers kicking up the soft sand. I head to the dunes, racing up the first one, and almost falling into a knoll.

"Hey, watch what you're doing!" Two lovers sit up from their blanket, brushing sand off their faces.

"Sorry!" I push on to the next dune, breathing hard. At the top of the fourth one, I bend over, hands on my knees, trying to catch my breath. It's almost dark, but I see them, Maggie's shoes, with knee socks draped over them. Immediately I look out to sea. A dark inert blob in the water.

"Maggie!" I scream. Kicking off my Keds and tossing my coat to the ground, I shoot into the water, ignoring the icy burn. Her face is submerged, but the yellow-gold hair floats out in a circle like tentacles. I throw my head back and reach under her armpits as my legs tread water. I kick hard, straining to maintain my hold. Our faces touch. "Maggie!" I yell into her ear. Water sloshes over me but I spit it out and keep kicking. Her body weight overpowers me and we begin to sink. With one final push I propel us to the surface. I continue to kick, holding Maggie's head up with one arm, and pulling with the other. Yards seem like miles, but finally I feel the sand beneath me. Once my feet touch bottom, I pull as hard as I can until Maggie lies on the sand. I try to remember what I'd seen the lifeguards do. How long has she been in the water? I roll her onto her side, pound her back, and watch the water gurgle from her mouth. I slap again, and then roll her onto her back. There's a slight cough, and her body quivers.

"Maggie? Maggie? It's me, Petey." Her eyelids flutter, and I see her chest move. I begin tugging on her wet clothes, stripping her down to her underwear, and then covering her with my warm wool coat. "We have to get you warm, Maggie. Can you hear me?" Once again her eyelids flutter, and there is a slight nod of her head. "You're going to be all right, Maggie." My knees press into the sand. I begin rubbing my hands together quickly until I feel warmth. Then I rub her hands in mine.

"Petey?"

The sound of her voice brings me to tears. "Maggie! Oh, Maggie." I press my face against hers and cry. "You're all right. We'll get you home soon."

She nods again, and there is a soft whisper, "Petey?" I look into her eyes. "I wanted it all to be over. I didn't know what to do. I'm sorry." She coughs again. "My throat hurts."

"It's okay. Maggie. It's okay."

"You, you saved me, but how . . . did you . . . are you alone?"

"I came with Jimmy."

"Jimmy's here?" Her voice is barely audible.

"He's back at the parking lot with Dad."

"Dad?"

"I'll explain later. Everyone was looking for you. We were all so worried. Can you sit up yet?" I reach behind her. "Here, lean against me."

Her head rests on my chest, my legs wrap around her, and I whisper in her ear, "I was so afraid, Maggie. I thought I'd lost you." I was crying, rocking her in my arms.

She sways to the side and wretches on the sand. I hold her head up.

"Hey, you guys all right?" They stand a few feet away from us, the two lovers from the dunes.

"It's my sister. She almost drowned."

Maggie

hills racked my body despite the layers of quilts and the body warmth from Mom. I lay in my parent's bed, my mother's arms wrapped around me. Dad brought a hot water bottle for my feet and sat next to the bed. I kept telling them both how sorry I was, but they said, "Ssshhh. Don't talk now."

I asked about Jimmy and was told Dad had taken him to the emergency room. He had a mild concussion but would be fine. Dad had driven him to his parents' house and promised to pick up Jimmy's car in the morning and bring it to him.

I closed my eyes, but sleep rolled in slowly, like a late day fog. My teeth chattered.

"Does she have a fever, Rose?"

"No, I checked."

"Her lips are purple."

"I know."

Even with my eyes closed, I could sense them staring at each other, gripped in worry.

"John, maybe a little swallow of whiskey would help."

I heard chair legs scrape the floor and slippers shuffle to the kitchen. The whiskey was kept in the cupboard above the refrigerator. I'd only seen Dad take it out a couple of times. Once, when his father had died, he'd pulled out the bottle, poured a drink, raised it and said, "Here's to the old man."

Dad brought me the glass and held it to my lips. I sipped, and coughed.

"It will burn a little, Sunshine."

A wisp of a memory of the first time I'd heard my nickname came to me. We were on the front porch, Dad and me. There was another man there, with bushy white hair and a beard. I'd never seen a beard before. I pulled on it and the man laughed. I asked Daddy if he was Santa Claus. Daddy said, "No, this is your grandfather."

I sat on his lap, and he made funny faces. I laughed, and he tousled my curls and said, "She's a ray of sunshine, if there ever was one. Little Sunshine, that's who you are, Maggie Donovan." It was after that Daddy started calling me Sunshine. I never saw his father again.

After another sip of whiskey, my teeth stopped chattering. "Where's Petey?"

Mom spoke in my ear. "She's in her bed. Kitty and Gramps are tending to her. She's a very brave girl."

"Is she all right?"

"Yes, she'll be fine, just like you'll be. Go to sleep now, Maggie."

I closed my eyes again. Inside my head there was this constant whooshing sound. I nuzzled against my mother's bosom and focused on the steady beat of her heart. Her words sounded like a distant echo.

"I think she's asleep now, John."

The touch of a rough hand on my brow and a tender kiss on the cheek told me that Daddy was still there, even before he spoke. "When I think of how close we came to losing her. . ." Even over the thick covers I could feel their hands grasp each other and squeeze. "I was such a fool. How could I have not known what was happening?"

"You only did what you thought was best. I'm to blame. I just didn't think a priest would . . . I mean . . ." Her heartbeat quickened as her sobs came. The mattress shifted as my father crawled into bed, his heavy arm draped around my mother and me.

Petey

itty put warm towels on my sheet and then piled blankets on top of me. She stuck my hair under her plastic bagged hair dryer, but my thick hair still lay damp on the pillow. My arms were like sodden deadwood on the mattress, while my legs throbbed. She propped me up on pillows and then spooned hot chicken soup into me. I slurped a long fat noodle. Gramps sat at the foot of the bed.

"Can I get you anything else, sweetie?"

"No, thanks, Gramps. Is Maggie okay?"

"Thanks to you she is. Your Mom and Dad are with her. Just like you, she needs to get warmed up. But she'll be fine."

"I think I want to sleep now."

Kitty took the bowl away and set it on the nightstand. "How many pillows do you want?"

"Just one, thanks."

"You just close your eyes. Gramps and I will be right here if you need anything."

My eyes stung from the saltwater, and my throat was sore. I had swallowed some water when a wave came over us. "I'm so tired, but I keep ... thinking..."

"Try not to think, Petey. You just lie back and close your eyes."
Gramps patted my hand.

"But I can't seem to sleep."

"I used to sing your mother to sleep sometimes when she was little.
My voice might be a little rusty, but you want me to give it a go?" I nodded, closed my eyes and heard my grandfather's deep tenor voice . . .

> *"My wild Irish rose, the sweetest flower that grows.*
> *You may search everywhere, but none can compare*
> *With my wild Irish rose. . ."*

— ~

The nightmare woke me. My legs kicked the bed sheets, trying to push
away the kelp. My body was sinking deeper and deeper. Maggie was calling for me, but even as my arms flailed, I continued to fall, as her voice
grew more distant. The water darkened as I pushed upwards, my hands
touching a mushy lump. Opening my hand, I saw a red pompom attached to a biretta. Dropping it, I continued to kick in the darkness
until surfacing, spitting and gagging. I saw him then, in black cassock
and cape, the back of his balding head pulling away as he rowed further
out to sea. He turned and grinned, as my pale-faced sister gripped the
side of the boat. My mouth opened to scream "No!" but instead I awoke
to the sound of a ticking clock and whispering voices in the bed next to
mine.

"What did you say to him, Joe?"

The clock continued to tick, and I began to perspire under the quilt.
It was the heavy stillness I heard before his voice finally responded.

"I'd kept the secret ever since she died, but he had to know."

"Had to know what, Joe?"

"Kitty, if I tell you, it will be your secret too. Rose is never to know,
especially now, after what's happened to Maggie."

"What is it Joe?"

"Eleanor left me a letter before she died, telling me that Bob Neelan was the father of her child. I told him and demanded that he never have anything to do with his granddaughter again."

"Oh my God! Rose is his daughter? Then Maggie is. . . I mean . . . he raped his own granddaughter."

"Please, Kitty, don't ever say that again. It may be the truth, but it's not a truth I want to hear."

"I'm so sorry, Joe."

I felt a tickle in my throat, but pursed my lips and held back my cough. Kitty was shaking her head. "I understand why the man hung himself."

"You never should have gone there, Kitty."

"But the gun was missing. I thought you might have. . ."

"I must admit that I thought of the gun, even briefly looked for it, but thank God I couldn't find it."

"Would you have used it?"

"I like to think not. I swore to uphold the law, but I don't know... what he did..."

"It was such a shock to see him hanging there, Joe. My screams brought Father Thomas from the church. He calmed me down, called me a taxi, and said he'd take care of everything. All I could think about was getting home to you.

My coughing interrupted them.

Kitty rose from the bed and stood by me. "Petey, are you all right?"

"Would you get me a glass of water?"

"Of course, dear."

A sudden low rumble told me the furnace just kicked in. The heat register ruffled the window curtains. Gramps squatted next to me, his hand on my brow. "Did you just wake up, Petey?"

I lied. "Yes. I was having a nightmare. . . that I was in the ocean. . . and Maggie was calling to me but" . . . I began to cry.

"Hush now. You're all right. You're home, in your own bed. It's all over now." Gramps patted my hand again.

But it didn't seem over.

Maggie

When morning came, I knew I had a fever. First came the chills, then sweating. I was back in my own bed, with Petey in hers. I could hear her coughing and sneezing. Clare, too, still had a fever. Mom didn't go to work. Neither did Dad. I couldn't remember a day that Dad had ever skipped going to work. I'd seen him force himself to go even when his back was bad. He would just put his back brace on under his work clothes and head out the door. Another time he had the flu, but told Mom that he'd take aspirin all day to keep the fever down. She'd argued with him about it, but he just said they couldn't afford for him to lose a day's pay. But today, Dad sat by my bedside, frequently sticking a thermometer in my mouth or putting on more covers. Mom brought me soup, but I only took a couple of sips.

The doctor came at four o'clock. The metal stethoscope felt like an ice burn on my chest. As instructed, I took a deep breath, only to go into a fit of coughing. My head fell back onto the pillow as I stared at the ceiling. There was a cobweb in the corner with a small spider. I was too weak to call out to Petey, my spider killer. She knew how much I hated them. Besides, she was now breathing for the doctor as his stethoscope moved from her chest to her back.

"Petey should be up and about in a couple of days. No fever, and her lungs are clear. Keep up the fluids and bed rest until she's feeling better. Looks like Clare has a virus that's been going around. She should be fine. Maggie is the one that needs watching. Give her aspirin every four hours, and let me know if the fever gets any higher. You may have to bring her to the hospital for x-rays. She could have pneumonia."

My eyes burned and there were pink spots when I closed them. The grown-ups had all gone downstairs, and Petey was talking to me, but she sounded far away. I think she was crying, and saying she was sorry. . . something about Jimmy.

— ~ —

Dad and Mom came to visit me in the hospital every evening, but we only talked about little things. Mary had learned to use the hula-hoop. Genny wanted to play the guitar and was bugging Mom for lessons. Clare sent in pictures that she had drawn for me. I still hadn't seen Petey as she stayed home to watch the kids. I longed to hold her in my arms and thank her for rescuing me. Gramps and Kitty had come to say goodbye before leaving for Florida but their visit was a blur to me. I couldn't focus on anything. Instead, a slide show of images kept flashing through my head: Monsignor Neelan pressing against me or blood trickling down my legs. Each set of footsteps in the hospital corridor paralyzed me with fear. No one mentioned his name. If only sleep would bring me peace instead of nightmares.

My screaming brought the night nurse. "Shush, it's all right. Just a bad dream." Her round face bent over mine as she placed a soft hand on my forehead. "You're all right, Margaret. Just relax. Just a bad dream. Probably your fever. Do you want some water?"

I watched her pour water from the pitcher, stick the straw in, and hold it to my lips. Taking a long sip, I looked around the room, remembering the ivory blinds on the window, the curtain drawn beside my bed, the dull beige walls. I was in a hospital. I was safe. *He* was not here. My body was shaking. I looked at my hands clenching the sheet. There was no blood, no knife in my hand. His body was not on top of mine, yet I could still feel its weight. I took a deep breath and loosened my grip, wishing Jimmy were there to hold me.

Petey

"When's Maggie coming home?" Mary clamored into bed with Genny.

I leaned over to give her a kiss goodnight. "Soon, I think."

"I miss her."

"I know. We all do. You read very well tonight, Mary. What book are you starting next?"

"I don't know. How come Mom didn't come upstairs to tuck us in?"

"She's spending time with Gramps and Kitty downstairs. They're leaving tomorrow, remember?"

"Yeah. I'll miss them too."

"Except Kitty's smoking." Genny sat up in bed and rubbed her nose. "It makes my nose itch."

"SShh, Clare's sleeping." I looked across the room at Clare, curls falling into her eyes, her thumb in her mouth. Much as Mom tried to get her to stop, Clare still sucked her thumb at night. She wanted me to tell her leprechaun stories like Maggie did, but she had to settle for my reading to her. I could never compete with Maggie's stories.

"Can't you read another book?" Mary pleaded.

"It's getting late; already past your bedtime. And I've got studying to do. Scoot down. I'll tuck you in. Did you both say your prayers?"

They nodded. "I said a Hail Mary for Maggie."

"Me too. I said *two*." Genny was never to be outdone.

I turned off the light and shut the door. Walking back to my bedroom, I dropped on the bed and opened my Algebra book. We had a quiz tomorrow, and I needed to review some equations and finish that essay for Religion class. Dad said Maggie might come home tomorrow. I glanced over at her empty bed. How strange it was to be alone in the bedroom. Slamming the Algebra book shut, I stretched out on the soft quilt. My fingers pushed through tangled hair. If she were here right now, Maggie would be brushing it, talking and laughing with me. Or would she? Maybe things would still be all messed up. Maybe Maggie would still be unhappy. I lifted my head at the sound of voices.

Creeping down the stairs, I stopped before they could see me. I sat on the steps, peering through the first rail opening. Mom, Dad, Gramps, and Kitty were all sitting in the living room. Gramps was talking.

"I think it would be good for them."

Mom sat on the arm of the couch next to Gramps and Kitty. "I don't know. They've never been away from us before. And it's so far."

"It would just be for the one week, when school vacation starts."

"What do you think, John?"

Dad leaned back in his armchair and sighed. "Well, the doctor says she can come home now. Her lungs are clear. But she's not herself. I don't know what it's going to take to get her back, but we have to do something."

Kitty spoke. "We'll pay for the train ride for both of them, if cost is an issue. I can get a good rate with my discount pass."

Gramps took my mother's hand and said, "They'll get some sun, relax, go to the beach with us. You know we'll take good care of them."

Mom kissed him on the cheek. "I know you will."

Dad was nodding. "The doctor says she needs rest at home for a while. Let's see how she does. See if she rebounds. Then give you a call, okay?"

Were they talking about Florida, like Gramps had said? I almost jumped on the stairs in excitement. Mom was walking toward the kitchen. "Now that that's settled, I need to finish that cherry pie I started for Maggie's return home. It's her favorite."

"I'm going out for a cigarette." Kitty stepped out to the front porch, closing the door behind her.

Just Gramps and Dad now sat quietly in the living room. I started to tiptoe back up the stairs as Dad turned on the television but stopped when I heard Gramps speak. "John, if you don't mind, can you turn that off so we can talk a bit?" I perched back on my step and looked into the living room. Gramps was standing in front of Dad.

"I ... ah...wanted to tell you I'm sorry. I was stupid to bring a gun into your house."

"You didn't use it."

"No, but I was angry enough to."

The room was so quiet. I was afraid to breathe. Dad was shaking his head. "I'm the one who was angry and stupid. Still can't believe what I did."

"Is he going to press charges?"

Dad shook his head. "No, I went to see him and his parents. Nice people. Surprisingly polite, considering."

At first I didn't know what that sound was; a throaty rasp and suck of breath. He was trying to hold it in, the sobbing. When it did come, it was almost silent, but his shoulders shook as his head dropped forward. "I don't know what came over me. I swore I'd never fight again, never hurt anyone else like I did in the fucking war."

Gramps put his hand on my father's back. "I've seen men do lots of things they never thought they would do. You had every right to be angry. It's your daughter, for God's sakes. I came damn close to taking a swing at Neelan."

"But I knew what my punch could do . . . what it did once before . . . I shouldn't ..."

"Best put it to rest, John. It's over."

My father straightened in his chair and looked in my direction. I shrank into the stairwell. "Thanks, and thanks for the offer for the girls. You're probably right. Some time away in the sunshine would be good for them."

I crept back to my bedroom and tried to study but all I could see on the pages was the look of pain on my father's face.

Maggie

I showered and dressed by myself this morning. No more sponge baths from the nurse. The hospital tray of food sat on my lap untouched, except the nibbles I took of the roll and a few mouthfuls of mashed potato. Shoving it aside, I swung out of bed. Still weak, I steadied myself against the bed. What day was it? I'd lost track. All I knew was that the doctor had signed my release papers and that I was going home. It felt good to breathe all on my own. I watched the clock. The minute hand moved to 6:05. I looked at the door. Was a watched door like a watched pot that never boiled? No one would come if I kept staring at it?

Petey burst through the door first. "Maggie!" She rushed into my arms and we hugged. Tears streamed down my face. It seemed I cried every day lately.

Dad kissed my cheek. "Are you ready, Sunshine?" I smiled. He hadn't called me that for a long time.

A nurse came through the door with a wheelchair. "Would you like me to wheel her down?"

"No, I can do it. Thanks." He pushed the wheelchair to me. "Your chariot awaits." Again I smiled.

"Would you get that bag of my things over there, Petey?"

Stepping out into the winter air, I zipped my coat up before climbing into the car. Petey and I sat in the back seat, our hands locked together. "I didn't expect to see you."

"Mom said she would stay home tonight so I could come."

I squeezed her hand. "I'm glad."

When I walked through the front door I was greeted with more hugs. Clare immediately crawled into my lap in the living room. "We missed you *so* much. Will you tell me a story before bed?"

Mom reached down and lifted her from my lap. "Not tonight. Maggie just got home."

"But she's been gone forever, and I wanted her to tell me the ..."

I reached up and pecked her cheek. "Maybe tomorrow, okay, Clare Bear?"

Everything looked different to me somehow. Had that sag in the couch always been there? Chips of paint were peeling off the window-sills. The edges of the rug were frayed. But I was home. I was loved.

Mom was still putting the others to bed when the doorbell rang. Petey answered it.

"Hi, Maggie." Jimmy stood in the doorway. Even with my father watching, I ran into his arms. His hair was damp. His neck smelled of soap. "I know it's your first day home, but your father invited me to come by."

I smiled gratefully at Dad and he smiled back. "Well, I promised your mother I'd pick up some vanilla ice cream to go with her cherry pie. Be back in a jiffy." He nodded at Jimmy as he left the room. "Good to see you, Jimmy."

"You too, sir."

We sat together on the couch and he reached for my hand. I waited for him to say something, but he just looked at me for the longest time.

I brushed my hair away from my eyes, remembering that I hadn't combed it or put on any makeup. "I'm sorry. I must look awful."

"You look beautiful."

I wasn't sure what to say. Did he know everything? "I... I suppose you know. I mean about..."

"Yeah, I know. We don't have to talk about that right now. You just have to get well, that's all, okay?"

I nodded and leaned against him until Mom came in with the cherry pie and ice cream.

This was the first morning since coming home that I had the energy to get out of bed. Tying my bathrobe, I shuffled downstairs into the kitchen. Mom had left a note on the kitchen table next to some toast and a soft-boiled egg. I nibbled on the toast and took a couple of bites of the egg, now cold. I still wasn't very hungry. Schoolbooks sat stacked at my bedside, but just the thought of studying tired me. I carried the plate of toast out to the living room, pushed the television on, and curled up on the couch. Local news and weather was being broadcast. I listened to the weatherman forecast snow flurries for tomorrow, before seeing the local news anchor flash his pearly white smile at me. I tried to work up the energy to get up to turn the channel, preferring a late morning game show. As I got off the couch and walked toward the TV, the news anchor's voice stopped me.

"Let's go to St. Peter's Catholic Church, where Mike DeFusco reports on the memorial being established for recently deceased Monsignor Neelan."

Deceased? Monsignor Neelan? The bishop was the first person they interviewed. I listened to him recite a litany of Monsignor Neelan's accomplishments, followed by interviews with parish members, most of whom I recognized, all talking about how much their pastor would be missed and how tragic it was that he had died suddenly of a heart attack. Then his picture was on the screen. Those deep-set eyes I knew all too well. My hands started to shake, and the plate of toast fell to the floor. I must have turned the television off before fainting on the rug, where Mom found me when she came home during her lunch hour.

I finally agreed to go. Mom and Dad kept saying how good it would be for me to be in Florida enjoying a change of scenery and getting fresh air and sunshine. Petey, of course, badgered me constantly. She didn't understand how much I wanted to be with Jimmy. Finally Dad was letting me date, and I thought we would now have those fun times we'd missed. But it wasn't like that. He didn't kiss me like before. And I wasn't even sure I wanted him to. What did I want? I wanted him to hold me, to tell me how much he loved me, but instead he treated me like I was some kind of delicate flower. I wanted us to laugh like we used to. I can't remember the last time that we laughed together. We used to talk about the future, how I'd go to college somewhere near his med school, and we would study together. Now we struggled for conversation. Was his schoolwork really that demanding, or was he just making excuses for not coming home on weekends? Maybe if I went away, he would miss me. Maybe I would come back the girl I used to be and he would love me again.

Dad carried the suitcases onto the train for us, lifting them onto the rack above the seats. "Now, remember, stay together, and if you need anything, ask the porter. Call us as soon as you get there, okay?" He hugged us both, and got off the train just before it pulled out of the station. Petey took the window seat. I'd never seen her so excited. She rattled off the names of each town we passed, nudging me with excitement as we went through big cities with their high rise buildings and famous landmarks. The jostling of the train and clattering of the rails lulled me into a restless sleep.

The last night before our arrival I awoke in a sweat, having to go to the lavatory. I wobbled to the front of the car, grabbing backs of seats to keep from falling. My hand brushed something soft. I looked down to see a red pompom. I gasped and fumbled the last few steps to the bathroom. Sliding the door shut, I fell to the floor, shaking and woozy. My heart was racing. I put my head between my legs, trying to ignore the stench of stale urine. I don't know how long I sat there. Was I going crazy? Finally I stood, steadied myself and eased the door open. Smiling up at me from her seat was a little girl curled up against her mother's shoulder sucking her thumb. On her head she wore a felt hat with a red pompom.

Petey

Gramps and Kitty greeted us with big hugs at the station. I couldn't believe it. A whole week to spend in Florida! It felt like summer here. I could wear shorts every day. Gramps carried our suitcases to our bedroom. It was painted sunny yellow, with white chenille bedspreads on twin beds. I asked Maggie if I could have the bed by the window. She shrugged, "Sure." Kitty showed us around the house, which was small, but everything was so new and bright. There was a big picture window in the living room with plants set on the sill.

"Let me show you what I really love." Kitty took me by the hand and led us to their back yard. There was a small patio with table and chairs. She led us out onto the lawn and stood by a tree. Plucking an orange from it, she said, "Here, try one." Wow! An orange tree right in their backyard!

I was anxious to get to the beach, but Kitty said that Maggie needed a day of rest first. Maggie sunbathed in the yard while Gramps and I roller-skated on the sidewalk. The next day I excitedly helped pack up for the beach. Palm trees lined the roads. When we stepped out of the car, I inhaled deeply and surveyed the beach. Vast stretches of fine white sand led to the shoreline, while the sky and sea were such a bright blue; they almost blended into one. Tentatively, I walked to the water. There were no waves crashing onto rocks or gurgling shoreline pebbles, just a languid ripple tickling my toes. I took a deep breath and walked steadily forward. Soon, I was out over my head, turning to the right for each breath, tasting the salt as my head plunged under. I swam fast, pulling hard, until finally rolling over onto my back and stretching my arms out over my head. I let the ocean be my pillow. The salt and bright sun burned my eyes, and I pressed them tight. There were few people at the beach, and no one else in the water. Gramps said only people from up North ventured into the water this time of year. I saw him then, advancing slowly in. He waved at me, and I waved back.

As he swam towards me I thought about his secret, the one he told Kitty that night I lay in bed pretending to sleep. Sometimes I found him staring at me as if he suspected I knew. Maybe he thought I would tell, but I wouldn't. Could I ever tell him my secret? I hadn't been to confession in months. Mom had wanted me to go, but I could no longer unburden my soul to a priest, even if it was at St. Catherine's, where the family now went to Mass. No one ever talked about why we joined a different parish. No one ever talked about what happened with Monsignor Neelan, at least not in our house. At school there were rumors that his death was suspicious, that he was in some kind of trouble. Some boys were telling everyone that the mob was after him, that he had connections with the underworld. I wanted to laugh, but didn't. It didn't keep the diocese from creating the memorial at St. Peter's church, a place that Dad said he'd never set foot in again.

"You're quite the swimmer, Petey." He tread water beside me, his long legs bicycling beneath him.

"Thanks, Gramps."

"Did your Mom ever tell you about the summer I taught her how to swim?"

"No."

"She was still a little tyke, about six or seven I think. But I always thought that if you live near the ocean, you'd best know how to swim. She wasn't a natural, like you are — was afraid at first actually. The weather was calm, and I was holding her against me, encouraging her to relax.

There hadn't been much surf, but a freak wave came over both of us. I didn't see it coming. I lost my grip and the wave took her. When I burst to the surface, I could see her golden head bobbing up and down. She was kicking her little feet as hard as she could, spitting out water, her arms pulling furiously. Darned if she wasn't swimming all by herself. She was mad at me, accused me of letting go of her on purpose."

I laughed. "Yeah, Mom doesn't get angry very often, but when she does, watch out!"

"Yep. Just like you."

"You think I'm like Mom? But everyone says Maggie takes after Mom."

"True, in some ways. Certainly Maggie looks more like your mother, but you want things to be just right, will fight for it, and get angry when it's not, just like your mother. C'mon my little granddaughter, put your arms around my neck, and I'll paddle us both in, just like I used to do with your Mom."

Looping my arms around his neck, I pressed against his back and felt the strength of his arms pushing aside the water. He set me down knee high and took my hand. We had strayed quite a stretch from our beach blanket. I walked slowly, still thinking of Gramps' words.

"Gramps?"

"Yes, Petey?"

"Is it okay to be angry sometimes?"

"Depends. I mean everyone gets angry. It's what you do with that anger that counts."

"But what if you get so angry that you want to hurt someone?"

He stopped walking and looked at me. "Petey, what happened to your sister made us all angry. If you're talking about what your father did, I hope you've forgiven him for that. Jimmy has." The tears came unbidden. I sucked in deep breaths, trying to stop, but I couldn't. "What is it, Petey?"

"Dad isn't the... the only one who... who wanted to hurt Jimmy." My words spilled out in staccato. "I was so mad at him! I really hated him! You know, for what I thought he did to Maggie."

"We all felt that way, Petey."

"But I *really* did. I even . . ."

"What, Petey?"

I sniffed, wiping my nose with the back of my hand. "Remember you told me about your gun?"

"What about the gun?"

"I took it out of your suitcase."

"You? So that's why it was in the back in the closet."

I nodded. "It scared me, having it there when you were so mad in the living room, talking to Kitty."

"You heard that?"

"Uh-uh. So I opened the suitcase to hide your gun, but when I picked it up, the gun, it... it made me feel like, like I don't know, like I was changing into a super villain or something." I sniffed and licked the dripping from my nose. "The gun, it was so heavy, but I lifted it up and. . . and I thought of Jimmy and what he did to Maggie. I imagined shooting ... and seeing Jimmy, lying there dead. How could I be such an awful person? " Blubbering, I buried my face into Gramps.

"Oh, Petey."

Seawater dripped down my legs as my chest heaved with sobs. I could barely hear the soft "Ssshhh" of Gramps voice as he encircled me in his arms, and I smelled the mix of sweat and brine on his chest hairs that tickled my nostrils. I don't know how long we stood in the damp sand, or who passed by. Finally my tears were spent. He took me by the hand, and gently guided me to sit with him just shy of the dune reeds.

"You're not a bad person, Petey. You're human, like all of us. Thank goodness you did hide the gun so no one used it. I never should have brought it into the house. You've been carrying this secret a long time, Petey, haven't you?" I nodded. He sighed. "Well, I'm glad you told me. Carrying secrets hurts. You have to give them up eventually. And when you do, you have to let go of the hurt. Do you understand that, Petey?"

"I think so."

"But I shouldn't have hated Jimmy like that and... and pictured shooting him."

"You didn't shoot him, Petey. No one did. It was one bad thought. Everyone has bad thoughts sometimes. You love your sister and knew how much she was hurting. You were also afraid of losing her, weren't you?"

"I guess so. Do you think God will forgive me?"

"He already has, Petey."

"But I didn't go to confession."

"He still hears you, whether you're in a confessional or not, Petey. And he loves you, just like I do."

I looked at Gramps, and remembered his secret, the one he shared with Kitty that night, and knew that no matter what, he would always be my grandfather. "I love you too, Gramps."

He kissed me on the forehead. "You ready for that picnic lunch, now?"

Maggie

I squinted at the miniscule grains of hot sand sifting through my fingers.

"Do you want some suntan lotion on your back?"

"Huh?"

"Suntan lotion. Florida sun is pretty hot. Without it you'll burn."

"I guess." Kitty's cool fingers pressed into my back, rubbing up onto my shoulders. Last September, Jimmy had kissed each shoulder after putting on lotion. I ignored the tear dribbling down my nose. I'd seen him very little these past few weeks. Pneumonia kept me bedridden a long time. He'd come by some, and once I was well, we even went out on a couple of dates with Dad's blessing. But then he started coming less and less. He told me how busy he was with exams, and that he was now applying for medical school. Where would that take him? He never talked about what happened to me. He never talked about what Dad did to him either.

Dad was often by my bedside through my illness, tucking the covers for both Petey and me, just like he used to when we were little. One night I woke to see him standing by my bedside, staring down at me.

"Daddy?"

"Sorry. I didn't mean to wake you."

I rubbed my eyes. "That's okay." I saw his Adam's apple move as he swallowed.

"What is it?"

"I just, well, I never told you I was sorry, about what I did ... to Jimmy, I mean."

I knew about the knockout. Jimmy had told me.

"Can you ever forgive me?"

I nodded as my eyes watered.

"You're still my little Sunshine, right?"

He bent down and I wrapped my arms around his neck. "I'm trying to be."

Kissing the top of my head, he said, "You'll feel better soon. I promise."

Kitty squirted another dollop of sunscreen on my shoulders and rubbed some more.

"Are you getting hungry yet, Maggie?" I turned to see her haloed red head leaning toward me. Shading my eyes with my hand, I looked into her sequined sunglasses.

"Kitty?"

"Hmm?"

"Did you really have a miscarriage?"

She untwisted the top of her thermos and took a sip. "Lemonade. Do you want some?"

"Maybe a little." Kitty poured some into a paper cup and handed it to me as I sat up on the blanket.

"I was a lot older than you, but yes, I did."

"Is that why you don't have children? I mean, are your insides messed up or something?" The jeweled sunglasses came off. Crimped wrinkles fanned out from her green eyes, and I was afraid that I'd upset her.

"Is that what you think, Maggie, that you'll never have children?"

"I don't know. I don't know what to think."

"Maggie, lots of women have miscarriages. It happens all the time, and most go on to have children."

"But you don't have children."

"No, I don't, but it doesn't mean you won't. By the time I got pregnant, I was in my thirties. I was a nurse in the war and fell in love with a young sailor. He wanted to marry me after the war, but I knew it wouldn't last. I told him to go home to Wisconsin and marry his high school sweetheart, which I think is just what he did."

"But how could you let him go? You loved him!"

"Maggie, sometimes you can love someone and it's good, and you hold on as long as you can, because you know it's going to hurt to let go, but the time comes when you do. Marriage would have hurt us both more in the end. He was so much younger. I don't think his family would have approved, and I sure as heck didn't want to move to Wisconsin and live on a farm."

"I don't want to let Jimmy go, but I'm not sure he wants me any more after, you know..."

She set the thermos down, and put her arm around me. "Oh, Maggie. You are still just as loveable as you ever were. What happened to you was awful, wrong in every way, but it's over now."

"Do you think he will ever forgive me?"

"But there's nothing to forgive, Maggie. It wasn't your fault. You hear me? You have to believe that!"

Pulling my knees to my chest, I dropped my head forward. "I'd like to believe that."

"Give it time, Maggie. Perhaps Jimmy and you will part, but hopefully it won't be because of what happened. Your lives may just go in different directions."

"I wish I could start all over somehow. It's nice to come here, be away for a while."

"Your grandfather thought it would be good for you and for Petey, and your Mom and Dad agreed."

"Dad's been talking about Petey and I going to Gravor High next year instead of Holy Redeemer. My friend Samantha is transferring over there for her senior year. I know Petey would like it. They have a terrific science program and she could play softball. And I guess someplace new might be good for me too. I could take Chemistry again next year with a different teacher. I was already struggling and then after missing so much school this year, I don't think I'm going to pass."

"A good plan, Maggie. You might find you like it."

"But it's not a Catholic school, and even though I'm not going to be a nun or anything, I like going to chapel. I try to talk to God, even now, after what I did."

"And what do you hear, Maggie?"

"I think He still loves me."

"Of course He does. That won't change. And no matter where you are, you can talk to God, right?" I nodded. I clenched my toes in the sand and shoved, spraying a passing seagull. The buzz of a motorboat droned in the distance. I raised my head and gulped hot air.

"You didn't think I should be a nun, did you?"

"No. I saw a confused young girl nowhere near ready to make that choice, a choice I strongly suspected was one not made of her own choosing."

Trailing my fingers in the sand, I shut my eyes hard but still saw his face, heard his words. . . "I've been watching your sister, Agnes. . ." I wiped my tear-streaked face and sniffed.

"Maggie, are you all right? Is there something more you want to tell me?"

"The convent. I had to, you know, because of what he said."

"What, Maggie, what did he say?"

"That he'd take Petey too if I didn't go to the convent, but then I ran away. I. . . I never should have left her. I . . ." Tears streamed down my face.

Kitty encircled her arms around me, whispering in my ear, "It's okay, Maggie. He's gone. You hear me? He can't hurt you or Petey ever, ever again. She reached for some napkins, then took me by the shoulders, tipped my chin and looked directly into my eyes. "You're going to be just fine, Maggie girl, just fine. It's all over." I took a napkin and blew my nose.

She squeezed my shoulder. "Now, how about we put the food out for lunch? I see Petey and your grandfather coming."

Petey and Maggie

Kitty's picnic spread was surprisingly abundant and delicious. We ate pepperoni and cheddar cheese for the first time. Mom had only served American cheese. Nor had we ever tasted crabmeat, which Kitty had spread on rye bread, another novelty. We wolfed down the sandwiches, munched on potato chips, and drank lemonade.

"Now before I set out the cookies, your grandfather and I are going to lounge on our beach chairs for our afternoon siesta. I've got some beach pails, and I was hoping you girls would look for seashells. I've started a collection as well as making shell doodads. So whatever you find I'll put to use. What do you say?"

"Sure. I'd like that, wouldn't you Maggie?"

"Okay."

The sun sat high in the sky when we started, a luxurious heat a thousand miles away from the cool dampness of New England. We zig-zagged in the sand, eyes cast downward, searching the elusive whole seashell. Most were chipped or broken.

"Look, Petey, a pink and white one!" The shell was striped lavender pink and white with fluted edges, what we learned later was a scallop shell. Within a half hour we'd each found another pink scallop shell as well as some brown ones. We also found clam and mussel shells, some cowrie shells, and one small conch shell. Our yellow and orange striped umbrella was now a good distance away.

"Let's take a break. I'm getting tired." We sat and poked our toes into the soft sand.

We took turns picking shells from the bucket, examining each one. "I really like the lavender pink ones. I'm going to buy some hair ribbon that color for both of us."

"I'd like that, Maggie."

"I think Kitty will like all the shells we found. I'm glad Gramps married her. She was talking to me about when she was a nurse in the war."

"A nurse? Really?"

"She was in love with a sailor but didn't marry him."

We stared at our feet, both remembering that January night when Kitty revealed her lost pregnancy.

"It's hard to think of Kitty ever being sad, but I guess she must have been after, you know, what she said happened."

"Yeah, but she didn't do what I did. I'm sorry, Petey. Everything just seemed so hopeless, you know? And I felt like I couldn't' tell anyone about what was happening to me — what he — you know, did to me. It was like this awful secret that weighed me down. Can you understand?"

We pushed our toes deeper into the sand with heads bent low before turning to look at each other. "I wish you'd told me. I thought Jimmy was the one, just like Daddy, and I — I thought..."

"It's okay. It's what everyone thought."

The tide was coming in. The water now licked our toes.

"You haven't been in yet, have you Maggie?"

"It's a little chilly."

"Oh, come on. It's great once you get in." We held hands tiptoeing forward, finally submerging our bodies, ducking our heads under, and letting out a shrill of exhilaration.

"Petey, do you remember that synchronized swimming routine we invented as kids?"

"Kind of."

"I'll lead and you follow, okay, little 'sis?"

Our bodies curled up in a ball and we twirled counterclockwise. We stretched our legs outward, fanned our left arms in a rainbow arch, and then turned to make three diagonal strokes, aligning our bodies so that our toes touched. We were supposed to do synchronized leg lifts and submerge. Instead we both began kicking, splashing water on each other. The furious kicking and squeals must have alarmed Gramps and Kitty, who ran in our direction.

"Are you girls all right out there?"

We were laughing so hard we could barely answer. "We're fine, Gramps! Just having fun!"

We stumbled to the shore, arms locked.

Book Discussion Questions

1. Maggie pleads with her sister to understand her feelings for Jimmy. Why is it so important for Maggie to have Petey's understanding, and why doesn't Petey understand?

2. The word "secrets" is in the title of the book. There are a number of secrets that are eventually revealed in the story. What are they and how do they influence the events that take place in the story?

3. What family secret does Petey's father reveal when she is bedridden with cramps? How does it affect his behavior towards his daughters?

4. Describe the relationship between the two sisters. Give examples of how it affects their feelings and actions.

5. Describe the relationship of Monsignor Neelan with his mother. How does it affect his character? How do you think the secret about his sister affected his life?

6. What did Maggie's confession about 'impure thoughts' to Monsignor Neelan reveal about both characters?

7. Rose Donovan remarks that the bond between her husband and his daughters is a 'precious thing' and expresses concern that it's in jeopardy as a result of his forbidding Maggie from seeing Jimmy. Do you think this is correct? Do you think the father is reasonable in his decision? Why or why not?

8. The Donovan family is portrayed as devoutly Catholic in the 1960's. In what way does this almost become a character itself within the novel?

9. When Maggie's friend Samantha compares Maggie and Jimmy to Shakespeare's 'star-crossed lovers' is the comparison accurate? How were Maggie's parents destined to forbid her from seeing Jimmy?

10. Dreams may represent a repressed fear or a repressed wish. What does Petey's dream about Jimmy at the beach represent?

11. Did you admire Petey's refusal to be a 'tattle-tale' initially. Why or why not?

12. Rose tells Petey that her most positive memories of her father were of attending Sunday Mass with him. How might this have affected the course of her life?

13. John Donovan is portrayed as a loving and protective father. What motivated him to act the way that he did? Examine the choices that he made.

14. Maggie considers telling her parents about the sexual abuse by Neelan. What barriers prevented this?

15. To what degree is Bishop Feeley complicit in the sexual abuse that takes place?

16. How does religion play both a positive and negative role in the Donovan family?

17. Why did Rose think that talking to a priest would help her daughter? Examine how her faith influenced her decisions.

18. What made Maggie think that Msgr. Neelan would be on the side of her and Jimmy?

19. Give examples of the contrast in settings between Msgr. Neelan's office and the Donovan home.

20. How are Gramps and Kitty portrayed? What role do they play in the story?

21. There are numerous beach scenes in the story. What does the ocean represent to the two main characters?

22. Petey and Maggie both have nightmares after the near drowning. What are they and what do they represent?

23. The TV news reports that the death of Msgr. Neelan was caused by a heart attack. How does this detail echo the theme of deception?

24. What does the incident of the red pompom on the train suggest about Maggie and victims of trauma?

25. What does Petey's confession to Gramps about hiding the gun reveal about her? How does he respond?

26. Were the Donovans typical of Catholic families in the 1960's? At the end of the novel they do not abandon their Catholic faith but change parishes. Evaluate their choice.

27. There are a number of scenes that touch upon the subject of birth control. What do they show about the thinking on the subject in those times and the lives of Catholic women?

28. Find details in the story that reflect the difference in age and maturity between the two sisters. Explore how this difference affected the dynamic between them and the events that transpired.

About the Author

Theresa Schimmel is the author of three children's book, numerous stories, essays, and poems. **Braided Secrets** is her first novel. She is a member of the Association of Rhode Island Authors and has always had a passion for writing. A former teacher and educational consultant, she now spends her time writing in her home state of Rhode Island. She is married to her husband, Steve, and is the mother of two adult sons and grandmother of two children. For more information on her and her books, go to her website: www.tamstales.net

Made in the USA
Middletown, DE
01 July 2016